The Attic

by

Lynda Rees

A Flip or Flop Mystery

Cover Art by *Tina Lynn Stout*

The Wild Rose Press, Inc.
PO Box 708
Adams Basin, NY 14410-0708
Visit us at www.thewildrosepress.com

Publishing History
First Edition, 2025
Trade Paperback ISBN 978-1-5092-6146-8
Digital ISBN 978-1-5092-6147-5

The Attic, A Flip or Flop Mystery
Published in the United States of America

Chapter One

She showered in the mansion's crude, plastic, one-piece bathroom stall, trying her best to wash guilt and terror from her pale skin. Red goo on her flesh mingled with water flow, her tears, and then drizzled in streaks down her legs into the rusty drain.

The warmth eased her sore muscles. She closed her eyes, trying to block out memories straining to take possession of her spirit. Someone stole part of her soul. She desperately wanted it back.

She puffed an exhale and inhaled fresh oxygen to cleanse her insides. Her heart ached in her chest, trying to burst free. She held her breath for a count of four, then breathed in for a count of eight. She held it, counted slowly to four, and then breathed out to the count of six, repeating the process four times. With each repetition, her heartbeat slowed more. She'd learned the technique eased anxiety when it struck.

She scrubbed her hair for the third time with lilac-scented shampoo, still pulling bits of dried leaves and twigs from the long, blonde tresses. She'd finally gotten used to the shade, which looked oddly natural on her. The lilac scent helped remove the crude odor of his heavy cologne—clearly an attempt to postpone bathing—combined with foul-smelling breath tinted with alcohol, onions, and tobacco.

She still sensed his rough, calloused grip on her

bruised arms. Her hips burned from scrubbing where welts had developed from the friction of her jeans being ripped down. She forced visions away to still her pulse and avoid another panic attack.

The flow of water cooled, reminding her she'd showered long enough. She'd exhausted the supply of heated liquid from the inadequate, ancient, hot water tank. After stepping out of the rickety stall onto a towel, she buffed her flesh with soft terry, continuing to rid herself of memories she certainly would dream about later.

She mustn't catch a cold. The Lord knew she had enough problems. Besides, she couldn't afford the cost of a doctor or the attention such a visit might bring to her.

A noise from the street signaled the slam of a vehicle door in front of the building. She gazed through grime undoubtedly accumulated over at least a decade of neglect on the thick pane. Voices drifted upward to her high observatory.

"Oh, crap, I've got to get this mess cleaned up...quickly."

She scrambled to finish drying, slid her slightly damp body into sweats, and donned a tee shirt she'd brought to the bathroom. She'd been diligent about returning personal care items after they were used to the tote she'd carried them in so she could make quick work of it.

Nasty clothing was crammed inside. Her tattered hoodie missed a zipper pull. "Well, it's trash."

Should she keep it? "Nope. You're gone, baby." She might like the jacket, but not the recollections that came with it.

She wiped the creaking, paint-flaking, metal shower as dry as possible with her damp towels. With a final once-over to make sure she didn't leave evidence of her presence, she snatched her things and rushed to the safety of her private sanctuary.

As she entered, she eased the door shut. Voices from outside on the portico filtered upward. A key was inserted into the front door. Very carefully, without making noise, she tiptoed barefoot up the solid oak stairwell. Finally, at the last door, she slipped inside, closed it behind her, and hoped to shut out the recent past along with other events that haunted her.

Mid-morning sunshine streaked through ornate, stained-glass windows to coat her rusty, metal bed and its yellowing white blanket with glistening light, as though answering her prayers, assuring her it would be okay.

Would it? *Will things ever be okay again?* She barely recalled when they were. Now, she had this latest fiasco to deal with. Could she escape it? Ignore it? Doubtful. Her only hope—delay the inevitable. Then what?

It would be found. If nothing else, decomposing flesh would draw the attention of animals, possibly vagrant campers along the riverbank.

Homeless…like her. Only she had shelter, a roof over her displaced head. Did that make her one of them, scavenging for what they could? For food? A place of shelter? For security? What did that even mean? It had been so long, she couldn't recall. Was there even such a thing as security?

Doubtful.

Chapter Two

Eli Lange pulled his pickup truck to the curb in front of the deserted 1798 mansion. "It's cool how the middle-class neighborhood sprouted around this old mansion."

Charli Owens-Lange admired their prize. "Yes, but ours has a bronze plaque for the house's link to the Underground Railroad when the owners helped slaves to freedom across the Ohio River "

He nodded. "Makes me wonder what is in store for its future." He bit his lower lip. "Your grandmother told me they used the tunnel system as a secret entrance and exit to a speakeasy operated here during Prohibition."

She snickered. "Funny, liquor being illegal. No wonder Prohibition only lasted a few years. Still, how did they get away with hosting lavish parties serving contraband booze?"

He cut the truck's engine. "Of course, police were paid off to look the other way. Those who frequented the establishment preferred their identities to remain anonymous, given they were among the local societies' most wealthy and powerful." He glanced upward at the walls. "I can't wait to restore this baby back to her former glory."

Charli smiled at her business partner and fiancé. "Me either. She's a work of love. I wish we could afford to keep the house once our work is done, but we need the profit to keep Owens Construction afloat. The sooner we get started renovating, the quicker we'll get this place sold."

Eli smiled knowingly, and a plan revealed itself in his mind. No time for that now. "Well, it's too late today to get any work done."

Charli nodded her pretty head. Her copper curls bounced and shined in the late afternoon sunlight.

Eli stepped out of the truck and rushed around to open the door for the love of his life before she could do so herself. His tiny woman, a petite 5' 2" tall, possessed an independent soul and liked fending for herself. He preferred to do what he could for her.

"You're right about that." She stepped out onto the path that wrapped three sides of their almost-an-acre property. Gazing down at it, she snickered. "You know, this is the only cobblestone walkway remaining in town. The city commissioner said they left it intact for historical reasons. All other sidewalks in Sweetwater have been modernized with concrete." She strode around to the truck bed to lower the tailgate. "We only have time to take these cleaning products and tools inside. Then, after dinner, we can move your belongings and furniture in."

He loaded his arms with tools. "Yep, I wouldn't want to miss out on Irma's dinner. She's making my favorite meatloaf."

Charli laughed. "Gran does love spoiling you. She likes feeding people and misses Kyler, but he's doing well at university. Having you around helps."

He blew her a kiss. "Yeah, I miss that young man myself. I adore your brother."

Her head tilted as she eyed him. "Are you sure about moving out of Amanda and Frank's house? I know you'll miss Abbe, and they told you you're welcome to stay as long as you want."

He smiled. "The key there is as long as I want. Frank's back home from Afghanistan and trying to settle in. Abbe needs to defer to him now, instead of me. It's taking some getting used to. They need privacy…without me in their faces every day. I'll see them often enough. It's not like I'm moving back to Cincinnati. I'll be just a few blocks away."

She turned toward the house. "I guess you're right. I hadn't considered that."

He blew her a kiss. Both had their hands full.

She reciprocated and then eyed him curiously. "You did a good thing—selling your construction company and relocating here to help Amanda with Abbe while Frank worked for the military."

Eli had gotten a hefty sum in the low millions for the profitable business he'd created.

"Thanks, but I got more from it than they did." He'd adored spending the last couple of years with his sister and niece. "I didn't know what all I missed out on. A man can't live on work alone. Now I have you. I want a family like Amanda, Abbe, and Frank. I want a home and to belong. You, Irma, Wes, and Kyler are all part of that now. I'm more than happy to be here in Sweetwater. Besides, I'd burned out on management. Now, with you in charge as the official boss, I can relax and focus on the creative work I love. I missed the craft part of it as my company grew so large."

Her smile told him she thought the same thing. Charli glanced at her engagement ring, glistening in the sun's rays. "Are you sure you're okay with living out of a suitcase, with only a chair, a bed, and a television set?

We could buy you some real furniture."

He shrugged. "Absolutely. It feels wasteful to purchase good furniture until we're married. Staying here while we renovate the place is perfect. This gives me somewhere to land without undue expenses. It will deter break-ins and vandals while we have equipment and supplies stored inside. A place to rest my head with a comfy chair to zone out when I'm exhausted suits me fine. The kitchen appliances in the house may be ancient, but they work. That's all I need—that and you in my life."

Chapter Three

They had moved the last of his personal belongings into the house the evening before. Eli met Charli at her truck the following morning in front of the mansion. He took her into his arms, and her world fell into place.

"Morning, babe. How are you?" He gave her a long, passionate kiss.

She snickered up at the tall man who owned her heart. "I'm good, better now. The real question is, how are you?"

He released her from the hug and stepped back with a shrug. "As good as you'd expect. I'd have been better if you were here by my side. Sleeping in a new location is always a challenge for a few days until you get used to all the sounds. Believe me, this old house has its share of creaks and bumps in the night."

"No worries. I'll be sleeping with you soon enough. Then I can protect you from the groans and moans of an old house."

He treaded to the truck bed to unload another batch of supplies. She did the same. The yelp of a small poodle interrupted their chatter. A plump, middle-aged woman dressed in jeans and a sweatshirt held a dog's leash. The animal stretched his guide tight to get as close to them as possible. He sniffed their legs.

"Oh dear, I'm sorry about that. Pookie is so curious. Don't worry. He's just anxious to make new friends."

Blushing, she yanked gently on the line, pulling the little fella backward a step. "He doesn't bite."

Charli and Eli smiled. Eli stooped to stroke the feisty animal, who craned his neck to get a better petting.

"No problem. I love dogs. He probably smells my sister's German shepherd on me."

Charli stuck out a hand. The woman shook it limply. "Nice to meet you. I'm Charli Owens. This is my fiancé, Eli Lange. We just bought this place. We're getting ready to remodel it."

"Wonderful, it sure can use some loving care. It will be good to have actual living neighbors inhabit it for a change." *Something lived there that wasn't alive.*

Eli stood and shook her hand. "So, you live in the neighborhood?"

She nodded. "Yes, that's me over there. I'm Nancy Underwood." She pointed to a small, two-story Tudor with a postage-sized lot.

Charli's brows lifted high. "I take it you've heard the rumors."

Again, the woman blushed. "Well, of course. Hasn't everyone? They're not exactly rumors. I've seen things. Most everyone around here has witnessed at least one oddity hereabouts." She waved her hand, indicating the vicinity.

"I realize there's folklore…but oddity?"

"Absolutely. We've all seen shadows around the grounds. People witnessed silhouettes through curtained windows. Several incidents have been reported. The police always investigated; they've never found anything suspicious. There's a long history of this house being haunted."

Charli laughed it off. "I'm sure there's a logical

explanation for everything. They've just not been here at the right time, is all. I don't really believe in ghosts. I'm sure if you do, you have good reason to."

The woman flicked a brow with what looked like a forced smile. "To each his own, I always say. I wish you luck and much happiness in your new home." She led the poodle toward their house. "Pookie and I enjoyed talking with you."

"Thanks, Ms. Underwood. It was good to meet you."

Eli waved a free hand, then carried his load toward the heavy, carved wooden front door. Leaded cut-glass windows, each as tall top-to-bottom, flanked the entrance.

Charli finished loading hers. Then she caught up with Eli at the stoop. "Strange woman, but she seems nice enough. Don't worry, Eli. I'm sure the ghosts won't bother you too much."

Eli opened the door, juggling his bundle. He held it for her to enter and then followed her inside. "Don't worry, babe. I'm sure it's just your average spook. I ain't afraid of no ghost." His last words mimicked the famous line from the comedy, sending them into hysterical laughter. "Of course, it could be a chilly ghost. I tried to shower last night, but the water turned icy cold. The haunt probably used all the hot water."

She nearly lost her load she giggled so hard. "Funny guy! Guess we'd best get a plumber to check it. New water heater, first on our list of to dos."

Chapter Four

Soon they had stowed equipment and supplies. Charli stood back to admire the foyer.

"Beauty of this building blows me away. Everything original about it is extremely high-quality, exceptional for that time. Just look at this marble tile on the floor and steps. The Mahogany banister and spindles are hand-carved—works of art—priceless."

He looked upward. "Take a gander at that enormous crystal chandelier. That thing must weigh a ton. When we get around to it, cleaning that baby will take forever."

She snickered. "Yep, I can see a big, old guy like you tenderly polishing each individual crystal pendant with those massive hands of yours."

He snaked an arm around her waist and pulled her against him. "Aw, Charli, I thought you loved what I can do with these big, old hands." His lower lip drooped into a pout as he feigned, inspecting his free paw.

"Don't change the subject, mister. If you get me all horny, we'll never get this place in livable shape. You want the kitchen or the bathrooms?"

"No contest. I'll take the kitchen. It might be larger, but there are three bathrooms in this monstrosity."

"Awesome! I was afraid to open the refrigerator. It's likely a mess. Do me a favor. Wait until I'm out of range before you crack the door on that ancient machine. You might need a gas mask."

She strolled into the room where they'd stored them previously to gather supplies to tackle her chore and then reappeared in the kitchen. "That butler's pantry is almost as large as my bedroom at home. Or it would be if it wasn't lined with deep cabinets and drawers on both sides. It's a cook's dream come true."

Eli stared inside the antique, green refrigerator that had probably occupied its space since the early nineteen-fifties.

"Oh, Eli, you promised to let me get out of puke-invoking range before you opened that door." She held utensils in one hand and a large bucket of supplies in the other.

He grinned toward the machine. "Get a load of this, will ya?"

"Don't tell me it's not operable." She strode toward him.

"Nope. Not gonna do it. Looks clean. All I need to do with this is give it a once over and then move on to the oven."

Her jaw dropped. "Hum! Even the light bulb inside still burns. Go figure."

Eli opened the oven door. "This thing is clean as a whistle too. I'm surprised."

She puffed out an exhale. "What do you know? Usually, a management company doesn't bother with the upkeep of appliances at an abandoned property. They barely keep the lawn cut at best. Maybe they spent more time here than normal and needed to use the appliances occasionally."

He chuckled. "That, or we have ourselves some exceptionally clean ghosts. Either way, I'll take it. Looks like my job isn't so bad."

She surveyed the bottom and top cabinets that stretched all the way to the high ceiling and lined two long walls. The old sink's porcelain had pitted. Countertops were marble-looking laminate with ill-fitted marble strips nailed around the edges that peeled away in places. Black and white squares of stick-on linoleum tiles were chipped. Several blocks were missing and exposed black undercoating over wooden planks she hoped were oak. Layers of painted-over wallpaper peeled in a few places. The fireplace had been left filled with cinders, and the hearth was dusty. Tall windowpanes over the sink were so dingy with buildup they looked pearlized. One could hardly see the gorgeous backyard view they were meant to exhibit.

"No, I believe you still have a full day's work to get this kitchen usable." She spun on her work-booted heels. "Have at it, Hunky Daddy."

A few minutes later, she dropped her materials outside the first-floor bathroom, the one off the dining room, and set up a step ladder. She stood on the top rung to strip off triple layers of thick, ugly, antique wallpaper where it had begun to peel free. Once she finished that, she scraped loose areas for anything still clinging to the surface. She swept the walls and ceiling down and then gave them a wet-mopping.

Surveying her work with hands on the hips of her jeans, she smiled. "That will have to do until we have time for remodeling."

Charli scraped up partial tiles where she could, then swept the floor. After wetting down the pitted porcelain tub and sink, she applied cleaning powder in thick coats. She'd leave them so the solution could do its work. It would soak into crevices to pull out the gunk that settled there.

While solvents did their best dirty work to make her chore easier, she fixed the broken chain on the ballcock. She poured bleach inside the water receptacle and then cleaned the too-tiny, antique medicine cabinet with its beyond-repair mirror. Next, she pulled out a stainless-steel pad to scrub the tub and basin. After several rinses to rid them of cleanser, she stood back to observe her handiwork.

"Not too bad. At least Eli can take a bath without coming home with me." She pulled a pad and pen from her bib pocket to write a list.

#1 Bath: Molded metal ceiling tiles—fine. Claw-footed tub—resurface porcelain, remove paint from outside. Recoat. Build shower stall. Install high-energy, low-water usage toilet. Pedestal sink—fine. Remove wallpaper. Paint walls. Refinish chair railing and shiplap board. Remove tile. Replace. Reseal stained glass. Install storm window.

She slid the pad and pen back into her pocket, picked up her supplies, and trudged upstairs.

On the second floor, she repeated the process. This time, she noted only clear, leaded glass in the window. This bathroom was in much the same condition as the first. A couple of hours later, she strode to the third floor, to do the same for the last bathroom in the big house.

Pausing at the top of the stairs, she observed this level. The first floor consisted of a huge sitting parlor on one side of the front, a music room the same size on the other side, and an enormous foyer in the center. Behind those were a sizeable, square dining room, a bathroom that had been added at some point, and the butler's pantry. To the back, a giant kitchen housed a rock fireplace with a hearth along one side wall. The other side had a back door that led to a small covered porch.

The second floor had four substantial, square bedrooms, each with its own fireplace, and a walkway all around the center staircase. At the middle of the back wall, a bathroom had been carved out of parts of the two back bedrooms.

The third floor differed. One huge room took up most of the space to one side along the front of the house. On the other side were two small bedrooms previously used for house staff.

Along the back, sat another small room for that purpose. The fourth had been converted into a tiny bathroom but had previously been a birthing room. The walk-in-closet-sized space had been used primarily so women giving birth to their children could be kept away from the rest of the household while they spit infants from their hoo-has.

Charli snorted at the thought. She wasn't sure if the audacity that screams might offend the sensibilities of others was the reason for the special rooms, or if they were meant to give consideration for the mothers' privacy. Either way, the whole idea irked her. She wasn't against childbirth and found it strange that it had been considered distasteful. She could hardly wait to become the mother of Eli's children.

"Enough, girl. You've got work to do. Get it done before your body realizes how tired and hungry you are." She laughed at the habit she'd gotten into. "Ghosts, if you're listening, I hope you don't mind me talking to myself. I'd speak to you, but you haven't presented yourselves yet."

She surveyed the last bathroom to be cleaned for the

day. Thankfully, it was smaller than the others. The area consisted only of a cheap porcelain basin attached to the wall with exposed plumbing beneath it. A rickety, chipped toilet from the fifties. A scrawny, rusty, dingy shower stall completed the fixtures. No shower curtain hung from its frame.

"This will take a complete teardown. We can fix the plaster cracks and then paint. The fixtures must all go. Flooring needs replacing."

She took notes. The window frame needs repair; but the wavy, antique glass panes of the upside-down, cup-shaped window looked fine. They'd just need to seal the panes. Floor board and window trim remained in amazing shape, though they obviously had been painted several times. A good scraping, some paint thinner. A fresh single layer would do the trick. No shiplap here, just plaster to be repaired and painted. A built-in, tile, wall-to-wall shower stall would be more efficient and elegant than the rickety insert that forced her to cringe. Surely, she could find an antique dresser that could be converted into a small vanity. They'd have to install a fresh, new toilet.

Once she finished her list, she began the chore of cleaning. Being smaller, it took much less time than the others had. She'd saved scrubbing the shower as the last chore. As she worked top-to-bottom, it nearly appeared usable. She knelt to do the base. Something caught her eye in the trim at the stall's entrance.

A stick stuck in the grimy space. She used her scraper to flick it free. The item landed in her gloved hand.

"What the heck?"

After discarding a strand of blonde hair stuck to it,

she examined the pencil-shaped object. Dragons carved along its length appeared to be hand-painted scarlet red and gold. The pointed end wasn't overly sharp. A sliver about a half-inch long had broken off. Even damaged, the object spoke to her. Way too beautiful to simply discard, she washed it clean in the vanity and dried it with a paper towel. Then she stuck it in her bib pocket.

She gathered her equipment, lumbered downstairs, and stored it in the butler's pantry. Arriving in the kitchen, she beamed. "Wow! Look what you've done with this place. It nearly sparkles. Way to go, Eli. That's some fine work."

He wrapped an arm across her petite shoulders. "Thank you, ma'am. I'm so glad you approved. I aim to please. It wasn't nearly as difficult as I'd anticipated, only lots of it. This room is enormous."

"Yes, I think it's large enough to accommodate a sizeable center island, like we discussed earlier. We could use those discarded antique windows in my garage to build the base. There's plenty of that beautiful wood we reclaimed when they tore down the old bowling alley. It would be strong and sturdy. Material from the lanes would make a gorgeous countertop."

He smiled. "Yes, we should build it wide enough so there's plenty of workspace on one side, with seating for at least six on the other. Maybe we could put shelving on one side for cookbooks and such."

She gazed around the cabinetry. "Great idea. I wonder if we'll have enough lane boards to do all the countertops."

"Doubtful, but maybe. If not, we can have wooden ones with a thick finish created, or we can use granite. Either way, the cabinets are perfect. The wood is unfinished on the insides and just dusty. We might need to fix or replace fixtures. Otherwise, I believe we can refinish or paint them. They're just too good, too fabulously old to discard."

"Yes, the same goes for the butler's pantry. The floor, like this one, needs replacing, but the cabinets are glorious. That's a huge cost saving on our budget."

He pointed to the stove. "Another thing, this range is a pleasant surprise. It's got a couple of character nicks, but otherwise, it's in pristine condition. It's massive and weighs about a ton, so it would be difficult to move anyway. We should keep it. It's got a warmer, a deep well for frying, a small oven, a large one, a cast iron griddle, and six burners. What more could a cook want?"

She curled her nose. "Really? That old clock on it doesn't look too good. The cover is yellowed."

His head rocked. "You're right. It doesn't work. I bet we could replace the guts with a fresh one. We can get glass to cover the front. It would look good as new."

"Yeah." She bit her lower lip. "But wouldn't a buyer want a nice, modern stove?"

He shrugged to one side. "Maybe, but we could put a flat, glass-topped four-burner stovetop on the island. The kitchen needs a garbage compactor and a wine cooler as we design it."

She smiled up at him, her shoulder cradled beneath his arm. "Good thinking, hunky daddy. I like the way that brilliant mind of yours works."

He fingered the red item sticking up out of her bib pocket. "What 'cha got there?" Pulling it out, he examined it. "Looks like a Chinese hair pick."

She smiled. "Awesome! I figured it was a chopstick. I found it in the third-floor bathroom. Maybe I'll use it in my hair."

Chapter Five

Charli strolled into the great room early the next morning to find her grandmother sitting on a barstool, nursing a cup of coffee. No surprise she was dressed for the day. As usual, Gran never left her bedroom without her silver hair coiffed to perfection and her makeup done. Today she wore an ivory pants outfit. Pearls hung below the cowl neck of her silk shirt. Matching earrings topped off her ensemble.

Gran put the newspaper down and nodded toward the pot. "Coffee's ready. I put creamer in your go-cup."

"Thanks, Gran. What are you up to today?"

Her regal head tilted. Charli admired her lack of wrinkles—an oddity for a woman of her age. But then again, Gran was an oddity in all ways. She poured herself a full mug of hot brew.

"Yum. Smells delightful."

"You look different today. I kind of like it. What made you decide to wear your hair in a bun instead of your usual ponytail?"

"Oh, thanks…I think. Actually, I found this adorable Asian hair pick at the house yesterday. It inspired me to try something new."

"Speaking of your new remodeling project, are you sure you don't want to move into that house with that sexy fiancé of yours? Or Eli could stay here. You'd both be much more comfortable." Gran's gaze bored into her.

The woman knew her better than anyone.

"Gran, you know how I feel about shacking up. I don't want to influence Kyler to disrespect women and the sanctity of marriage."

"Hell, honey. Kyler is a grown man. He's in college now. You've had your chance to mold him into the fine young man he has become. Be proud. He adores Eli. Eli feels the same about him. Take my word for it. Your brother wouldn't think twice about the two of you living together before you're married. You've been engaged for more than a year. The wedding is planned for December 20. What the heck difference would it make to the boy? He knows better than to disrespect a female."

She and Gran had gone over the same disagreement several times since she'd first brought Eli home for dinner. The woman wasn't wrong, but Charli didn't want to argue the point. She'd decided and stuck to it. "You're probably right, Gran. I'll just feel better, waiting for the next couple of months to officially live together. I'm not as open to these things as you."

Gran sighed, clearly accepting her defeat. "Well, you did lead a more conventional life. Being on the road with my band since the age of fourteen opened my eyes to a lot of things you weren't subjected to. I led a more glamorous, adventurous, wicked experience than you did, but we both grew up much faster than normal. You took on adult responsibilities at sixteen for raising your baby brother. I led the life of a touring rock star."

"At least you have some normalcy now that you've retired. It still feels odd, though, a grandfather in my life after all those years—not in a bad way." Charli took a long sip of her brew, letting the silky heat wash away any doubts about the three main men in her life.

Kyler did incredibly well at university and as he quarterbacked his team. Eli turned out to be the best thing that had ever happened to her. She couldn't wait to become his wife. Wes, well, he shocked the whole clan when he arrived on the scene. He'd proved himself a wonderful addition to the family. She welcomed her surprise grandfather with open arms, happy to finally form a relationship with him. Wes made Gran happier than Charli had ever seen her.

Gran beamed, not a blush in sight. Nothing phased that woman. "Yes, well, I never expected my baby daddy to reappear, or that he might want me and a family. Funny how time changes things. I just wish your dad had been more open to meeting his father before he passed away. If he'd wanted to get to know Wes, you would've all met much earlier. Then again, Wes is much more the family man, now he's ready to settle down. When I'd learned of my pregnancy, Wes had been otherwise focused—all about business. He tossed me aside like yesterday's trash. His excuse—he believed I'd slept with my best friend Jimi. Wes knew full well, Jimi and I had become close as brother and sister after our one fling at Woodstock. Wes tried running from his fear of rejection and commitment. It took him five failed marriages, tons of therapy and alimony to learn that for himself."

Charli drew her backpack off the hook by the door and slung it over a shoulder. "And he's still madly in love with you, Gran."

Gran glowed and flashed her pearly whites. "As I am with him, sweetheart. Don't expect me to be as prudish as you." She strolled to Charli and tapped her granddaughter lovingly on the nose. "When Wes returns to town, he will move in with me…at least until he finds

22

a place of his own. If I have anything to say about it, we'll never be apart again. Your sexy grandpa and I have wasted enough time, and I intend to make him so happy in my bed he never wants to leave." She sighed longingly. "I miss him like mad."

Charli rolled her eyes, not the least surprised at the subject of sex, used to her wacky grandmother's ways. "I'd expect nothing less, Gran. Do whatever makes you happy."

She would anyway.

Gran nodded. "I'm glad he's decided to retire to Sweetwater. It will be good for all of us to have him here with us. Fortunately, he found a new business partner willing to take over management of his entertainment agency."

"Yes, I'm excited to have Wes around and thrilled he's agreed to walk me down the aisle with you at Eli's and my wedding." Charli glanced at what Gran had been reading. "Anything interesting in the paper today?"

Gran strode back to the countertop. "Check this out. There's been a murder." She pointed to the headline. '*Sheriff Wyatt Gordon confirms body as a murder victim.*' It goes on to say a lady taking her dog for a stroll heard a couple of wild dogs fighting in the forest. Her animal broke free of her leash and scrambled into the woods toward the animals. As she appeared, they attacked her pet. She carries an eco-safety horn in her sweatshirt pocket when she goes out. You know, like an aerosol hairspray can. They are used for emergencies on boats and such, to get help. Anyway, she blasted it. The loud noise sent the creatures scrambling. She snatched her pet's leash and checked him for wounds. The standard poodle wasn't harmed badly, but as she stood, she realized what the critters were fighting over. They'd been nibbling on human remains. She ran back to her house down that dead end street leading to the woodland and called the sheriff's office." Gran read from the paper. "'*Sheriff Gordon, and deputies Jaiden Coldwater and Leo Sanders were on the scene, as reporters arrived. They confirmed the victim died under suspicious circumstances.*'" She looked up from the paper again with a sneer. "We all know if you read between the lines, that means murder."

Charli shook her head wearily. "I knew things were getting a little too peaceful around here."

Gran nodded, brows high. "Indeed, but Charli, please promise you'll stick close to Eli until they nab whoever did this. They found this dude not far from your and Eli's mansion. From the correspondent's description, it sounds like the dead-end street just over the hill from the back end of your property. You know, those woods behind the house go all the way down to the river. Be careful, babe. There's a killer on the loose. Who knows what he's after or why he targeted that fella?"

"That goes for you too, Gran."

Charli glared at her frisky grandmother, knowing full well the woman would do whatever she pleased anyway. She'd been known to play hero and investigator before, and she'd faced her share of stalkers during her singing career. It came with the territory as a famous rock singer from the seventies through the last decade.

Gran patted the center of her breasts. "Don't worry about me. I always have my two best friends handy— Mr. Smith and Mr. Wesson."

Charli snickered and shook her head in awe. Gran never fully dressed without her hidden artillery. "Do the police know who he is, Gran?"

"Not sure. The article said they didn't find a wallet on the guy. I'm sure they'll identify him soon."

Charli frowned. "Jaiden and I are meeting for coffee this morning. I'll see what I can learn from her. Surely, the authorities would've already reached out to me if this happened on our land."

Gran stood and poured herself another cup of Joe. "You're probably right. It might not have been on your stretch of the woods, but sounds awfully close to it, only lower on the hillside."

Charli kissed Gran goodbye, grabbed her keys, and tool belt from the peg by the door and headed out to go meet her best friend. Jaiden would know more.

****

A half hour later, the uniformed, exotic deputy sat across from the rehabber in a booth at Sadie's Royal Diner. Having relocated to Sweetwater after leaving the Texas Rangers and healed from a gunshot wound suffered while taking down a drug ring, Jaiden had taken a role as Wyatt Gordon's deputy. She'd come to stay with her retired-veterinarian mother, who moved here to be near her son, Jaiden's brother, Calvin Coldwater.

Cal, a twenty-year veteran Navy Seal, had taken a job as horse trainer for Levi Madison at Mane Lane Farm. Charli and Jaiden had formed an instant bond upon meeting and had become besties ever since.

Sadie Carson, a sixty-something redhead with her white-trimmed, pink, retro dress and white apron, short sleeved cuffs, and broad grin, stood beside their booth.

"Well, if it ain't Mutt and Jeff. I'll be darned if the two of you aren't as opposite as a couple of young ladies could be." Her chuckle emphasized her overly Southern twang. "You're as purty as a picture, Jaiden, with your dark skin and eyes, and that silky black mane of yours. You're the spitting image of your gorgeous, Choctaw mama. Except Brightleaf's hair has turned silvery now. No one would suspect a tiny little thing like you as a ferocious lawperson. Or that your papa was as redheaded and Irish as they come."

Sadie turned to her other customer. "And you, Charli, with those copper curls and fair skin. You're the prettiest little imp I've ever seen, even if you do dress like a lumberjack in flannel shirts and bib overalls. Say hello to that stunning granny of yours. Tell her to bring lots of cash to card night. Jaiden, you tell Brightleaf to do the same. I intend to take them both for a bundle." Sadie cackled. She paused to let her compliments take effect. "So, ladies, what'll it be this fine day?"

They thanked Sadie for the compliments, assured her they'd pass along her messages, and placed orders for coffee and her special blackberry croissants. Once their food arrived, the twosome dug into the delicacies.

Charli chewed her first bite and eyed her friend. "Gran showed me the news. Sounds like you had an exciting yesterday. Please, tell me you didn't find that corpse on my land."

Jaiden smiled, knowingly. "I figured you'd heard by now. The Sweetwater grapevine usually travels faster than the media in this town, but it's still early. And, no, we don't believe it's your property. That woman discovered the body just shy of your piece, given remains we noticed an ancient fence line beyond the parameter we marked off. You might want to check, though. I didn't compare the deed, but it appears he died on city land once earmarked for a road extension. You know, the section I'm talking about. It goes all the way down the hill near the bridge, and it butts up to your property line running downhill there." Her Texas accent resonated almost as strong as Sadie's.

Charli frowned. "Yeah, aren't there some homeless camping in that area and under the bridge?" That strip along the Ohio River had been known as a vagrant haven. "I'll check the deed. Maybe Eli and I will hike down there and get a look from our side. We had it surveyed before we took possession, but we never walked the borders."

Jaiden nodded between bites. "Good. We didn't find any surveyor marks in the area we roped off. Be careful if you decide to do that."

"Did you identify the victim?"

"Yes, but only after we discovered his vehicle parked a couple blocks down the street. We're not sure why he entered the forest, but he might've been tailing someone or looking for something. We traced his registration. The out-of-towner came from Cleveland."

Charli frowned and sat her cup down. "Why would a man from Cleveland look for someone or something in the middle of nowhere in Sweetwater, Kentucky?"

Jaiden pursed her lips. "Yep, that's a quandary. It turns out the guy worked as a shady private detective. He's a suspicious character, suspected of working with the Mob."

Charli's eyes widened. "Oh, hell, no. Not in our quiet little town. Not again."

Jaiden grimaced. "Sorry, Charli; no place is immune to crime. If it were, I'd be out of a job. You've had a couple of bad experiences with The Syndicate. Hopefully this one has nothing to do with you."

"Wonder why he came to town." Hair stood on end at the back of Charli's neck.

Jaiden stared at her down her nose. "Stay out of this, Charli, and be careful. We don't know who did this or why yet. There's a killer on the loose." Jaiden leaned to the side for a better view of Charli's messy bun. "What's that in your hair?"

Charli's hand touched the hair pick she'd cleaned up and used to secure her ponytail in a bun. She slipped it free and showed it to Jaiden. "This? I found it in the mansion yesterday. Cute, isn't it? There's a chipped piece in the red and gold paint, but the design is so intricate. I didn't have the heart to toss it. It's just too pretty."

A scowl clouded Jaiden's face. She took the slim, red object between two fingers and twisted it slowly. Her fiery gaze seemed to penetrate the wood the stick was carved from.

A chill ran down Charli's spine, and she shivered. "What's wrong, Jaiden?"

After a long pause as she continued to inspect the tool, Jaiden met Charli's gaze. "It's oddly like a piece of evidence we discovered at the crime scene. It might mean nothing, but would you mind if I kept this? I'd like to take it to the station and do a side-by-side comparison."

Baffled, Charli frowned. "No, guess not. Go for it…though, I don't know how a Chinese hair pick found in the shower at our long-vacant house could be tied to a murder."

Jaiden's expression turned serious as she blinked and gave her head a jerk. "It's probably not. I just want to rule it out. No worries. I'm sure it's nothing." She obviously remained purposely vague.

Clearly she had gotten all she would get from her friend today. "Yeah, sure, have at it." Charli might be agreeing, but she continued to be intrigued. She stood to go and tossed a twenty on the table where their bill lay and placed the saltshaker on top of it. "So, are you and Clay meeting Eli and I tonight at the Ten Mile House? We want to talk through some wedding stuff with you guys."

Jaiden picked up the red stick. "Sure thing. It's a rarity for Doc and me to have the same night off these days. I'm looking forward to the evening with y'all."

They left the diner. Charli strolled toward the paint store.

Jaiden waved as she crossed to the sheriff's office. "See you there, and thanks for breakfast."

Chapter Six

Charli brought in the paint cans she'd purchased after coffee with Jaiden and sat them on the kitchen counter. Eli appeared from the butler's pantry.

"Morning, sunshine. Thanks for picking up supplies. I can't wait to freshen up these antique cabinets. A fresh coat of paint will make them shine." He pecked Charli on the nose.

She raised her lips to receive his next sweet kiss. "How'd you sleep your first night in our haunted house?"

"No worries. Guess our spiritual inhabitant must approve of me. I slept like a rock."

He opened the freshly mixed paint can and selected a brush. Having already set up two step ladders at opposite ends of the rows of cabinets, they were ready to begin their chore.

Charli followed suit and climbed one of them. Eli handed her a brush and paint tray full of the soft shade of ecru she'd selected.

"Thanks for removing all the doors, knobs, and hinges. Painting them outside will keep the mess in here down and make drying quicker. It's gorgeous outside, a fresh autumn day."

While they worked, she told Eli about her conversation with Jaiden and the deputy's interest in her found object.

"That is a bit strange. I'm sure it's nothing. Those

hair sticks are probably fairly common, and it didn't appear to be an expensive piece. Likely many people have them."

"Yeah, I guess so. I'm sure you're right. Still, weird my best friend thinks I could have anything at all to do with that dead guy."

A few hours later, they'd finished with the cabinet bases. Eli washed his hands and smiled.

"I'm starved. How about I run over to the Royal Diner and pick us up a couple of burgers and some fries?"

She rubbed her growling stomach. "I'll research that hair pick while you're gone. It's got me curious."

He kissed her on the nose, grabbed his wallet and left. "Back soon."

Charli sat outside on a bench soaking up early afternoon sun while she logged online and scanned through hair implements. It didn't take long before one similar to hers popped up. They were cheap, as expected, and were normally purchased in bundles of ten or twos.

Satisfied hers was likely not connected to Jaiden's investigation, she decided to take a stroll. She'd tucked a copy of the property plat in her overall's bib pocket before leaving home that morning. She pulled it out, then carried it to the back of the yard where the cut lawn ended in woodland and sloped downhill.

She quickly located the border side of the plat and a few yards downward in the woods, stumbled on remains from an ancient, barbed wire fence. This side would be closest to the dead-end street way down below the mansion.

She followed ruins of fencing and took care of her steps so as not to get tangled in brush grown thick over many years of neglect. Thankfully, she'd worn work boots, as always while on the job. The utilitarian shoes were comfortable for long hours on her feet.

Eventually, she reached the riverbank. Ohio River water lapped gently against a stretch of sandy shoreline about ten feet deep. The only footprints she found were those of small animals. Homeless vagrants tenting closer to town didn't appear to have invaded her land, at least not yet.

Charli picked up a muddy, plastic soft drink bottle and a water-soaked candy wrapper that looked to have washed up in the current. After pulling a plastic grocery bag from her jeans pocket, she stuffed the refuse inside and tied it to a loop on her pants. "Why the heck do people have to litter?"

Then again, those items could've escaped someone on a boat in the wind.

She walked the borderline again, this time uphill. Stopping at about where she figured the hillside would line up with the dead-end street, she climbed carefully over rusted wire and rotting posts. Trekking softly, she eventually discovered crime scene tape that roped off the vicinity around where Jaiden and her cohorts searched for clues concerning the homicide.

It gnawed at Charli that the deceased had been identified as a known associate of gangsters. Sure, Kentucky had strong historical ties to mob activity. Why did it keep rearing its ugly head in quiet Sweetwater? Hopefully, it would have nothing to do with her this time. At least she satisfied herself the body hadn't been discovered on her and Eli's property.

She returned from her hike as Eli strolled out of the kitchen door with two paper bags in hand. One emitted a delightful fragrance of freshly fried potatoes and mouthwatering burgers. He sat them on a bench, opened one and handed her an icy bottle of water.

"Where have you been?"

She wiped sweat from her brow with the back of a hand, then opened the bottle and took a long swig. "Thanks. I needed that." She sat on the other end of the seat, the food bags between them. "I was curious about the borderline of our land. So, I decided to take a little journey down toward the riverbank to makes sure that dead guy wasn't killed on our property. There's an old fence that seems to follow the surveyed plat perfectly. I followed it, and on my way back up, I located the CSI yellow tape. He wasn't, though the perimeter they marked is nearby."

Eli sighed heavily as he closed his eyes. "Babe, I understand your curiosity, but a man was killed there. Not only that, who knows what criminals live in that homeless camp along the river? You shouldn't have gone down there alone. If you were that intrigued, you could've waited for me to get back. I'd have been happy to go along and humor you." Eli knew better than to tell her what she should and shouldn't do, and his expression showed it as soon as the words came out of his mouth.

"I really didn't give it much thought. I sat here sunning, and curiosity got the better of me. I decided it was a better use of my downtime." She reached for a burger.

His eyes were sharp and serious. "You might've put yourself in danger. I can't bear you being in harm's way. Please, stay out of that murder case. We've got enough on our plates without getting involved in something that doesn't concern us."

She gave him a conceding nod. He wasn't wrong, after all.

"Fine, and you're right. I looked up that hair thingie. Apparently, they are cheap and popular. The one I found most likely had nothing to do with Jaiden's case."

He unwrapped his sandwich. The delectable aroma made her mouth water. "I figured as much."

Chapter Seven

Charli and Eli strolled into The Ten Mile House. Jaiden and her fiancé, Dr. Clay Barnes, sat on barstools chatting with the owner, paraplegic ex-biker, Justin Henderson, and his wife, Corrie, CEO of her family's conglomerate, Adelle Industries.

Charli took the empty stool beside Jaiden. "Hi, guys, what's shaking?"

Handsome, straight-laced surgeon, Clay smiled. "We were discussing the dead guy they found in the woods the other day."

Jaiden's dark skin turned a rosier shade of bronze, but she didn't contribute to the conversation. Clearly, treading water, Jaiden stayed diligent about protecting an ongoing investigation.

Justin's dark complexion and raven hair complimented his handsome features. Though short for a man, he was known for his strength. If he didn't work out daily with weights, the guy would be in a wheelchair. Instead he loaded cartons of beer into the bar's cooler daily.

"That dude came into the tavern a couple days earlier. Said he was looking for someone—a brown-haired young woman. Didn't say why and didn't give her name, but he showed me a photo and passed it around to a few regulars who were here at the time. No one recalled seeing her. At least, if they did, no one told him so."

Justin continued, "He didn't stick around long. Just bought a round, asked his questions, drank half of his, and took off. Never saw him again."

Charli looked over Jaiden's shoulder, as the jean-clad deputy pulled her phone out and noted what Justin said. Justin watched Jaiden text the information to Sheriff Gordon and Deputy Sanders, and then he smiled.

Corrie's locks curled sexily down her slim back. The spicy blonde had a figure that could stop a stampede of wild horses and a spicy character to match. She snickered. "Looks like we're in for a rodeo, fellas. Just when peace was restored to Sweetwater another mystery is in the works. Jaiden, looks like you've got your work cut out for you."

Eli pointed to the cowboy and sunglass-wearing prosthesis sitting on the bar in front of Justin. "I see Bubba is joining us tonight."

They all laughed. Justin had a habit of pulling his prosthesis off for a rest and dressing it up ridiculously to get a laugh out of customers.

Justin dusted the snakeskin boots on the false leg. "Yep, just until Corrie is in a dancing mood. Nothing stops me from dancing with my gorgeous wife." He paused for their laughter. "You know, I love these cowboy boots, but shoes are just a whimsey for old Fred here."

Charli put a hand on Jaiden's arm. "So, did you learn anything from the hair pick I found?"

Jaiden gazed down and inhaled slowly. Obviously choosing her words with care. "Actually, the coroner found DNA on it, but it was distorted. Did you clean it with bleach?"

Charli nodded. "Sorry about that, if I destroyed

pertinent evidence. It looked disgusting. I found it lying in soap scum and grime and didn't want to put it in my hair in that condition. I cleaned it up as best I could."

Corrie sneered. "Yuck! I don't blame you."

Jaiden eyed Charli. "Bleach can destroy DNA, but it needs to be immersed in it for a couple of hours. When you scrubbed that stick with bleach cleaner, you might've altered but not completely removed it."

Charli's nose curled. "I found it in our renovation house. I couldn't trash it—too pretty. I don't see how that lovely thing could have anything to do with your case. The mansion has been vacant for years."

Justin chuckled. "Except for ghosts."

Eli laughed. "Yeah, the neighbors ensured we heard the rumors right away."

Jaiden rolled her eyes. "We've had several calls from witnesses who swear they either saw someone roaming the grounds in the dark or shadows that moved around inside. We checked on the place when incidents were reported but never found anything to substantiate the claims. It's always been locked up tight…until you two bought it." She nodded to Eli, who sat on the other side of Clay, and then to Charli to her right.

Charli bit the side of her lip, and an eerie sensation came over her. "No biggie. I just kept it on a whim. It was pretty, but it had a sliver missing anyway."

Jaiden's head tilted, and her ebony hair rocked to the side over her shoulder. The deputy frowned. "Yeah, about that…Coroner Baker discovered something else in it. A tiny strand of hair was stuck in that crevice where the sliver broke off."

There's more to this than Jaiden's sharing.

"My hair? That would make sense. Must've gotten

caught when I stuck it in my bun."

Jaiden winced. "Afraid not."

One of Charli's brows curled. "Seriously? Gross, I assumed I got the yuck off it." She cringed at the idea of someone else's hair in her mop of wild curls.

Jaiden scowled. "A minuscule bit stuck beneath the cracked wood where the sliver broke off. Apparently, its owner had bleached blonde hair. The fragment wasn't noticeable to the naked eye. Baker found it under a microscope and sent it to be tested for DNA. We'll check it against a strand discovered at the crime scene on a nearby branch. Chances are it won't match."

Corrie rolled her eyes and shivered. Her hand raked through her long, blonde curls. "It wasn't mine...thank the stars. I have never been in those woods."

Charli cringed, sorry she'd even found it. "Mine either. Far as I'm concerned, you can keep the darned thing. I don't want it back. So, the other blonde hair you have in evidence wasn't on the dead guy but was near him?" She ran a finger through her honey-colored curls.

Jaiden shook her head.

Clay looked at his woman. "Does that mean you're looking for a blonde-haired woman?"

"Let's say an unidentified blonde female is a person of interest."

Eli's nose squirreled up. "Why did you have interest in the hair pick in the first place?"

Jaiden sighed. "I might as well tell you. We discovered a similar hair pick in the vicinity of where the corpse was found. We're trying to determine the source of a certain wound on the body."

Charli gasped. "Holy crap! Are you saying that pretty thing might've been the murder weapon?"

Jaiden sighed heavily and stared at the bar in front of her. "I didn't say that. A similar item was located nearby. We found quite a lot of things in the roped-off perimeter. Mostly items like empty beer cans, bottle caps, discarded rubbers, and evidence of bonfires. You name it."

Charli shivered. "I would guess it's a convenient location for kids to park and do whatever. Party. Make out. You know, the last house on that dead-end street is half a block away. It's quiet and private."

Jaiden looked at Charli, a bland expression on her face. "Apparently."

The group nodded their heads, and Eli scowled. "I'm not sure I care for that kind of activity so close to our property line."

Justin's brows rose. "And that homeless faction camps near there along the river."

Jaiden sighed. "We'll go down there tomorrow to question everyone we can find. Maybe someone living there saw or knows something relevant."

Corrie's brilliant blue eyes grew larger. "Good luck with that. I'd suspect those people won't be happy to have cops show up. They're probably avoiding y'all." Corrie spent a lot of time in her New York City headquarters, but her Kentucky accent hadn't waned.

Jaiden shook her head. "Baker sent the hair to be tested for DNA. The victim was not blonde. They ran it through the database to see if there was a match. So far, we've found none." She gave Charli a pointed gaze. "Could we talk about dress fittings? There's less than two months before your wedding. I'm not sure how long it will take for the seamstress to make adjustments."

Charli understood Jaiden's need to change the

subject. "Sure, and I can't wait to see them. They finally arrived from the dressmaker's New York shop." It would be a pleasant relief to think about a topic other than a murderer—one who had likely gained access to their house...still on the loose.

There was more to this pick thing than Jaiden could admit to. Charli would bet on it. What was her friend hiding?

Chapter Eight

The following morning, Charli and Gran sat at the counter in the great room and touched base over morning coffee. Gran pointed to a fresh article in the newspaper. "Sheriff Wyatt stated to the press they are looking for a person of interest. Evidence indicated a blonde female had at some point been near the crime scene. Wyatt said that clue was not on the corpse."

Charli scowled. "That doesn't mean my hair pick was involved. Jaiden said it only appeared to match one found near the crime scene. She also mentioned they would compare to see if it, or a similar weapon, might've created a wound."

Gran scowled. "Wound? You mean it could've been the murder weapon?"

Charli shrugged. "Don't know. Jaiden wouldn't say. Apparently, the guy had a puncture wound. It had to do with a shard of wood she thinks came from that stupid hair thing I found. She didn't say where they found the splinter."

Gran put the paper down. "I wouldn't worry too much about it, Charli. It's probably completely unrelated. You know how these things go—especially after that debacle where they accused Wes of murdering his partner and assistant. The police must check every scrap of evidence. Otherwise, the wrong person could be convicted, and a killer might go scot-free. If it weren't for us, your grandfather would be rotting in jail now instead of finalizing his retirement at his New York corporate office."

"Yeah, that was one gigantic mess." Charli eyed her grandmother curiously. She'd come up with an idea during her restless night. "Gran, what are your plans for today?"

Gran shrugged and stood, then poured more coffee. "I don't know. I was thinking of attending water aerobics. Tonight is my card club meeting, but nothing's set in stone for the day." The woman never missed poker night with the ladies. She sat the pot down and put a hand on her hip. "Why? What's up your sleeve?"

Charli snickered and stood. "How would you feel about making some of your special chocolate chunk cookies? We could go visit your pal, Sam Baker, and take him a plateful."

Gran glared at her granddaughter with a snicker. "I'll be happy to. It's been a while since I've seen Sam. He's a sucker for my cookies. Poor baby has an insatiable sweet tooth."

Charli pulled a jar from a cabinet. "He likes your blackberry jam. We have several left. Let's take him one." She chose a red ribbon from a drawer and tied it around the neck of the pint glass container.

As Gran set about selecting ingredients to bake the cookies, Charli chose a serving plate. She sat a sheet of cellophane beneath it and another ribbon to tie the dishful with once the aromatic delicacies cooled.

Charli chuckled. "That poor man is putty in your hands, Gran. You know, he's madly in love with you."

Gran nodded sadly. "I do, but he's always known Wes owns my heart. Sam is the best of friends, and he's okay with that. As much as I cared for him, I was open with him from the start. I never told him who that person was until Wes showed up. Sam and I were longtime friends-with-benefits, as they used to say. Once Wes forgave me, Sam knew I only had eyes for him."

Charli found a gift bag to put the plate and jam in. Once the gift was ready, the twosome set out for the coroner's office.

****

Gran knocked and then opened the door. Dr. Sam Baker wore a white jacket over his clothing and sat at a desk with his hands on the keyboard of his laptop.

"Ladies, come on in. This is a pleasant surprise."

Charli eyed a table beside his desk lined with filled evidence containers. She spotted a bag of clothing, one with socks, others full of things like beer cans, candy wrappers, and assorted strange pieces of what seemed to be trash. These were clearly from the murder scene.

The balding man stood and covered the evidence with a sheet as he smiled at his guests. His short stature made him only about a couple of inches taller than Gran, probably around five-foot-six. His wide grin showed sparkling whites and plumped his cheeks even more, and his eyes expressed genuine joy.

Gran handed him the dish. "We brought treats."

Charli set the jar of jam on his desk. "I hope we didn't choose a bad time."

His computer showed a data screen, and a file lay open on the desktop. A report stuck out of it, and only the top fourth of the page was visible. Good thing Charli had total recall and good eyesight. The information she viewed became appropriately filed in her brain.

He glanced over his shoulder at his desk and shook

his head. "Not at all. I'm just entering some forensic data into the computer." He smiled down at the plate and sniffed the aroma with closed eyes and a broad smile. "My goodness, Irma, you gals sure know the way to an old man's heart."

Gran grinned. "It's been a while since we had a visit, so I decided to just drop by. Charli was free, so she came along."

Charli tried to act like it was a spur-of-the-moment thing, but they all knew she had an ulterior motive. "I hope you don't mind."

Doc placed the cookies on the desk and quickly closed the folder. "Not at all." He unwrapped the treats, selected one, and indicated they should join him.

Both women waved his invitation away.

"Enjoy." Charli smiled and noted the sparkle in his eyes as he gazed lovingly at Gran. No hiding his adoration.

Meanwhile, Charli strained to read what was visible in the medical examiner's report. Certain words caught her eye—puncture, COD: GSW. A chill zipped down Charli's spine. She shivered, and then confusion hit. *GSW—gunshot wound?*

After chewing, Doc eyed them as though not fooled. "So, ladies, what can I do you for today?"

Charli chuckled, and her face heated. "Well, actually, I was curious if you could tell us what you've learned about the hair pick that I gave Jaiden. She said it was related to the murder case she's investigating. I assume you're working on that."

His head rocked up and down. "Indeed, but first, let me tell you about another guy I know with a penchant for sweets. Poor fella was on his deathbed when he smelled his favorite chocolate chip cookies. With his last strength, he got out of bed and dragged himself to the kitchen. His wife of fifty years baked those beautiful delicacies." Doc picked up another cookie and waved it in front of him as he pretended to sniff it. "She plated four of them, fresh from the oven. With his last human strength, the man reached for one. She slapped his hand and said, '*No, they are for the funeral*.'" Doc stuffed a bite into his mouth and slapped his leg with a hearty laugh.

Gran chuckled. "Oh, Sam, you've got fresh material."

Charlie gave him a boisterous laugh to humor the funny little man. "Doc, you never fail to supply a captured audience with humor. Your jokes may be grim, but they're always entertaining."

He cackled. "Well, when a guy faces death each and every day, he has to find humor in life to stay sane."

Charli laughed. "I suppose that's true."

Doc eyed her with a more serious look. "So, when will you and Eli tie the knot?"

Happy to take the subject off mortality for a few minutes, she smiled. "We've set a date of December 20. It's a holiday wedding."

Doc's smile grew wide. "Oh, that should be lovely. I suppose you'll use holiday colors. Just think, the church will already be decked with poinsettias and Christmas décor."

"Yes, and Wes will walk me down the aisle. He and Gran will give me away."

Doc didn't smile. "Good, I'm happy for you."

Doc's soberness was understandable. Wesley Drake had swooped into town with his silver hair, square jaw, and pale green eyes and taken over Doc's place as Gran's main man.

Wesley Drake, Gran's promoter and agent since the sixteen-year-old singer had gone on the road with her band, The Terrestrials, had helped her become famous as Starr Bright for several decades. They'd briefly been lovers before a traumatic breakup. When Wes swooped into town, Doc and Wes had tried to become friends. Charli could only hope. She wanted a relationship with her newly discovered grandfather, and she respected her lifelong friendship with Doc Baker.

Doc snickered, like he knew about matrimony, though he'd never taken the step himself. Had he pined for Gran all those years?

"Let me tell you something. What's the difference between marriage and death?"

Gran chuckled. "I'm afraid to ask."

The doctor resumed with a snide grin. "When you're dead, you don't wish you were married."

Gran swatted his arm jokingly. "Now, Sam, don't go putting marriage down. Charli's about to take that big step."

The doctor laughed at his own humor and smiled at Charli. "Sorry, sweetie. I'm sure that young man of yours will keep you very happy. He'd better, or he'll answer to me."

He cupped his hand around Gran's ear and whispered, "How do we know death is a man?"

She cocked her head and furrowed her brows. "Don't know."

"He comes quicker than expected."

It was impossible to make Gran blush, but she pushed out a huff of laughter. "Oh, Sam, you're incorrigible."

He shrugged. "I'm afraid it's incurable, a fatal flaw." He paused while they laughed at his corny pun. "Now, what may I assist you with, Charli?"

"I hoped you could tell me what you've learned about the hair pick I gave Jaiden. She said it might be connected to her murder case. You know, the guy they found in the woods."

His head rocked back, and his mouth opened wide. "Ahh, I figured as much. I'm limited as to what I can share since it's an ongoing investigation."

Gran put a hand on his knee. "We realize that Sam. No one wants you to discuss case evidence, but Charli is involved in this thing. We have a right to know to what extent."

"Well," he glanced over his shoulder at his computer and then back to her. "I understand you washed the item several times before you wore it. Even though bleach marred DNA, trace blood evidence remained. That doesn't mean it was the victim's blood. It could've been that of the owner—the wearer. The bleach you used destroyed the possibility to obtain clear DNA from it, so we were unable to do a viable comparison of it and that of the dead fella."

Gran stared intensely at his face. He twitched—a sign he hid something.

"So, have you ruled it to be of no use in the case?"

He hesitated. "Not exactly."

Charli tried to relieve his anxiety about oversharing. "Jaiden said there was a blonde hair in the thing's crevice."

She touched her honey-colored locks. Maybe if he realized they knew that much, he would share more.

His expression looked more relaxed. "Yes, indeed. There was a tiny piece you'd been unable to see or remove. I extracted it with tweezers after I viewed it under a scope."

Charli filled in more of what Jaiden had shared. "She said there was another blonde hair found at the scene. Not on the body either. Right?"

She and Gran sat in guest chairs across from him. His back faced the desk, which butted against a wall. Over his shoulder, Charli noticed a small plastic bag stuck out of the manila folder on his desk. It contained a slice of something red—the color of her hair stick.

Coincidence? Hell no.

He nodded, expressionless. "No, it was on a nearby branch. There was a lot of evidence at the scene. We've been through every article and tried to determine what was there prior versus what had to do with the murder. It's been a difficult, time-consuming chore."

Gran helped relieve building tension. "The paper said Wyatt had shared with them that the blonde female is a person of interest and not a suspect. Do they think she's the murderer?"

Charli tried to read more of the coroner's computer report. Disappointingly, the screen went black from non-use.

He grimaced. "Yes, at this time, that is true."

Gran grinned. "What you do is fascinating, Sam. You're the coroner, but you're also a medical examiner, right?"

He smiled. "Indeed. As county coroner, I'm responsible for determining what cases require autopsies. I do my fair share of them, mostly just for Sweetwater Township. Five medical examiners in the county report to me and do autopsies required in their assigned areas. Of course, in times of disaster or overwork, we help each other out."

Gran's eyes widened. "That's a lot of responsibility on your shoulders. I'm duly impressed. So, what's all that stuff in evidence bags on that table? I apologize. You know how inquisitive I am. Can't help myself. I couldn't avoid noticing it before you covered it up."

He shrugged, shook his head, and blinked. "No worries. The CSI team was here earlier. They boxed items to take to their lab and will be back soon for the last of it. Sometimes, evidence is attached to the body, like clothing or jewelry. Sometimes, it's picked out of the corpse's hair, off their skin, or from under their nails. Other times, items close to the body end up in my lab first. They are cataloged and taken to the CSI lab for further examination."

Gran purred. "Oooo, a very heavy burden you have, my friend."

Gran's little chatter with Sam gave Charli time to consider what she'd seen and read on Sam's screen, which he obviously assumed was out of her sightline.

Charli glared down her nose at her old friend. "You don't believe that the blonde woman is the murderer. Do you, Doc?"

His eyes squeezed shut, and his lips pursed. He opened them with a sigh. "I can't say. That pick ties the female to the victim. If you tell anyone I told you this, I will adamantly deny it."

Naturally, Gran was the bold one. She shot straight to the question on their minds. "Was it the murder weapon?"

The poor man's face blushed to a reddish shade of

purple. He blinked several times as he stared at his shoes. "I cannot divulge critical information on an ongoing case. That item resembled a chopstick, and it is critical evidence." His shoulders slumped as he gave Charli a grave, sorrowful expression.

A chill sped down her spine. She shivered. He didn't want to tell her the thing that had corralled her honey-colored mop into a bun had been the murder weapon. Or had it? The report said COD: GSW. That meant the cause of death was a gunshot wound.

Charli breathed an inhale of relief. Her hair pick didn't kill the victim, but it still had to do with the dead man…and the mysterious, missing blonde.

"Was he stabbed to death?"

Doc flinched. "No, a puncture wound was not the cause of death."

Gran blushed. "Thank you for sharing that with us, Sam. It puts our minds at rest…somewhat."

Charli winced. Clearly, this was all they would get out of their old friend today. Was the stranger stabbed—just not to death?

"No worries, Doc." Charli paused. "It's been interesting to learn more about your work. I appreciate your time today and hope you don't take offense to all our questions. I feel close to the situation since I seem to have stumbled upon a clue in that hair thing."

Maybe no worries for Sam Baker. Charli was not as lucky. She stood to go.

Gran did likewise. "We'd best get out of your hair. I'm sure you have work to do, and we've got a wedding to plan."

He pushed a smile back onto his face as he followed them to the door. A hand rested gently on each of their backs. "You know, it's October. You don't have much time left to arrange that marriage ceremony of yours. I guess I'd better shake my tux out of mothballs and have it cleaned."

He chuckled and returned slowly to his normal jovial self. "Did I tell you about my friend who rushed into the kitchen and told his wife, 'I stabbed a vampire, beat zombies to death, and killed the devil himself.' She gasped, 'You were supposed to give them candy, sweetheart. It's Halloween.'" His head lolled backward as he burst into laughter. Clearly, Doc enjoyed his own humor.

Gran pecked her old friend on the cheek. "Good one, Sam."

"Doc, you're hilarious. Don't ever change." Charli chuckled.

Why had that silly stick been in her house?

Why did she find it?

What the hell was going on?

Chapter Nine

Of course, Charli shared what they learned with Eli. She kept no secrets from him—not anymore. Her man was trustworthy. He'd proven more than once her life was safe with him.

What about his life? He lived in their project house. Had a cold-blooded killer—the mysterious missing blonde woman—broken into their property to take a shower and wash away evidence of a murder she'd committed?

"Eli, you could be in danger."

"Look, Charli, you know I can handle myself. Besides, we've gone over this monstrous structure with a fine-toothed comb. It's locked up tight as a preacher's wallet on Sunday morning. This murder happened, according to the paper, just before we took possession of the place. If someone committed homicide, they could've washed up here without being caught. They would be long gone now. You must admit, if this blonde gal did the deed, cleaning up in a vacant house was pretty smart. When they find this person, and they will, there will be no blood evidence at their home."

Charli rolled her eyes. "I'm not prepared to admire the wits of a cold-blooded killer. That woman stabbed that guy and then shot him. Doc's report said he was killed by a gunshot wound. I tried to pry it out of Jaiden at the dress fitting, but she wasn't about to give out any more information."

"Of course not. Any facts she shared might prevent them from catching the culprit. We'd best stay out of it. Charli, babe, we don't know this female did it. She's only sought as a person of interest, not a suspect in the killing. Either way, she isn't in this house now, and it's locked up tight."

"Yeah, you might be right. That agrees with what Wyatt told the press. What Doc said is much more sinister, and what I saw on his report just about floored me. It makes me almost sure that the thing I found was used in the murder. It might not have been what killed the guy, but it exonerates me—not that they seriously considered me involved. The police believe it could be the object used to stab the man. Doc's report contained data I couldn't read about a puncture. Bloodstains on the pick were distorted but not completely gone. My washing it only keeps them from identifying whether it was blood from the victim or someone else. An evidence bag stuck out of Doc's file. It appeared to hold a sliver of red-painted wood. It might've been the missing piece that had broken off my hair pick. I wanted to ask him outright, but we'd already put the poor guy through the wringer. It looked like he became nervous talking with us, but there's more he's not telling. I have a feeling it's enough to implicate our uninvited guest as the culprit. That person was in our house. It frightens me…more for you than for me. You live here."

He pulled her into his arms in a hug that warmed her breasts against his belly. Her head rested on his chest. His heartbeat on her cheek comforted her racing mind. She remained in the safety of his embrace for a while to relish the closeness.

"Just promise me you'll stay alert and be careful. I couldn't bear it if something happened to you." She'd lost enough people in her lifetime.

"I promise. I'll be fine. We've checked the windows as we resealed them. We changed the locks on the house. Whoever might've had access to the place before we took residence, I'm certain they can't get in again—not without breaking a window."

He lifted her chin with a gentle finger, and she melted into his lingering kiss. "Now, if you feel better, we've got tons of work to do." One hand playfully patted her rear.

"Okay. Keep that up, and we'll never get started. Paint is dry. I'll put doors and fixtures on the kitchen and butler's parlor cabinets. You want to refinish mantles in the dining and living rooms?"

"Sounds like a plan." He released her.

They set about completing those chores for a full day's work and then had dinner with Gran at her and Charli's home. Afterward, Eli returned to the project house—alone—or so they hoped.

****

At the mansion, Eli once again inspected doors and windows to ensure the place was locked and he was by himself. He took stock in the elaborately carved, enormous, floor-to-tall-ceiling chifforobe built into the end wall of the second-floor hallway. It was a truly unique piece, and he was happy previous owners had seen fit to leave it intact.

Not only was it one-of-a-kind and gorgeous, the wardrobe was utilitarian. Historically, such homes had none or only a couple of actual closets. People then didn't maintain as abundant a wardrobe as most do these days. Much of their clothing was stored in drawers. Very few items needed hanging. Since construction, various inhabitants had erected a handful of crude bedroom closets. Eli and Charli planned to modernize those, make them more usable, and add a couple more.

The only other wardrobe in the house was a smaller, but similar one on the third floor inside the old nursery area that took up most of the top floor. It, too, was finely crafted and beautifully carved. Both pieces were works of art. Luckily, they had remained as part of the house— probably because it would've been too much trouble to detach and move the large, heavy items.

Oh, well, our win.

****

The following day, Charli and Eli worked together to remove old layers of varnish from the curving mahogany staircase, careful not to drip chemicals on the beautiful marble steps. Charli applied the first layer and removed it. Eli stood and stretched his aching muscles, tired of bending, hunched over.

"How about a break? I'm starving. Let's get some lunch."

Charli rolled her head from side to side. "Good idea. I could eat."

He started down the steps. "How does leftover lasagna sound? Irma sent some home with me the night before last. It's in the refrigerator."

Charli admired his long, lean legs and his easy stride as she followed him downstairs. His tight buttocks provided a pleasant view. Damn, she loved that man. Just the sight of him gave her heart a thrill. Working beside him every day was a dream come true, and the reality of spending her life with him filled her with enough emotion to take her breath away.

"Suits me fine." Not only Gran's cooking—

She followed her man to the kitchen. While he peeked into the fridge, she washed her hands in the sink. He moved things around and around, continuing to search with a huff.

"What's the matter?"

He stood tall, hands on hips, and shut the door. "I can't find it."

Her brow furrowed, as she dried her hands. "What do you mean?"

"I mean, I moved the contents around in there twice. That dish of lasagna isn't in there. I recall Irma handed it to me as we left. I *think* I put it in the truck."

"Are you sure you didn't sit it down when you gave me that incredible goodnight kiss at the door?" She winked.

He snickered. "I don't think so."

"Maybe you forgot to bring it in from the truck."

"I'll go check, but I would've sworn I stored it in the refrigerator when I got home." He left her to go out and look for the food in his vehicle. "It was in a disposable tin covered with foil. I recall it distinctly." He looked confused.

She pulled dishes and silverware from the cabinets and set the table. They had to eat something. She was starving.

Eli returned minutes later with a baffled look on his face. "I checked under and behind the seats, in the glove compartment, and even in my toolbox. Not there."

She shrugged. "Maybe it fell on the ground as you got out. Animals might've carried it off and eaten it. No worries, I can run down to the deli and pick up a couple of salads. Sound good?"

Eli shook his head at the dilemma, strolled to the sink, and then washed his hands. "Sure. Guess so. Sounds good. Whatever you want."

"Look, Eli, maybe one of the workers came in and helped himself to the leftovers. Who knows? One of them asked to use our microwave yesterday, to heat his lunch up. I said sure."

Workmen had erected scaffolding around the perimeter of the house so they could sandblast the bricks. Another crew moved a lift from wall to wall as they repaired the slate roof. Having all the extra people around was inconvenient, but Eli and Charli had decided to deal with it.

Her pal, Bubba Larson, had gone out of his way to get his roofers on the job as quickly as possible. Sometimes getting contractors was difficult, but Charli had the in with most businesses in town. People in the community practically raised Charli and Kyler. They all looked at her as their girl and her younger brother, Kyler, as their little guy.

Funny because now he was grown and in college, the long, lanky youth stood as tall as Eli's six-foot-six inches. Since working out with weights, the kid had finally bulked up some muscles. That worked well as he quarterbacked the college football team.

****

The partners avoided the increasingly sensitive subject of their mysterious invader, the murder, and the red Chinese stick as they ate a quick lunch. They then reassumed the task at hand. Tension was there under the surface, where Eli preferred it to stay. What was past was past, and he didn't like it to interfere with their present or their priorities.

Safe in the house, hopefully, he'd alleviated Charli's concern for him. They needed to focus on work and not things out of their control.

Irma had followed their lead and didn't bring up the subjects. The aging rock-n-roll star had obviously picked up on his and Charli's moods and steered dinner conversation toward wedding plans and progress on the renovation.

As he'd kissed Charli goodnight at the door, she'd held onto him tightly—not passionately, but like she was hesitant to release him. He jokingly tweaked her nose and planted a kiss on the tip. "See you tomorrow, sunshine. Don't forget the bagels."

She swatted his behind with one hand, the other remaining wrapped around his waist. "Wouldn't dare. I know the routine. If I expect any work out of you, I have to feed the monster in your stomach first. Bagels and cream cheese it is; just make sure you have the coffee ready. That's my go-fuel."

"Yeah." He released her and backed toward the door. "No worries, sunshine. I'll feed your caffeine addiction."

As usual, he hated to leave the little minx who had stolen his heart. Nights were long without her petite body curled inside his arms. He could barely wait for December 20 to come.

The laborers were gone when he arrived at the mansion. Once he'd ensured the place was sealed and he was alone, he settled down for a lonesome but much-needed sleep.

A snap sounded from somewhere upstairs. Eli's eyes shot wide, and he cocked an ear to listen. The house emitted many a strange creak, as old houses did, but this was different. He flipped the covers off and set his bare feet into slippers. Snatching a hoodie sweatshirt jacket from a chair, he slipped it on and trudged to the foyer. He tried the handle. The door proved to be locked, as he'd left it. No windows appeared to have been opened.

He continued to listen with a keen ear as he slowly took one step at a time up the stairs. Nothing. No noise. Only the sounds of his house shoes as they gently landed on the marble steps.

On the second floor, he checked windows and doors in all four rooms and opened closets to ensure they remained empty. The bathroom was clear, as was the hallway that circled the central stairway. He opened the massive wardrobe. The inside was void of trespassers.

He took the same journey to the third floor and repeated his search in the bathroom, maid quarters, bedrooms, and nursery area. The only thing left was the second, slightly smaller wardrobe. With a deep breath, he stilled his pounding heart, snatched the knob, and whipped the door wide.

Nothing.

"What the hell was that noise?" He shrugged, closed the door, and stood for a moment.

There was no sound to be heard inside. He leaned on the windowsill. Outside, a slight breeze whispered through trees and whipped colorful red, yellow, and orange leaves from the autumn spectacle they'd created on the grounds.

"A branch must've fallen and landed on the roof or hit the house." His shoulders rocked up and down.

"What the heck? I'm getting into the habit of talking to myself. Man, I need our wedding over and Charli by my side." He twisted his neck around to relieve the tension that built there. With a sigh, he gave up the search and fell into his lonely, solitary bed.

Chapter Ten

Charli arrived with the sunrise, as promised, with breakfast fresh from the bakery. As he poured her a cup of hot coffee, she sat at the card table they'd put in the huge kitchen. The temporary fixture would soon be replaced with the island they planned to build and would leave space near the fireplace at one end for a table area for future residents.

"So, what's on the agenda today? The banister could use another layer of paint remover before we stain it. Should any other chore be a higher priority?"

He plopped into the chair beside her. "Actually, I'd like to explore more of the basement. We did a walkthrough before the sale, but I'd like to take a closer look. The rest of the house is sufficiently locked. I want to make sure the basement is as well."

Her head leaned a tad, and her brows crunched together as she stared at him as though trying to read his intentions. "Why the sudden interest in security? You've been so confident the place is as safe as Fort Knox whenever I've brought up the subject."

He shrugged one shoulder, and his head rolled to that side to avoid her gaze as he chewed a bite of his bagel. He finally swallowed. "Oh, nothing much. I just don't want to go on assumptions. We really should check out the tunnel system the Underground Railroad used. It would be a shame if it wasn't locked properly, and some animal got in. A wild creature loose in a house like this could cause major damage. We need to protect our work and supplies from that possibility."

"Uh-huh." Obviously, she didn't buy his confident act and knew something else bothered him.

He took a sip of his coffee. Only his slurping broke the silence between them. "Maybe we should consider installing a security system. It could be a great asset to advertise and might increase the value more than its cost."

She sneered, leaned against her chair back, and crossed her arms. "Ah, yeah. What gives, Eli? Something happened, didn't it?"

He couldn't fool Charli. She knew his tells, like she knew every inch of his six-foot-six body. A chill shivered through him, not sure if it was passion or premonition. He took her soft, delicate hand in his huge one and brought the exquisite, silky appendage to his lips.

"It's nothing, babe. I didn't want to alarm you unnecessarily. I just heard some weird sounds last night. One really—a loud thud upstairs. I checked and found nothing out of the ordinary. A branch must've hit the house. There was quite a bit of wind, you know."

"Yeah." She took a final swig of coffee to swallow down her remaining bagel bite. Then she stood, hands on hips. "Come on. We'll check out the perimeter to see what it was."

Eli followed her out the back door. She nodded to the left. "You go that way. I'll go this direction." She set off to the right.

As he edged around the building, he looked up and down and made sure all was fine. No broken branches lay on the ground that might've fallen during the night. Scanning the scaffolding, it looked fine.

He rounded the front corner as Charli came from the other side. Trucks filled with workers parked. Men stepped out. Charli greeted them and inquired whether any of them had been there during the night. None had.

Eli joined her, said good morning to the workmen, and slid an arm around her waist. "Nothing strange to that side of the house."

"Yeah, I found *nada* either. The guys all said they hadn't been here since they left yesterday. Whatever you heard hit the house must've blown away in the wind."

"Yeah, I guess you're right. Or the scaffold could've wavered in the breeze. It might've knocked against a brick wall. Still, I want to inspect the basement."

Bubba Larson showed up before they could do that. "Morning, Charli, Eli. I just came to inspect the work and make sure we're on schedule."

"Good to see you." Charli gave her old pal a friendly hug. "Thanks for putting our house as a priority. Time is money, as they say. The sooner this place is completed, the quicker we can sell it and move on." She didn't look convinced about that.

The idea of selling the old mansion caused a heavy sensation in Eli's chest. The old girl might have a decadent, mysterious history, but it grew steadily on him.

He could tell by the way Charli acted as she refinished the magnificent staircase banister, she'd begun to fall in love with the house as well. Still, he would never consider they might keep it, unless they resolved a few cryptic oddities about it. If all was well, once it was restored, the house would make someone a fine home—a great place to raise a family.

Bubba grinned. "Girl, you know I'd do anything for you. Your work is always a top priority to my team." He nodded toward the house where his men had ascended to the rooftop. Workers climbed the scaffolding to finish their job. "The guys need another couple of days to finish. They have to tuckpoint and resurface the outside windowsills. The roof will be finished by noon. Before I let the roofers go, we'd like to look inside the attic, if you don't mind."

Charli's brows shot up, and she met Eli's gaze. "Attic? I don't believe there is one. We haven't noticed a door to an attic."

Bubba's mouth curled to one side, and he glanced at the roof. "Well, from up there, it sure looks like there's room for one."

Charli squinted. "Maybe we'd better take a closer look. There could be some entrance to it in the ceiling somewhere on the third floor. Maybe inside a closet or something."

Eli nodded. "Sure, we'll take a gander and let you know before your guys leave today."

She shrugged. "No problem. Let's do it."

"Great." The big man strutted toward his workers.

Eli followed Charli toward the house. "First, let's check out the basement, though."

"But you said the sound came from upstairs."

"It did. Guess it was nothing." He strode toward the back door. "Let's go check downstairs."

Moments later, they stood in front of the heavy wooden door with its z-shaped brace on both sides, the entrance to the lower level in an alcove off the kitchen. It had an old-fashioned rusty metal knob and square key block.

"The original one must've not been safe enough for the previous owner. Looks like they installed a brass lock with an antique finish." It hit at Charli's eye level. "Isn't this lock gorgeous?" she gushed. "Check out the double fish design, one to each side of the keyhole."

She pulled the key from the lock. The attached brass ring also held a second key of the same design.

Eli's brows rose. "I've never seen one quite like this." He took the keys from her and inserted the second one into the hole. It fit perfectly as well. "So, they're duplicates. Good."

"I've never encountered one like it before either. It's so fancy, an elegant design, like a sculpted cross with a circle on each side and two at the top. Even knobs on the bottom that work the mechanism are intricately crafted." She flipped the items over and over, then returned them to Eli.

Eli slipped the keys into his shirt pocket and opened the heavy door. He reached inside and flipped a plastic switch. A single bulb lit up stone steps dipping downward. "Let me go first."

He slipped inside the narrow stairway. Turning, he took her hand, and together they descended. At the foot of the steps, they stood on a layer of concrete while he swatted his hand above them until he found the string that hung from another single light bulb attached to a sixty-something-era fixture.

She sighed. "We really need to get the electrician here. I'm sure none of this wiring is up to code."

They stood in a vast space the size of the floorplan above them. There were shelves built into nearly every wall around the two rooms. The walls were stone, sealed with concrete between them.

He nodded toward the floor. "These cracks in the poured floor appear minor. None looked to be leaking. The rafters are thick and deep. The subflooring and braces of wood have darkened over the ages."

He stood on tiptoe and stuck a fingernail into one. "Hard. No visible termite damage. Seems solid as a rock." That was a relief.

A tingle sizzled at the base of his nape and slithered down his back.

Charli shuddered as though she shook off a similar sensation. She pulled her flashlight out. Turning right, she inspected the walls, ceiling, and floor. "Nothing appears to be messed with. Windows are dirty. Prowlers could never see inside. If they did, they'd find it not worth breaking in."

The space held an eerie atmosphere. Dust in the stale air stored secrets from a long ago, tragic, and illegal past. Whose feet had tracked the residue into the area to linger to modern days?

Desperate people had hidden here. They'd fought for their lives and ran for freedom. Others had slipped past watchful eyes to party gaily and indulge in prohibited beverages. Dusty powder reached out to penetrate lungs, like it wanted to grab you and whisper its secrets in your ears. Maybe draw you into it like a ghost on the prowl. Eli shivered.

He followed Charli into the room. His arm rose, and his hand lay on the sill of one of the four high windows. "They still let in some light, but they sure need cleaning. They're too small and far up for anyone to want to crawl through. Maybe we should replace them with insulated glass blocking."

"Yeah, sounds good." She ambled to the huge brass

and timber door that dominated a wall on the northern side of the room. "This is the door you mentioned. It was supposedly bolted shut way back in the fifties. I doubt anyone would've come through there since then. Tale has it that the tunnels were unstable. The historical society and city government funded having them sealed to prevent anyone from getting trapped in there. You know, kids, animals."

Eli nodded as he slid a hand across the brass metal fixtures that had aged to a beautiful green hue from oxidation. "Or curious explorers. I wonder what relics lie hidden in whatever remains of this old tunnel."

She nodded. "I'm sure there are many who would love to give them a last shot. Not on my watch. The last thing we need is to have some history buff get trapped or, worse yet, killed in there. Another scandal would not help us get this old monstrosity sold as soon as we fix her up."

He chuckled. "Yeah, the Underground Railroad and then the speakeasy, illegal booze, and gambling ought to be enough."

She frowned, as though a yearning had come over her. "It must be my maternal instinct kicking in. The idea of losing my baby once I've put my heart and soul into it always bothers me. This time, more than usual, and the job is barely started." She shook her head with a sigh.

How would she feel when it came time to sell the mansion?

They inspected the second room to the other side of the stairs. She flicked her flashlight around, and Eli used the one on his phone. "Nothing here, just a bunch of old shelves, some dusty jars, and lots of rooms. Wonder what they used this area for."

She shrugged and headed back up the steps, Eli on her trail. "Looks to me like it was mostly storage for food and supplies. Makes sense. It's large and dry. Shelves along most walls would hold a ton of crap."

"Yeah, I guess people had to store a lot of goods back when this place was erected. There wasn't a convenience store on every corner like there is nowadays."

Her head rocked to the side, as Eli relocked the basement door. "Guess we can rule out intruders coming through the basement. I don't see any sign there's been much activity down there in the near past."

He pushed the key back into the antique lock. "Yep. That bolted door downstairs is substantial and seems secure. The only thing we might do for now is find a new lock for this door that looks antique but with more modern fixtures in it. I don't much care for the skeleton key type of traditional lock, even if it is pretty."

She quivered when he used the word *skeleton*. "Maybe we should leave those on there and install a new one that works easier with a better-locking device. It should be an upgrade, look antique, but provide modern convenience and access."

He puffed his lower lip out in a pout. "Okay, I'll search the internet for a replacement tonight…alone in my bed…while I fend off ghostly creatures that go bump in the night." His voice teased as he pulled her into his arms for a lengthy kiss that threatened to distract them with more fun physical activities for the rest of the day.

She swatted his chest playfully. "You devil, we've got work to do and a schedule to keep."

He skimmed a hand across her firm, little buttocks and released her reluctantly. "There you go, entice me.

You know, being in my presence is all it takes, boss lady."

She pecked his lips. "Hey, hunky daddy, remember, you were tired of bossing people around. You're the one who insisted I lead this business partnership."

"Slave driver," he called after her as she moseyed toward the foyer.

Chapter Eleven

Before lunchtime rolled around, the twosome was hard at work. The door chimes sounded throughout the tall foyer, wafting its mellow tones up the full three stories. Charli called from where she stooped beside the banister near the second floor.

"Come in. Door's open." She stopped sanding, stretched her back, and strolled down the marble steps as the enormous oak door crept open.

Eli dried his hands as he entered from the back of the house. "I applied the last coat of stain remover to the spindles." He dried the hands he'd washed residue from. A bright smile showed on his handsome chiseled face. His sandy hair flicked back from his forehead with a twitch of his head and rested against the back of his neck.

Sheriff Wyatt Gordon held the door wide for Jaiden to enter. His deputy shoved thumbs in the thick utility belt around the waist of her deputy uniform. He motioned to a couple of guys in tan coveralls to stay put on the stoop.

Eli grinned and shot a hand toward Wyatt. "Nice to see you, Wyatt, Jaiden." He nodded toward them. "I'm surprised to see you here. What's up?"

Charli sprinted down the steps and gave her friends each a hug. "Good to see you handsome as always, Wyatt."

Wyatt winced and drawled, "Much as I'd love this

to be a social visit, I'm afraid it's not."

Jaiden took over. "We're here about the hair tool you found in this house. You're both aware of its connection to our recent murder case."

Charli snorted. "Who can miss it? It's all over the paper. The press is having a field day, between what you've divulged so far and their own speculation. How can we help?"

Wyatt glanced up the stairway. "We'd like to search for more evidence since we've confirmed the red stick you found here was connected." He looked pointedly at Eli and then Charli. "Question is, do we need a search warrant?"

Jaiden shrugged to one side. "We have enough to get one by later today, but if you're amicable, we'd like to just go straight at it."

Wyatt nodded. "With your consent, of course."

Eli's brow rolled up. "We've got nothing to hide, and we're not involved in that in any way. Jaiden already told us that the murder and the assailant's visit to this house happened just prior to our taking possession of the place. What do you want to do?"

Wyatt waved a hand toward the closed door behind him. "We've brought along a couple of guys from the forensics team—our CSI men. We'd like to assist them in a search of the whole house, to see if the trespasser left any other evidence."

Jaiden screwed her nose up. "In fact, we need to take the shower stall and drain back to the lab for testing. Maybe even the vanity drainpipes. We suspect that since the intruder took a shower here and cleaned up from her encounter with the deceased, there could be additional residue stuck in the s-curve of the drain, possibly even in the shower stall itself."

Charli shivered. "I had that thing in my hair, and I handled it over and over. My fingerprints are all over it, and I probably washed off critical evidence. Does this make me a suspect?"

Wyatt chuckled grimly. "We don't believe you had anything to do with this. We ruled it out. You've verified your whereabouts when the murder was committed."

Charli mulled it over. "Yeah, I was with Eli all day. We closed on the house and then took some supplies over to it so we could clean the next day."

The handsome, silver-haired sheriff nodded and drawled in his deep-throated southern twang, "Our crime scene unit will go over the house to see if we can find any other clues related to the case. In the meantime, halt work on it and vacate the property."

Charli twisted her lips. "Wyatt, I looked up those hair picks online. They're inexpensive, usually bought as a set of two, and anyone could obtain them. They're common."

Wyatt snickered toward Jaiden. "Yeah, I know, kiddo. Deputy Coldwater did the same research."

Charli frowned. "You guys know I cleaned that whole bathroom with bleach cleaner." She went on to explain all the work she and Eli had done on the house so far.

Wyatt nodded. "Still, there could be minute evidence stuck in the areas around the drain."

El shook his head, standing shoulders back and hands on hips. "Hell, Wyatt, take the whole freaking shower stall if you want. It needs to be removed and replaced anyway. The top floor is our lowest priority. You'll just save me the trouble of hauling it out of here."

"Good, then you won't mind if we take any items we deem might be of help from that area?"

Charli scoffed. "Not at all."

Jaiden smiled. "If we need to remove anything else besides fixtures in that bathroom, we'll give you a call."

Eli smiled. "Have at it, and I appreciate that."

Jaiden frowned. "You won't like this, but we need you two and your work crews to vacate the premises during our search. We should complete our search here by the end of the day tomorrow."

Wyatt chewed the side of his lip. "Eli, I understand that you live here. Can you find somewhere else to stay for the next couple of nights? If not, you could bunk at my and Sage's house. Our guest room is vacant with our daughter away at college, and you're more than welcome to it." Wyatt's daughter, Haley, wasn't really Sage's daughter, but she had grown closer to Sage than her own mother.

Charli smiled at her dear pal. Wyatt was like a brother to Charli. She had lived with his family for a while as a teenager. "That won't be necessary. Eli can stay at my place. Kyler is away at university, so his room is free."

Jaiden leered silently toward Charli. She didn't fool anyone.

Eli escorted Wyatt out the door and left it open wide. "You can tell your guys to proceed. I'll vacate once I pack a small bag. First, I've got to tell Bubba to have his men leave and to reschedule the work they tried to finish today and tomorrow. Hopefully, they can jiggle some jobs around to return in a couple of days."

"Man, I really hate to put a crimp in your work life. It's unavoidable." Wyatt shrugged.

Eli rolled his shoulders. "No worries. We'll manage." He went to break the news to Bubba Larson. Wyatt instructed his officers with what he wanted them to do.

Jaiden and Charli were alone. "I'm really worried about Eli living here if a murderer broke into the house. Is he safe here?"

Jaiden placed both hands on Charli's shoulders. "I'm sure he is. This unfortunate incident happened before you and Eli obtained this property—even though immediately prior to possession. Besides, you've changed all the locks, sealed all the windows, and inspected every inch of this place yourselves. Whatever evidence we're able to uncover on the premises is from beforehand."

Charlie frowned. "But you are looking for blood evidence. That person must've stabbed the victim. She's a killer. What if she comes back?"

Jaiden's gaze met Charlie's. "Eli can handle himself, and he seems fine with living here. I wouldn't worry too much. Besides, I didn't say she murdered the guy."

"But she did stab him?"

Jaiden nodded. "We believe that's the case."

Charli's chin lifted high. "So, the sliver of red wood that you have in evidence came from my hair thing-a-ma-bob, but it didn't kill him. She also shot him. That was the cause of death."

Jaiden's brows stiffened. "Yes, COD was a GSW. How did you know about the sliver of wood?"

Charli shrugged to one side. "Oh, forgot to mention, Gran and I visited Dr. Baker the other day. He didn't realize that I saw the shard." No need to get Sam in trouble with the sheriff.

Jaiden shook her head and puffed out some air. "Of course, you did. I told you not to get involved."

Charli glared at her buddy. "I am involved. That murderer broke into my house. I wore her bloody stick in my hair." She flinched from a cold shiver.

Jaiden placed a hand on Charli's arm. "We have nothing to confirm this female did the shooting. Until we can prove otherwise, she's just a person of interest."

Charli emitted a cynical laugh. "Yeah, sure. That makes me feel all better." She shuddered.

Jaiden let go of her and stepped to the foot of the stairs.

Charli placed her hands on her hips. "The press has been all over this. Gran told me she read in this morning's paper the victim had some missing items the police are searching for."

Jaiden sighed and puffed air out with a huff. "I might as well tell you. Otherwise, you'll stick your nose in where it doesn't belong…again. The victim's shoes and wallet were missing."

"I understand the wallet. Maybe she took it for his money. You think it's a robbery gone bad?" *Too confusing*

"Females aren't usually muggers. Mostly male thugs do the muggings."

"Yeah, but she could've robbed him, if she had a gun pointed at him." *Possible*.

"Feasible but doubtful. It could've been self-defense. The guy might've lured her there to rape or kill her. Or they could've been lovers and had a spat that turned violent. We don't know if they were acquainted or strangers and have no idea who this woman is. It's not possible to rule anything out at this point."

It was difficult for Charli to understand any of this worrisome information. "Maybe she didn't want you to find out the victim's identity, so she took the wallet."

Jaiden gazed upward and back at Charli. "His cell phone was clipped to his belt. We located his car a few hundred yards along the street where it ends in the forest. It was possible to identity the victim that way. We're investigating the man to determine why someone wanted him dead."

Charli's mouth screwed up. "He wouldn't wander around in the woods barefoot. Why would she take his shoes?"

Jaiden shrugged. "We're not sure what happened to them. Look, Charli, that's all I can say at this time. I want you to know enough to convince you to stay out of this, but it's an on-going investigation. You understand. I must use discretion."

Charli gave her pal a quick hug. "Yeah, I get it. I'd best go help Eli pack since he's bunking with me."

Jaiden winked. "Enjoy!"

Charli threw her head back and laughed. "Gal, you know I will."

Chapter Twelve

After a night in Eli's arms, exhausted and completely satisfied, Charli fell asleep while he showered. The bathroom door creaked opened and shut. Figuring him done, she rose, showered, dressed, and finally strolled into the great room.

Eli sat on a barstool, drinking a cup of coffee. Gran stood and sipped hers. Her slim frame propped against the counter at her back. They talked casually.

His head twisted around at the sound of her work-booted footsteps. "Morning, sunshine." He flashed her a grin that wet her panties, as she recalled how he'd pleasured her last night…several times.

"Morning, Eli." She gave him a long, sensual kiss.

Gran drawled, "About time you got up. I'd call you Lazy Bones, but with this guy in your bed last night, I doubt that would be the case. I figured you needed every second of your little beauty sleep."

Charli's eyes rolled, and she ambled to the carafe for her own deep, dark fortification. "Gran, I know it's hard for you, but could you try to behave yourself?" She giggled at Gran's wag of her brows. "Coffee smells wonderful."

Eli leaned back in his seat. "Tastes that way too."

The poor guy had grown used to Gran's ornery teasing and wacky personality by now. Charli figured he even liked it. She knew how much the two of them enjoyed each other's company. It pleased Charli that her family loved Eli almost as much as she loved him.

"So, we can't work today." She leaned against the countertop like Gran did and stood beside her beloved grandmother. "What should we do?"

Eli tossed his shaggy, dusty-blonde hair. "We should take a trip to the courthouse and research the history of the McGregor House."

Charli's brows lifted. "Brilliant minds think alike. That tracks for me, too. We might find some information at the Sweetwater County Historical Society. It's a couple doors down from the courthouse."

****

Charli glanced at the municipal building at the end of the turnaround which circled a grassy section of parkland that divided the street, where town functions happened. Jaiden's cruiser was parked in front of the sheriff's office on the right side of the courthouse. Sadie's Royal Diner took up space on the other side of Main Street.

Men relaxed on benches in the park, probably waiting while their wives shopped in nearby stores, did business at one of the four banks on nearby corners, or attended to business at the county seat. The gazebo provided shade and a bandstand for events like caroling during the holidays. Mature oak trees shaded the whole area.

Charli sighed. "I adore this lovely town center."

Eli smiled. "It is pretty and atypical of a small, southern township."

He parked behind Jaiden's cruiser, strutted around the truck, and opened the door for Charli. "Ready?"

Charli laughed as she stepped to the curb and slung

her backpack over her shoulder. "Yeah. Let's do it."

He smiled as he closed the door. "Remember, Irma told us to stay out of trouble. We'll just research the house's history today."

She laughed. "Yeah, right. I promised her nothing. Gran knows better. I seem to find trouble no matter where I go. Probably get that trait from her."

Her grandmother acted the part of a feisty old gal. One never knew what mischief the famous, retired, rock-n'-roll singer might get into. Who knew what she and her cohorts at Gran's yoga class might come up with? It was a sure thing, she'd find some.

Charli and Eli arrived at the county clerk's office at the Sweetwater Courthouse. Built in 1802, the imposing, classic, red-brick structure had modern conveniences and electronics. The character of the original construction had not been altered but played up to its advantage. The building became a treasured facility for the county seat.

Charli waved and greeted clerks and residents who did business in their bullpen office. She and Eli passed through waist-high swinging doors to the Records Room. Workers in the front room continued to help customers purchase license plates and pay taxes.

Charli and Eli used a comfortable, high-topped counter space in the center of the back room where huge volumes of data books were stored on ancient wooden shelves of surrounding walls. More enormous tomes rested beneath the island workspace where Eli and Charli sat. A professional printer occupied one corner. Beside it, a computer sat on a small table. Mortgages, liens, deeds, plats, and other pertinent property data were stored in this regal chamber.

Charli had done her own title search before the closing, so she knew the deed book and plat information from their purchase of McGregor House. They'd also contracted their title company to do one so they could obtain title insurance at purchase. Of course, they only researched back fifty years for this purpose, sufficient for the sale. The deed was in order, and no liens had been posted against it.

This data allowed them to quickly find paperwork to back up what they already knew about the residence and to locate deeds all the way to the first filing of property ownership—as far as it could go back.

Eli searched through book after book, as deeds referred to prior filings, then more through the history of ownership. Charli did the same research for land plats. As they worked and located previous data, they used the printer to copy documents. Soon each of them had a stack of legal paper-sized evidence of their project's history.

After an hour of exploration, Eli sat back and pointed to the first deed. "Look here. Enos McGregor and his wife, Hannah, built the McGregor House in 1802 and passed it down through heirs. Owners just prior to the Civil War and through that time were Emory McGregor and his wife Josephine. We should research their time of ownership at the Historical Society. I'll bet they were the ones involved in the Underground Railroad."

Charli's chest filled with elation. "Awesome. We'll go there next. Put a yellow sticky on that document, so we can find it later."

"Will do. Here's another interesting fact. Owners during the early 1900s through the time of Prohibition were Stephano McGregor and his wife Leona. I'll mark that paper as well. We should check. I'll bet they were up to something fun in the old place at the time."

Charli chuckled. "You're on a roll, babe." She gave him a peck on the lips and slid a huge plat book back into its nook.

Eli stacked his paperwork together neatly and pointed to the top sheet. "I've gone all the way to our purchase of the residence. I don't see anything out of order. We already know the heirs who signed it over to us." He read the top page, "Brothers, Carlito McGregor of Savannah, Georgia; Eustice McGregor of Seattle, Washington; heirs of Lucien McGregor of Dallas, Texas—his son Lucien McGregor the Second of Houston, Texas; his daughter Louise McGregor-Myers of Phoenix, Arizona; and his son Michael Lawrence McGregor of Detroit, Michigan."

"Yeah." She curled her nose. "That's why it took several extra days to get the deed back. It had a lot of traveling to do to get an original of all the heirs' signatures."

Eli put the volumes he'd read through into their designated locations. "Guess we're done here. Next stop, the Historical Society."

He picked up his pile of records, and Charli did the same. They exited into the bullpen area and paid a clerk for copies they'd printed before the couple left the building.

As they strolled past the sheriff's office, Jaiden and Deputy Leo Sanders strode down the short rock steps to the sidewalk by her cruiser.

Charli beamed at her friends and stepped into Jaiden's arms for a loving hug. "Hey, gal, good to see you. Does this mean you're done with our house, or are you two heading there now?" She accepted her friendly hug from the tall, red-headed deputy who reminded her of a grownup, muscular, blond-haired Opie from the old television show she'd enjoyed as a kid.

Jaiden pursed her lips. "Not exactly. The crime scene crew is there. They should finish up later this afternoon."

Leo backed away with a smile. "We're going to the homeless camp down along the Ohio River."

Charli gave Jaiden a pointed glare. "Still looking for the wallet and shoes?"

Leo flinched. "You know about that, huh? How?" He glanced at his partner.

Jaiden shrugged with a head twitch.

Charli patted the deputy's arm. "I have my ways. No worries. The secret is safe with Eli and me. We will not interfere with your investigation. We know that information is not to be leaked."

Jaiden's head rocked forward, and she stared at Charli beneath her brow. "That means tell no one—especially your grandmother. You know Irma is part of the Sweetwater grapevine. Those people mean well, but the community in this little town has a way of passing information around faster than the media."

Charli chuckled, and her face heated. "You've got that right. No worries. We won't share the info with anyone. Gran and her cronies will not gossip about this at their weekly poker games."

Leo rested a hand on Charli's shoulder. "I'll hold you to that." Easygoing Leo winked.

Eli shook the deputy's hand. "No worries, pal. The secret is safe with us. We're just eager to get back to work on our project. So, have you learned anything about the victim that might lead you to whomever killed him?"

Leo nodded. "Not much, only that he worked as some sort of security person—not sure what type. The big guy may have been employed as a watchman or bodyguard."

Jaiden added, "We couldn't find much on his company though. The listing for it had a phone number that rings at the county jail. The address on his business card turned out to be a parking lot. Wyatt drove up there this morning to talk with the locals—police, neighbors, his landlord. You know the drill."

Charli brows elevated. "Sounds fishy."

Leo sighed. "Yeah, but Wyatt will get to the bottom of it. Whatever the guy did, he probably had a reason for being vague about his work.

They said goodbyes to the deputies, who jumped into their vehicle and drove away. Then Eli and Charli continued their stroll to the Historical Society building next door. Inside a clerk helped them locate areas where they could research the town's history and specifically that of their mansion. A couple of hours later, they sat with a stack of papers they'd copied.

Eli sighed. "We've exhausted everything we could find. I'm beat."

Charli nodded. "Yeah, me too. Let's go over what we found."

Eli flipped the computer off. "I located newspaper records to indicate Emory McGregor and Josephine being instrumental in the Underground Railroad's rescue of people to escape slavery from the South. They have been credited with ushering many a soul into their mansion, where they hid them until they could move them to the riverbank, where they were ferried to freedom across the river under cover of darkness. Their daughters, Ellory and Phoebe, and their son, Daniel McGregor, were apparently involved as well."

Charli's eyes widened. "Wow, what an exciting time. Can you imagine the thrill of helping thousands of those poor people? Not to mention the terror of avoiding capture for operating outside the law."

Eli nodded. "Powerful stuff." He blew out a sigh and sat back in his chair. "What did you learn about the illegal sale of alcohol?"

She patted the copies she'd printed from newspapers and the very few arrest records she'd located. "It seems the McGregors had an affinity for defying the law—or at least they acted on the fringes of it."

Eli's brows rose. "And?"

"I found that Stephano McGregor and wife Leona were 'suspected' of running an illegal speakeasy during prohibition, but they were never convicted. An arrest never went to trial."

Eli laughed. "Not surprising. I'd guess it was easy to dissuade authorities, since they were likely customers or friends."

Charli chuckled. "Friends in low places, maybe high ones?"

"Exactly." Eli snickered. "What else did you find?"

Charli pointed to a news article. "Stephano and Leona had three grown children who were likely involved as well—Joy Jacob McGregor, Harlan McGregor, and Myrtle McGregor. They passed the property down to their children—the elderly ones who we bought it from—Carlito McGregor, Eustice, the heirs of Lucien McGregor, his son Lucien McGregor the

Second; Lucien's daughter, Louise McGregor-Myers; and his son, Michael Lawrence McGregor."

"All of that is interesting, but it doesn't help us figure out what causes neighbors to believe the property is haunted."

Charli blinked wickedly. "Well, lover, you heard those weird sounds upstairs—the thudding. Maybe it is haunted."

Eli shrugged. "Doubtful. Not to say I don't believe in ghosts. Anything's possible. I just don't think that's the case. That house might have a lot of notoriety, but every old structure has a history. Even if owners died in residence, I found no indication brutal incidents occurred there. Did you? Aren't spooks supposed to only inhabit locations where they died under tragic circumstances—get stuck, as they say?"

She nodded and glanced at her stack of pages. "Yeah, that's the consensus. I'm with you, though. I don't believe the old gal is haunted. Even so, I might ask Sage to stop by and smudge the place. She believes that helps drive off any unwanted entities."

Eli snickered. "Yeah, the sheriff's wife is a character. Didn't she live in a commune or something?"

Charli relaxed in her seat. "Yes. Born a flower child in an upper New York State seventies commune, she lived there until she became school age. Her hippie parents named her Lemon Sage."

"Benton? Wasn't that her maiden name?"

She shook her head. "Actually, no. Benton was her married name. first husband' was murdered when they were brutally mugged in New York City. She survived and moved here a couple years later, looking for a fresh start."

Eli bit his lip. "It's okay with me if you have her smudge or whatever you want, but please try not to draw her into this mystery. Wyatt calls her a trouble magnet and has enough problems just keeping Sage out of harm's way. You're kind of like that, if you ask me. I worry about you. You're a bit impetuous and fearless. Don't go looking for trouble."

Charlie moaned. "I know, babe. Look, Eli, I won't do anything without you."

"What did you discover in the property's plats and templates?"

She pulled a sheet from her pile. "This is the original master floorplan the owners filed. A skilled draughtsman designed it. That makes sense since the McGregors who had it built were wealthy. They could afford the best."

Eli leaned toward the document to get a better look. "So that would be Enos and Hannah McGregor. Clearly, they had expensive taste. Everything about the structure is of quality."

Charli bowed her head and pulled out more manuscripts. "Yes. This is a topographical drawing of the landscape orientation showing elevation, and this diagram is a scale of the house setting."

Eli examined the graph and pointed to the stack he'd printed in the county clerk's office. "According to what we've found, the property originally amassed two-hundred-twenty-three acres. That is about a fourth of the whole town. As time passed, pieces were sold off. As the town expanded, the neighborhood around the mansion grew—mostly in the fifties."

"This diagram outlines the tunnel that leads to the river, which we were aware of. Many years ago the owners, township, and Historical Society sealed it for safety. It happened when they declared the place an historical landmark."

Eli's head dipped. "Yes, that's the huge, thick, iron and wooden door we saw in the basement. That's good. Otherwise, our insurance would be astronomical."

Charli pointed to the diagram. "According to this, there's another entrance to that tunnel, and a second tunnel that leads toward that old fishing lake on the other side of the woods behind the back yard of the house."

Eli bent over the scale drawing. "Wow, that place has been a pay lake for years, from what I've heard."

Charli looked at the same sheet. "Yes, but it was originally part of the mansion's land. From what I found, around 1917 the owners leased the lake to someone. The guy charged people to fish and camp there. He used that old cinderblock building beside the lake as a bait shop. Eventually, he sold snacks, essentials, fishing tackle, and even ice. That property later went to his grandson. I found where he obtained a beer license in 1967. Soon after that, this part of the property deeded off—must've been handed down to him."

Eli examined the paperwork. "Wow, that second tunnel comes out just about one-hundred-and-fifty yards behind that building."

Charli looked at the chart again. "Yes, I'll bet that's where they brought slaves into the mansion. It's a long distance, but the scale of landscape orientation doesn't appear to be steep."

Eli sat back in his chair, and his eyes opened wide. "Holy crap. There's no record here of that tunnel being sealed. I'll bet everyone long-forgot and overlooked it. That old house is designed with secrets in mind. Wonder what the original owners were up to."

She smiled, enjoying how Eli and she thought alike. "I found no evidence to indicate why they did that, unless they had already decided they'd get involved as unrest about the injustice of slavery divided the country."

Eli frowned. "We may never know, but I'd say that's a reasonable explanation." He bent over the draft again. "Looks like the opening is a small structure in the woods behind the fishing lake."

Anticipation swelled in Charli's chest, made it rise, and pushed a smile on her face. She eyed Eli with expectancy that burst from her senses. "It would be diligent as responsible owners for us to explore that tunnel. We should make sure personally that it is not a hazard to potential buyers or the community."

Eli's eyes squeezed closed as his head rocked back. His shoulders hunched and then relaxed. "I somehow knew the second you mentioned that tunnel, that you would want to explore it." He blinked. "What the hell." His hands lifted. "If I don't go with you, you'll check that freaking place out yourself. I can't let you do this alone."

She bit her lower lip and grinned. "I knew you'd see it my way."

He huffed. "Woman, you'll be the death of me yet."

She shrugged playfully. "Maybe…but not just yet. I'm not finished with you, Mr. Lange."

She leaned forward and kissed him on the lips. They were soft, pliable, and open to her probing. She melted into his arms as they came around her. Nothing bad would ever happen to her as long as her man was around. Eli had proved time and again, he would do anything assure her safety and that she was happy…and satisfied.

Eli let her go. "Let's grab some grub and take a

hike." He stood and picked up his documents.

"Sounds great. Burgers at the diner?" She picked up her things, took those he handed to her, and stuffed their new treasures into her backpack. "I put the tunnel profile on the top, so we can use it when we hike. We'd best pick up some bottled water at the diner. It could be a long, thirsty hike."

"Yeah, there's no telling what condition that tunnel is in. We might not get through it if it has fallen in over the years. Hell, it's been over a hundred and twenty years since its construction."

They paid for the copies they'd printed and left together. Jaiden's cruiser remained absent from the street or tiny parking lot beside the sheriff's office. Only a couple of cars sat there—one, Sheriff Wyatt Gordon's.

As they rounded where the road curved in front of the courthouse, their neighbor Nancy Underwood strolled down the steps to the sidewalk.

"Hello, Mr. and Mrs. Lange. How nice to see you." She accepted Eli's hand in greeting.

"Same here. How are you, Ms. Underwood?" He let go of her hand.

"I'm good. Just doing a bit of business."

Charli shook her hand. "Us too, checking out lineage and history of the McGregor House. No ghosts have appeared yet though." Charli snickered. "How's Pookie?"

Nancy smiled at the mention of her adored poodle. "He's well but probably irritated. I usually take him everywhere with me, but they don't like animals in the courthouse."

Charli and Eli laughed, and Nancy continued, "If you want to know history of that house, I could tell you a few scandalous stories."

Eli's hands lifted to his hips. "That right? We'd love to hear them if you have time to share."

"We're about to have some lunch. It would be great if you could join us." Eli smirked.

Clearly, he read Charli's mind. "Indeed. We're just going over to Sadie's diner. Please come. Our treat."

Nancy's chin dipped to one side. "Well, I never can resist lunch at the Royal Diner." She acted eager to spill whatever tidbit of gossip she knew about the McGregor House.

Chapter Thirteen

Spunky, red-headed Sadie Carson escorted the threesome to a table beside the window. Sunshine caught her all-but-orange tresses pressed into a large French twist at the back of her head and topped with a white waitress crown. Hairspray lacquer added to the glint of her coif.

Sadie had become a legend in the area, a hilarious character. Her accent flowed as thick as hare skin, and she stayed as goodhearted as they came.

"Well, ain't it just a blessing to have y'all in my lil' ol' diner. I didn't even know y'all knew each other." The owner and proprietor handed them menus in plastic slips trimmed with black. "I'll just go get y'all some water whilst you take a gander and decide on what ya want ta day." She spun around on her sturdy, white, leather, nurse's shoes and strode to the drink station beside the counter bar. A row of round, red and white vinyl stools lined the front of it, so customers could sit there to order and eat.

As they made themselves comfortable in the bench seats, Charli slipped in beside Eli. Nancy took the other side. Substantial cutlery sat atop paper napkins on the glitter-flicked tabletop.

Eli clasped his hands and rested them on his menu. Charli slid hers beneath his, knowing the food list printed on it by heart and already sure what she wanted.

Sadie sat three tall glasses of ice water down along with three straws sealed in paper. "All righty then, what'll it be?" She pulled a pen and pad from her white apron, poised to write.

Eli nodded for Nancy to go first. "I'll have the house salad with Sadie's dressing and the fish sandwich."

Charli and Eli followed with their order of burgers and fries. Sadie looked up from the pad. "Okie-dokie, I'll be right back with your grub in a jiffy." She picked up the unused menus, spun around again, and strutted behind the lunch counter where she placed their ticket on a clip hanger for the cook to prepare.

Eli shook his head with laughter. "That woman is a gem."

Nancy nodded. "A Sweetwater landmark to be sure."

Charli laid her hands together on the tabletop. "So, Nancy, tell us what you know about McGregor House."

The elderly woman acted thrilled to have what she clearly considered the scoop of century. "Well, my parents used to party at that house. The owners were quite wealthy; and, as you know, money buys power. They hobnobbed with all the politicians, county officers, business owners, and such. My daddy became a judge after the war—the first World War, you know. That didn't mean he didn't enjoy a little fun. Right after the war that awful plague hit the country. Thousands died. I believe they called it the Spanish Flu. Some call it the deadliest pandemic in history. I read that more than five-hundred-million people were infected globally, about a third of the population. It caused around fifty-million deaths—over six-hundred-seventy-five-thousand in the States alone. I was too little to give it much thought at the time."

Charli frowned. "Yes, I heard of it when COVID started. The newscaster called it some sort of influenza virus troop movements partially spread during World War I. They must've carried it home."

Eli grimaced. "I guess they misnamed it. I don't believe it started in Spain, though it is widely known as the Spanish Flu."

Nancy's smile looked sad. "Yes, and they had no vaccine or effective treatment, so it caused massive social disruptions. Just about every business closed, even schools, theatres, churches. Lots of businesses shut their doors for good. People were ordered to wear masks. Bodies piled up in makeshift morgues all over the place. That deadly virus ended around 1920."

Charli wiped a tear from her eye, as she recalled her own experience with COVID and sympathized with those who lost their lives and loved ones in both crises. "It's so sad."

Nancy agreed with a nod.

Sadie delivered their order on a pink plastic tray. She sat plates on the table, plopped a bottle of ketchup and an additional stack of napkins between them. "All righty, can I get y'all anything else?"

Eli smiled up at their retro-diner waitress. "No, thank you, Sadie. This looks amazing."

"Okie-dokie. If you change your minds, just holler."

Charli smiled. "Will do. Thanks." She squeezed a hearty dollop of ketchup onto her plate beside the aromatic pile of fries and looked at Nancy. "So, I take it your parents didn't contract the disease."

Nancy sighed and talked between bites of her meal. "Thank goodness, no. They were among the lucky.

People were restless, cooped up, practically imprisoned in their homes. Everyone became fearful. The government did what they could, but to add to the public's frustration, they instigated Prohibition. That pissed people off even more. You can imagine, in that situation, folks must've craved an outlet. It seemed to be the last straw that they outlawed alcohol."

Eli smirked. "Yes, the Eighteenth Amendment outlawed intoxicating beverages thanks to deep-pocketed political groups like the Anti-Saloon League and the Women's Christian Temperance Union, both with strong political connections. They pushed for anti-alcohol legislation on Capitol Hill and were successful. Prohibition became all but established by the time the States entered the war. Joining the conflict in 1917 happened to be the last nail in the coffin of legalized alcohol consumption. One could have enough alcohol on hand for personal consumption, but it became illegal to produce, sell or transport it."

Nancy smiled. "Yes, and some affluent drinkers built enormous wine cellars. Some even bought whole liquor store inventories so they could stockpile legal hooch. Only drug stores were allowed to sell it for medicinal purposes."

Charli laughed. "I can imagine how it must've been. Businesses flailed and failed as COVID spread. I read that during Prohibition, many manufacturers went under, but some breweries refitted facilities to produce ice cream, which became extremely popular. One Colorado company produced pottery and ceramic goods."

Eli swallowed a fry. "Also, that's when some breweries produced 'near beer,' a point-five-percent alcohol drink."

Nancy grimaced. "Yes, and drinking proved dangerous. Bootleggers invented a concoction they called 'bathtub gin.' Others produced rotgut moonshine, a foul-tasting, illicit hooch that sometimes blinded the consumer or even poisoned them. The deadliest of those contained tinctures of industrial alcohol produced for fuels and medical supplies ordered by the government to contain additives of quinine, methyl alcohol and other toxic chemicals. Meant to deter its consumption, that clearly didn't work. Before the amendment was repealed, low-quality, tainted booze killed over ten thousand Americans."

Charli shook her head. "That's horrible. I read in high school about 1932 when Franklin Roosevelt's landslide win for presidency helped ratify the 21st Amendment that repealed Prohibition. Supposedly, Roosevelt honored the occasion, formally downing a dirty martini. Can you say yuck?" She shivered at the thought of it on her tastebuds.

Nancy laughed. "Yes, well, it's an acquired taste I suppose. Then came the 'Roaring Twenties.' My parents loved every minute of that wild time in their lives. Speakeasies continued to flourish out in the open, at least until actual bars and nightclubs were able again to operate successfully."

Eli snorted. "I understand our house was a speakeasy. Know about that?"

Nancy smiled. "Indeed, it was. My parents frequented that establishment during and after Prohibition, along with many other movers and shakers of the time. Of course, they had friends in local government. The McGregors found it easy to get away with it. A little money under the table made little difference to them. They recouped that 'investment' quickly by providing the only safe place for people to kick up their heels and let off pent-up steam."

Charli frowned. "With alcohol banned, where did they obtain what they served to customers?"

Eli laid his burger down and swallowed. "Most of the alcohol consumed in those couple of years came from stills hidden in the mountains of eastern Kentucky. Some imported from Canada. They disguised areas in vehicles to hide the goods. Then they sneaked the concealed cargo across the border to wherever it delivered in the States."

Nancy nodded. "Yes, difficult to get but very lucrative for the persons that transported it, as well as those who sold it to the public. Scarcity completely changed the way people drink alcohol. Due to the shortage, bartenders were forced to become creative. Not only that, whether smuggled booze, doctored up 'whisky,' moonshine, or bathtub gin, quality lacked desperately. To make use of undrinkable liquor, mixologists used innovative ingredients to turn them into fun, boozy beverages. This started the tradition of mixing alcohol with other drinks, spices, fruit, vegetables— whatever they could come up with to make what became known as cocktails."

Charli giggled. "Thank goodness for that. I'm not much of a drinker, but I sometimes enjoy a good Tom Collins."

Eli searched on his phone. "Hey, I found a list of the most popular prohibition cocktails online. Many of them are still popular today. Heck, you can find nearly anything on the internet."

Charli eyed Nancy. "Tell us more about the house. How did all those people sneak in to drink and dance in the mansion? I realize the cops were paid to look the other way. Surely, they didn't want to draw attention to what happened there."

"You're right. They couldn't allow that traffic to drive up the hill or have cars parked all over the yard. That would've been like sticking your middle finger up at the authorities. It had to be handled discreetly. Patrons snuck into the mansion, driving back that dirt road that now goes around the football field and into the woods where it ended at the pay lake. They paid the guy for a day's fishing, and he let them leave their automobiles there while they attended the mansion to party."

Charli tilted her head in wonder about the elderly woman. "Aren't you too young to remember all that?"

Nancy chortled. "Thank you, sweetheart. I wasn't even born then. Later in life, like we all do, my parents enjoyed telling stories of their youth. I became enthralled at who they'd been before my birth. I suppose they settled down once I arrived. Not so much fun to have a hangover when your infant wakes you early in the morning."

Charli grinned. "I suppose not. So, your folks were party animals before you were born."

Nancy smiled. "Evidently."

Eli directed the conversation back to where it had been. "So, how did they get to the mansion from the pay lake?"

Nancy's mouth formed a circle. "Oh, yes. Well, they carried their party shoes in a bag and hiked a short distance to the old icehouse in the woods. I doubt there's still a trail, but there must've been one back then. I've never been there, only heard about it from them. Prior to electricity, a hidden entrance to a tunnel allowed servants to push wheelbarrows filled with large chunks of ice to the mansion for household use. The speakeasy's patrons entered through that tunnel."

Eli's brows rose, as his gaze met Charli's. Clearly, he thought as she did.

Nancy took a last sip of her drink and dabbed her lips with the paper napkin. "Eli, Charli, it's been delightful chatting with you. I hope you found something interesting in our little talk. I really must get back home. Pookie will need to go out soon." She slid from the bench seat.

Eli stood to shake her hand. "It's been eye-opening and helpful."

Charli smiled up at the octogenarian. "Absolutely, thank you for sharing. Let us know if you recall anything else of interest about the house. I just love history."

Nancy picked up her purse. "Definitely, will do. Thank you so much for lunch." She exited the restaurant with a wave and goodbye to Sadie, who stood at the lunch counter.

Eli slid into the seat Nancy had occupied and reached across the table to take Charli's hands in his. "You know what this means. Right?"

"We're going for a hike. I can't wait to find this secret entrance to the tunnel."

Chapter Fourteen

Half an hour later, parked beside the cinderblock building that served as a lakeside store, bait, and tackle shop, Eli paid the day's fee. Charli loaded her backpack with four bottles of water they'd purchased at the Royal Diner.

They hiked along the forest's edge until Eli pointed to deer tracks and a slight parting of brush. "This is the only trail I've seen along here. It doesn't appear humans used the path for a long time, but animals might've continually used it as the easiest, cleanest access to water."

Charli stepped into the brush through the opening. "Let's give it a try."

Eli walked around her and broke off a leafy branch. "Let me go first. I can knock away any cobwebs."

Her man always considered her needs. "Go for it, babe."

She gladly followed Eli's lead as he tramped through the underbrush along the slightly inclined trail. She admired the view of his strong backside. Broad shoulders, muscular arms, a slim waist, and tight buttocks were only a few of Eli's best qualities.

He continued to swat unpleasant things out of her way and held back the occasional thorny bush or heavy branch so she could pass safely. About three-fourths of a mile, he stooped. "Here it is. This must be the famed icehouse."

A small clearing at the entrance lay in front of a rock and mortar building with a metal roof. The approximately ten-foot-wide structure's front wall had a solid oak door with thick, rusty, metal fixtures. Its olive-green paint had chipped badly over the years. Builders erected it so the back section of the chamber built into the hillside.

Charli took a deep breath. "Great. Before we go further, let's hydrate. I'm surprised the hillside isn't as steep on this side as it is on the riverside." She nodded to the right and retrieved a couple bottles from her backpack. "About how far do you think the property goes around that way before it reaches the riverbank?"

Eli stared at the woods for a few seconds as he sipped a bottle of water. "I'd guess about one-to-two miles, maybe. We can figure it out on the plat later."

"Yeah, right now I want to find that entrance into the house." She sealed her bottle and plopped it back into her bag. Eli did the same. "We can always hike that route another day."

Eli cranked the creaky handle and shoved the rustic latch to the side. A gap appeared as the door became unlocked.

"I'm surprised this place wasn't locked up—at least with a key."

Charli shrugged and slipped a pair of gloves from her rear pocket onto her hands, anticipating it would be cool beneath ground. Who knew what yucky things they'd encounter. "It's probably been long forgotten." She followed Eli inside the square, block building, as he swung the creaky door wide.

He stomped on the floor. "Concrete, this place is

well-built. It's hardly cracked at all. No water, so it is sealed tight."

A steel slab covered most of the floor, and three were bolted into and covered the back wall. On each side lay thick steel trays, about two-feet apart. They stopped a couple of feet below the ceiling. She laid a gloved hand on a shelf.

"They must've broken ice from the lake and stored it here."

Eli pointed to remnants shoved beneath the left-side shelving. "Looks like discarded parts to an old, broken wheelbarrow."

Charli stood, hands on hips. "Yeah, but how the heck did this provide entrance to McGregor House? There's no second doorway."

Eli put a hand to his chiseled chin. As he studied the construction, dimples formed on his handsome face. Charli couldn't help herself and reached a finger to push a strand of his shaggy blonde hair off his damp forehead.

"What'cha thinking, Loverboy?"

"Well, for starters, there were valid reasons to disguise the entrance to the tunnel. The original owners had intentions to join the Underground Railroad movement. A discrete entrance protected them and those people they ushered to freedom. Secondly, this functioned as an icehouse. They would not want to contaminate ice with dirt or cause it to thaw. Sealing the tunnel way from the storage area would help keep cubes stored here frozen."

She sucked in a breath. "Makes sense. So, where would the doorway be?"

Eli stepped forward and, on tiptoes to maximize his six-foot-six frame, reached up and ran a gloved hand along the top of the trio of heavy plates bolted to the back wall. "The two side metal slabs couldn't be opened. Stationary walls of shelves lined each side, and outside them was the forest. The entrance must be either through the floor section or through this back one."

"Right." Charli bent and tested the floor plate. "This is heavy. Maybe you can lift it, but I can't budge it. Unless it's on some kind of spring that makes it easier to lift, it's not a viable option." She heaved a heavy exhale.

Eli glanced at her over his shoulder. "If this doesn't work, I'll give it a try." He systematically ran a hand around the top edge, between the back wall section panels. He inspected the bottom the same way. "This must be it. I can put my fingers behind this pane all the way to where it shows a bolt on the front. It must be there to disguise this section, so it looks attached to whatever beams are behind here."

She stepped toward him. "Let me help you."

He shook his head. "No need. Let me try something first." He stretched his arms wide and slipped his fingers behind each side of the panel. It appeared to easily pull forward a few inches. He shoved the panel sideways, and it slid along the top. A fixture fitted over the section to its left.

"Wow," she gushed. "I figured it would be on a hinge."

Eli nodded. "They designed it so the door itself didn't get in the way of heavy loads pushed into the tunnel."

She shrugged. "That makes sense." She pointed to the ceiling of the darkened tunnel. "Cobwebs along the top, but they don't go all the way down."

Eli examined them. "They seem to have been

disturbed."

Charli shined her phone light inside. "The floor is cobblestone. Walls are rock with cement sealant. What is that deep ridge that runs through the middle of the floor?"

Eli nodded toward the broken tool beneath the shelf. "The center rutted design created an easier path to push a heavy load in a wheelbarrow, especially uphill."

Her brows lifted. "Wow, they thought of everything."

Eli pulled his flashlight from his back pocket, flipped it on, then used the branch to brush the webbing aside as he stepped inside the tunnel and flashed the beam along the incline. "Looks to be a nice, easy grade uphill. You ready?" He looked over his shoulder.

She slid a finger around the back of his belt and nodded. "Ready and anxious. Let's do it."

They trekked steadily upward. The only sound was the easy padding of their work boots against a barely damp stone walkway. Quiet allowed Charli's imagination to run the gambit of what they might find. The silence told her Eli did the same.

She whispered, not sure why. It just seemed appropriate. "This passageway is in remarkable shape. It's barely even damp and not broken at all so far."

"Like most of the construction we've encountered on this job, it is done with quality craftsmanship." His blond tresses moved up and down with his head bob, lifted and then rested against the back collar of his dark-blue, plaid, flannel shirt.

Finally, after about a ten-minute hike, they arrived at an approximately eight-foot-by-eight-foot level base. Stone walls on three sides were larger here, more like those used in the house's foundation. They were sealed securely, and the concrete floor remained sound. Large, wide doors took up most of each of the three walls. The wood appeared dry and sturdy, though worn from usage. Thick, rusty fixtures secured the doors to their frames.

Eli squinted toward Charli. "So, which door should we try first?"

She nodded to the left. "Let's see what's behind door number one."

He chuckled and slid the craggy bolt. With a push, it glided to the side along the guide mounted to the wall above it. A small, empty room came into view.

"The servants probably kept a supply of ice here for easy access."

"Sure. That would be handy." She marveled at the ingenuity of necessity from the past residents.

Eli closed the door and laid a hand on the middle one. This sat flush with the wall. No handle, only about a five-inch indentation carved into the frame of one side about waist height for Charli. With no slide guide along the top and no hinges they could see, it appeared neither part had a pocket to shove it into.

Charli frowned. "What do you think?"

Eli leaned and tested the door with his weight against it. It moved forward about ten inches, the depth of the wall.

Charli's heart skipped a beat, and she huffed. "Wow. Now what?"

Eli bit the side of his mouth and stared. "That's as far as it goes inward." He shoved it to the left, and it didn't budge. He tried the other direction. The door complied. "It's heavy, but it moves easily."

Charli flashed her light inside and gasped. "This is

the pantry room in the basement, the one with all the shelves."

They stepped inside, and Eli reached up until he found the string that hung from a single ceiling light bulb. Charli followed him inside and flicked off her phone light. The sturdy shelf unit had moved to the side, revealing the tunnel entrance.

Charli sniffed. "This is ingenious."

Eli waved his flashlight along the top, sides and then the bottom of the section. "No slide bar along the top." He knelt and bent down to look beneath the about five-inch gap between the bottom rung and the dusty floor. "This baby has a set of awesome, industrial-sized, steel wheels." He moved the unit effortlessly from side to side a few inches. "Amazing." He stood, dusted off his hands, and then wiped them on his jeans.

"I guess this is how they brought customers through to party upstairs."

He smiled. "Yes, and slaves to be hidden away until they could secure passage across the river."

She stepped back into the entryway they'd arrived from. "Let's see what's behind door number three." Her heart raced, and excitement gushed through her veins.

Eli joined her. "Let's leave this doorway open for the time being. We can shut it later. For now, it helps bring some light in here."

"Good idea." She eyed the large, heavy-looking door. "This one has a slide guide like the first one." She shoved it to the right, and it moved without difficulty. "It's a stairway."

Wooden walls and a narrow passageway, wide enough for them, enabled an easy hike through it. The ceiling, barely tall enough for Eli to stand erect, caused him to hunch as they ascended the steps.

"Someone has used this staircase in the not-too-distant past. Dirt on the steps has been disturbed."

"Maybe the previous owner used it as he cleaned out his stuff."

Charli shook her head. "I doubt that. He died at an old age. He probably wasn't up to that kind of a chore. Unless he hired someone to clean out the basement and these tunnel rooms, I would think it abandoned long ago."

"That depends on where this baby leads."

After the couple mounted about twenty steps, they came to a wooden landing. A door to the left faced the turn of the staircase to the right. "Let's try this one."

Charli stepped aside to accommodate him. Eli pushed the door on the right, but it didn't budge. Pushing his hand to the left, he pressed, and the doorway moved forward.

Light from the house's windows filtered into the room they had revealed. Wooden drawers and cabinets with beveled glass doors surrounded them. As they entered the room, Charli's excitement surged.

"It's the butler's pantry."

Eli joined her and examined the entrance they'd used. "Pure genius. The inside part of this door is the back wall's cabinets. He bent down and ran fingers beneath the section. "Yep, just as I thought. This one has steel rollers underneath it as well. That's why it moves easily, regardless of what they previously stored here."

Charli snickered. "Of course, if they were smart, the used that cupboard to store lightweight items like linens. I'll bet that's why it has mostly shallow drawers."

"That makes sense. I would estimate servants used

this entrance to bring ice into the house, and they probably used it to access food goods stored in the basement cellar area without interfering with the owner's privacy."

Charli gazed around her. "It's so convenient—a servant's stairway. I'll bet this stairwell goes all the way to the third floor. That way maids could access the bedchambers to change linens, clean, and whatever."

Eli smiled. "And the menservants could bring up wood, coal, or whatever they used to fuel the fireplaces."

"Yes, there's one in every bedroom. At the time of erection most homes had no central heating. There's that one area downstairs with the slanted part of the wall beneath the gap. I'd guess they dumped coal into the room for storage. Someone over time installed those block, glass panes in the window."

Eli snickered. "Yes, and it would've originally had a wood or steel door to cover the access. We see that in a lot of older houses. With central heating in homes these days, old fuel storage areas are converted for other uses."

"Let's go on up."

She entered the shaft, took one easy step at a time, and followed the beam of her cell phone flashlight. Eli's more robust steps sounded behind her. She stopped at another landing where stairs took a sixty-degree angle to the right and faced a door.

"Here we go again. Want to do the honors?" She moved aside. "You seem to have a knack for this."

Eli snickered and joined her. He examined the passage. "It's a pocket door." He placed a hand into a small indention that appeared to be for that purpose and slipped the barrier into a wall pocket to the right.

She didn't expect it to reveal only darkness. "What

the heck?"

Eli tested the floor of the entranceway to the small space with a foot. "It's sturdy."

He stepped forward into the abyss and did a little bounce to test it again. "It seems to be a box of some sort. A tiny room if you will."

His hands tested the sides, as he leaned left then right. "There's about four feet to the right. That wall feels solid. From where I stand, there's only about another foot to the left, and that one's flat as well."

He ran his hands around the front wall that started from top to bottom. Finally, he brought them to waist height and found what he sought.

Charli couldn't see. At the sound of a latch's click, she smiled with glee. "Another doorway."

Eli opened double wood doors wide and stepped out of the chamber into the second-floor hallway. He offered Charli his hand. "For a closet, that floor-to-ceiling monstrosity is huge. I figured that's why the owners left it. Now I understand the real reason."

"Yeah, assuming the family passed down the secret to their heirs." In the hidden hallway, she gazed around. "Let's go on up."

His footfalls tapped behind her as she mounted to the next level to face another sliding pocket door at what should be the third floor—the last one. Steps took another turn on this landing and continued upward into darkness. Confused, she glided the panel into its pocket with little effort. It opened to another dark cavity. Doing as Eli had on the story below, she searched for a latch. Her hands fell on a metal catch. As she flicked it, the fixture spun on a slant to the left. With a slight creak, double doors opened.

"This is weird. I figured this led to the third floor hall. It does and, like the one below, opens through a cupboard. It's strange, but the staircase keeps going up." She grinned at Eli's smile.

"Yep, guess this old gal really does have an attic."

Her chest filled with air that fueled a thrill. Her skin rippled with anticipation. "Oh, Eli, I can't wait to see what treasures might still be in an old, deserted attic."

Eli put an arm around her, and she snuggled beneath it. He drew her to his side, then tipped her chin upward and planted a sweet kiss on her lips. "Don't get so excited, babe. You look like you're ready to jump out of your flesh. If it's like the basement, they've cleaned it out. There might be nothing there, just another empty room."

She chuckled and squeezed him around the waist. "Or that could be where all the ghosts live."

He stepped back and threw his head back in laughter. "There could be a casket up there where a vampire sleeps and only comes out to torture the neighbors on his nightly strolls."

She swatted his dirty jeaned butt. "Don't be silly, Eli. A vampire would turn to a bat and fly around at night."

Another laugh burst from him, and his deep-throated voice continued to ring with it. "How about we find out for ourselves? Want me to go first in case the vampire is awake?"

She took the first step up the next flight. "Ridiculous. It's not dark yet. We've got a couple of hours before dusk."

He followed her upward. "I doubt they stored large items up here. This stairwell is even narrower than the last."

"Maybe they used the attic as a nanny or maid's quarters."

"Or a place to safely hide escapees during their stay here." His voice echoed in the tight space. "Surprisingly these steps don't creak badly. They're strong. Though, like the others, they're worn in the center from usage."

She reached the top small landing and found another door. "Isn't it awesome? They built this house to last."

Eli joined her. "And it has lasted through the ages. It's into its third century, and it's got lots of life left in it."

She put fingers to her lips. "Shh, listen. You hear that?"

He frowned and leaned toward the entrance. "Moaning?"

Her brows shot up. "Your ghost?"

He sneered. "Or your awakening vampire. Better let me go first." He stepped toward the barrier between them and the muffled sound.

Chapter Fifteen

Eli stepped in front of Charli, placed his head against the barrier, and twisted the knob. The door stuck but popped open as he pushed with his hip. The large room with slanted ceilings constructed with raw, unfinished timbers. Even the floor planks and beams were exposed. Dusty air filled the dark chamber and spanned what appeared to be about half of the house's floorplan.

A few filthy boxes and an antique travel trunk sparsely furnished the area. A door hung open slightly in the center of a wall. Dim, eerie light seeped from behind it, as did a shallow whimper.

Charli gasped against Eli's solid back. She resisted an urge to flee. Her mind raced, and her hand trembled against his shirt. "There's someone in there."

He gazed over his shoulder with a snicker. "Don't worry, babe. Human or otherwise, I've got your back."

Knees weak, she flinched and gave him a watery smile. She pushed aside her instinct to turn from the sound. "I know it, but if it's a vampire, you're on your own, buddy. I'm outta here."

His head rocked sideways. "Sounds human to me." He stepped inside the dank attic. "Let's find out. Stay behind me."

She gave him a stoic nod. Her arm hair stood on end as did that at the nape of her neck. "Don't worry about that. I'm game, but you go first." She eased resignedly across solid planks to the opened doorway.

Eli's broad hand gripped the barrier and swung it wide. The second area appeared to be about the same shape as the first. Several old, rustic cots spaced around the perimeter. A rickety table grouped with a couple of straight-backed, shabby chairs. The secluded chamber had obviously housed several people at some point.

A single, slight female lay listlessly atop one of the ragged beds. The figure didn't appear to register their sudden entrance but continued to ramble incoherently on the cot. Her pale face beaded with perspiration. Eyes were glazed as though they focused on otherworldly visions. Her low voice mumbled as though speaking to some unseen person in desperation. Blonde tangled tresses splayed across the dingy pillow her head rested on. She wore a purple tee shirt beneath a half-zipped pink hoodie, and her arms gripped a purple backpack. Its fibers had frayed at a torn seam. Well-worn cowboy boots covered small feet, proportional to her size, much like Charli's petite stature.

"She's sick." Charli rushed around Eli and knelt to the woman's side. Her hand touched the delirious female's forehead. "This girl is burning up, and she's got a fist-sized goose egg on the top of her head. It's all crusty with dried goo stuck to her hair."

Eli's mouth flew open. "Wow, that's a whopper."

Her glassy gaze stared at Charli. "Mommy, I hurt. My tummy aches."

Eli stood at their trespasser's feet. Charli gasped. "She's on fire with fever. We've got to get her to the hospital."

He pulled his phone from his hip and dialed for help.

He gave the operator the address and explained the girl's condition. "Yes, please send an ambulance immediately. Also, please alert the sheriff's office. I believe they're looking for this person." Eli clicked the phone off. "They've dispatched first responders. I'll go down and open the front door so they can get in."

"Good. I'll wait here with her."

The girl grabbed Charli's hand as though her life hung in the balance. "Mommy, don't leave me. Don't let them get me. They're evil. They want me dead."

Charli stroked her forehead gently. "No worries, sweetheart. I'm right here. I won't let anyone hurt you, and I won't leave you."

Charli called behind Eli as he ran out the door, "Bring her some water and a wet cloth."

His voice echoed as he descended the flights of steps toward the first floor.

The young woman appeared to be in her mid-to-early twenties with below-shoulder-length, blonde hair that hadn't been washed in several days. Her skin looked clammy, and sweat drizzled down her unwashed, unadorned face. Though her eyes were glassy, they appeared a dull, pale blue. She seemed weak as she clung to Charli's hand. Her unpolished nails pressed into Charli's palms.

She drifted in and out of consciousness. Each time, she woke frantically, gasped, and begged, never letting go of her death grip on Charli's hand. "Mommy, I swear, I didn't want to hurt him. He was…he tried to rape me and said he would kill me afterward."

Charli continued to coo softly and tried her best to calm the desperate woman. "I know, dear. Don't worry."

"I've got to go." The girl tried to rise, but her head

barely lifted from the rough pillow. "They'll find me now."

"Lie still. You're ill. Help is coming." Charli stroked her arm. "I won't let anything happen to you. I promise."

"They're coming!" Tears streamed down her already striped face from sweat that rolled across dirty cheeks.

"Be a good girl. The doctor is coming. Not the bad man." Charli's mind wracked as she tried to figure out what to say to ease her patient's fears. "I won't let the bad men come. They don't know you're here."

"They know. I'm sure he told them." She fell asleep again, jerking, and restless.

Finally, Eli brought four bottles of water and a wet hand towel. He gave all but one to Charli.

"Thank, babe." She smiled sadly at her man.

"No worries. The door is open downstairs. I'd best go down and wait for help, so I can show them how to get up here." He looked back at her before exiting the door. "Don't let her hurt you in her delirium."

"She's not dangerous."

"I don't think she'd do it on purpose, but sometimes people in her condition can have extreme surges of adrenaline and violent outbursts." He winced. "All I'm saying is, be careful."

"Sure thing."

Alone with her again, the girl stirred to semi-consciousness. Charli lifted her head with one hand and pried the other hand from the girl's grip so she could use it. She tipped the bottle toward her lips.

"Here, drink. You need water. You look dehydrated."

The blonde's eyes eased shut. Her mouth opened to

accept sips of water. She swallowed and drank what was offered to her until she fell into another deep slumber. Each time she awoke, Charli coaxed a bit more water into her. Clearly, the girl needed hydrating, but Charli took care to only give her a little at a time. She didn't want the stranger to vomit.

The poor thing looked pitiful. She needed medical attention as quickly as possible.

Every time her barely cognizant ward came to, she stammered faintly not making much sense. Charli's heart ached to help her, convinced this pretty, young woman could not have brutally murdered the man found in the woods.

Possibly the sick female's confused state had Charli fooled. Unless her first impression of the stranger changed once the girl regained her wits, Charli would help clear the woman's name.

Before long, a bang and chorus of voices echoed from the stairwell. Eli entered the room. A procession of three EMTs followed. They carried a slim metal and fabric cot and were followed by Jaiden and Leo.

Charli attempted to stand and move out of their way. The woman became alert enough to clasp her hand in a deadly grasp.

"No…Please don't leave me. Don't let them hurt me." The poor thing panicked when the first EMT motioned for Charli to remain where she stood.

Two of the three rushed to the woman's sides. Each did initial tests. One slipped a blood pressure cuff around her arm. She tried to fight him off. Charli chattered quietly and soothingly to her. She urged the frightened girl to cooperate and assured her these people were there to help, not harm her. She finally became so exhausted from exertion; she succumbed and allowed them to do their work.

Eli talked quietly to Jaiden and Leo in the background, explaining how they'd found this strange woman in their house. The third emergency responder prepared the cot to be used. The blonde seemed as pliant as a wet dishtowel as they lifted their patient onto it and strapped her down, but even in her coma-like slumber, she never let go of Charli's hand.

At the doorway to the steps, Charli touched the girl's face. Her eyes opened, and she smiled sweetly but weakly back.

"I love you, Mommy. Thank you for coming."

"It's okay, sweetie, but I can't hold your hand for a while. You are very sick. You need treatment. These doctors will get you to the hospital, where you can get treatment you need. They'll carry you down these steps to their vehicle."

They weren't doctors, but the next best thing. Charli feared any other interpretation of their roles might frighten the stranger enough to make this trek downstairs even more dangerous than it was.

She picked her words carefully. "Just lie still now and let them help me get you to safety."

"Okay, Mommy." Her eyes closed again, and she drifted into another world.

Charli trailed close behind the three emergency workers. Eli and then Jaiden and Leo followed. It seemed an eternity as they strode carefully down three flights to the foyer and then took the few steps to the yard. The ambulance parked at the curb.

Already dusk outside surprised Charli. She hadn't realized how much time had passed.

Neighbors arrived home from their day jobs and hesitated outside on their lawns to watch. Those who were retired sat casually on their porches or stoops an gawked openly at this shocking production that played out in their neighborhood.

As the aides lifted the gurney into the ambulance and secured their patient in, one ran around to the driver's side and started the vehicle. One worker hooked the woman to equipment inside so they could monitor and better check her vitals throughout the short trip.

The woman wailed, left alone inside the cube with two strange men. "No. Mommy! No."

Charli gazed up at the female EMT. "Any way I can travel with her? She's calmer with me present."

"Are you family?"

Charli gazed over her shoulder at Jaiden. Jaiden nodded. "Close as you'll get."

"Okay, get in."

Charli didn't hesitate but climbed aboard before the woman changed her mind. Behind her Eli said, "I'll follow in your truck."

Without a glance back, Charli nodded. The emergency worker shut and locked the doors. Before they were barely closed, the vehicle sped away, lights flashing. Walls dimmed the siren's wail.

Charli sat beside the gurney and held the blonde's hand. What had brought such a lovely creature, so delicate and weak, to this point in her life? What had caused this woman to hide in the attic of an abandoned mansion? Why Charli's house?

Charli didn't recognize her. She knew almost everyone in town, at least by sight. How had the stranger come to brawl with the man in the woods? Had she gone there to kill him? Why—and why in Sweetwater? Who was she, and what relationship did she have to the dead man?

Charli liked this girl, unless her personality changed drastically once she got better…If she got better. *Please, let her survive.*

At the hospital emergency room, an orderly took over and helped EMTs pull the gurney out of the vehicle. They transferred the victim to a hospital bed and rushed it inside through automatic doors. Charli raced alongside, as the woman continued to cling to her hand with all the muscle she had in her weakened condition.

Charli sensed more than she saw, Eli followed them inside and down the corridor. Two deputies stayed hot on his heels. At the emergency room automatic doors, the cart stopped.

One of the men dressed in blue scrubs glanced around at his audience and then to Charli. "Miss, you'll need to go wait in the waiting room. Check in with the nurse there, and she will give you a buzzer. We'll alert you as soon as the patient is stable."

Charli peeled her hand from the desperate grip. "Sweetie, these doctors will take good care of you. They'll let me know when I can see you. Now you be a good girl and let them do their work. I'll be right out here. I promise."

The girl's brows furrowed, and a tear rolled from her eye. She looked so dehydrated. Where did she get enough moisture to cry? "Don't leave me."

Charli shook her head and backed out of the way. "I promise. I'll be right here. I won't leave you. Now rest. Be good."

A whimper sounded as the aides rolled the gurney

inside. Doors quickly shut behind them. "Okay, Mommy."

Charli fell into Eli's strong arms and let him power her down the hallway to a facility for family members with loved ones cared for in the emergency room. The space had been furnished with only three walls lined with uncomfortable, straight-back, cushioned chairs. A few tables held boxes of tissues. The television mounted to a wall played a mindless comedy sitcom. Eli sat her in one of the chairs that faced the TV and took a seat beside her. She drew comfort from his hand wrapped around hers.

A few minutes later, Jaiden and Leo entered the room. They sat on either side of the couple. Jaiden handed Charli one of the two cups of coffee she carried, and Leo gave Eli the second one he held. Jaiden took the lead.

"So, Charli, Eli filled us in on how you two found this woman, as best he could in the time we had."

Leo nodded. "It seems the two of you did a bit of investigation."

Eli stared at his buddy. "Look, we just tried to figure out as much as we could about the history of our house. By pure happenstance we came upon this gal. Who knew she was camped out in our attic?"

Charli swallowed a sip of fortifying hot liquid. "We didn't even know we had an attic, let alone a squatter in it."

Jaiden met Charli's gaze. "She is, apparently, the woman who sparred with the victim in the woods. Evidence makes it appear she stabbed him with the hair pick. We'll check her DNA, but I wouldn't bet against it matching."

Eli curled his nose. "We figured as much."

Charli's back stiffened, and her chin shot up. "Yes, she's involved somehow. Likely, she had a tussle with that man, but I'd bet my eye teeth, she did not kill him. If she did, I'd wager it had to be self-defense. There is no way in hell you will convince me that pitiful creature in there is a cold-blooded killer."

Jaiden placed a calm hand on Charli's arm. "Don't go getting all riled up. We didn't say she is. She's innocent until proven guilty. No one is going to railroad her."

"No, they're not. I aim to see to that."

Jaiden patted her arm. "It's okay, Charli. I hear you." She stood. "I guess you want to continue the charade with the hospital and pretend to be the girl's cousin. I told the nurse when I checked her in that's who you are."

Charli's shoulders relaxed. "Thanks, Jaiden, and yes."

Chapter Sixteen

About forty-five minutes later a doctor dressed in aqua scrubs stepped into the room. He glanced around at the police, which now included Sheriff Gordon and his wife Lemon Sage, who had arrived soon after her husband. A surgery cap covered most of the physician's short, cropped hair. He pulled his facemask down to hang below his square jaw and stuffed a pair of vinyl gloves into his rear pocket.

"Charli Owens, I'm sorry to see you and Eli here under such circumstances. I understand you are next-of-kin to the woman in our care."

Charli glanced at Jaiden then back at the doctor, surgeon Clay Barnes, Jaiden's fiancé. Jaiden slipped her hand around Charli's from the seat beside her friend, offering support.

"Ah yes, she's a distant cousin. Is she all right?"

Clay cleared his throat and pulled an empty chair to him, to sit and face them. His fingers interlocked, and elbows rested on his knees as he bent forward. "I'm afraid your cousin is in a state of delirium. That's a serious change in mental abilities which results in confusion and a lack of awareness of one's surroundings. This disorder usually comes on fast—sometimes within hours or a few days of whatever caused it. It can generally be traced to one or more factors, including long-term illness or imbalance in the body such as low sodium. Does your cousin suffer from any ailment that could've led to this?"

Charli swallowed hard. "Not that I'm aware of. We've not stayed in touch as we should."

Clay's head tilted. "I see. Well, it could be the result of infection, surgery, overdose, or withdrawal from alcohol or drug use, or certain medications could've caused her condition. Are you aware of any of those?"

Charli shook her head. "I'm sorry. I'm not."

Clay blinked. "She doesn't appear to have had recent surgery. However, she does have bruises on her legs, arms, and torso. There is also an abrasion with some swelling on the top of her head. There's a bit of crusty blood where something rough broke the skin. We pulled slivers of what appears to be bark and fresh maple wood chips from the injury."

Jaiden gave her lover a look which apparently told him not to ask questions, just do as she said. "Clay, please place the articles you removed from the woman's head into a sterile container and give it to me. It should not be handled about or trashed. Hopefully, she simply hit her head accidentally. I'd like to check to make sure she didn't sustain that injury from an attack."

"Certainly," Clay gave the deputy a wink. "Contusions on the arms and some of those on the legs are consistent with excessive force applied. Bruising left imprints of large human hands. I'm not a detective, but it's evident someone manhandled this woman."

Jaiden nodded. "Thanks, Clay. I suspected as much from what I could see of her at the scene. We will need to get photographs of those injuries."

Charli frowned. "Can you tell me more about this delirium state? Will she be okay?"

Clay cleared his throat again. "We certainly hope so. Sometimes the source is impossible to determine. Delirium may cause a lack of focus, constantly change topics, getting stuck on one idea, not responding to questions or environment, lack of interest, one to be easily distracted, withdrawn, fearful or distrustful, short tempered, elation, mood swings, personality changes. Or one might see visions others don't. The condition interferes with thinking skills, memory, especially recent events. Speech may ramble or be nonsensical, difficulty with reading, writing, understanding speech, restlessness, anxiety, or acting combative. A sufferer might make strange sounds, moan, or call out unduly. Others are quiet and withdrawn, sluggish or have trouble sleeping."

Charli's brows rose as she nodded. "My cousin is confused. She acts fearful, shouted people want her dead and they were after her. She cried and called me her mother. She seemed afraid of everyone. Only I could reassure her."

Clay smiled. "It's possible she recognized you on some deep level and realized even in her delusional capacity that you could be trusted."

Eli's hand stroked Charli's back. "So, Clay, what do we do for her?"

Clay sat up straight. "We're doing tests to determine if medication or withdrawal or concussion set it off. Delirium occurs when brain signals aren't sent and received properly due to a medical condition combined with medication side effects. A stroke, heart attack, lung or liver disease, an injury, or chemical imbalance could be the culprit. Exposure to toxins—carbon monoxide, cyanide, or any deadly poison, poor nutrition, severe loss of body fluid, lack of sleep, emotional distress, extreme pain, or being put into a deep sleep-state for surgery could cause it. Do you know if your cousin has experienced any of these?"

Charli frowned. "I'm not sure. I haven't seen her in a long time." A little white lie wouldn't hurt. Would it?

Clay's head tilted toward his fiancé', and his brows crunched together. "She's listed as Jane Doe on the paperwork. I assume that's not her name."

It was awful having to keep things from Clay, but for now it was necessary. "Of course not, but for now, the police don't want her identity revealed." Charli shot a glance at Wyatt. He shrugged.

Eli snorted. "What type meds would induce the condition?"

Clay explained, "Medicines to treat pain, sleep problems, mood disorders, such as anxiety and depression, allergies, asthma, swelling, Parkinson's disease, spasms or convulsions." His gaze met Charli's. "Are you aware if your cousin has been treated for any of these?"

Charli sighed, defeated. "I'm sorry, Clay. I haven't a clue."

"She had a very high temperature when she was brought in. That's our first concern—to get it down. So, we'll treat her for that. We're testing for the most common of these first. We'll find the reason…if that's possible. In the meantime, we treat her symptoms. We did have to sedate her, however, to get her to allow us to examine her. She clung to that purple backpack until she passed out. Then, finally, one of the nurses managed to pry it out of her hands.

Jaiden said, "We'll take that, Clay."

He smirked. "I'll send the nurse out with it when I go back in there."

Charli blinked. "Thank you, Clay. Is there anything I should know before I visit her? When can I see her?"

Clay sighed. "It will be awhile before we can get her stable and comfortable. I'll let you in as soon as it's feasible. Hospital settings present a special challenge for preventing episodes as much of the activity around here involves room changes, invasive procedures, noise, poor lighting, or lack of natural lighting. Any of these factors might trigger an episode. It is difficult to sleep in such a place, and lack of sleep can contribute to the condition. We'll administer medication to help her rest. Our goal will be to prevent or reduce the severity of her condition. Help promote good sleep habits. Keep her calm. Avoid further medical problems or complications. She should avoid medications such as diphenhydramine, popular over-the-counter allergy and sleep medications, and a few other kinds of drugs. We'll give you a list when she's released."

Charli's eyes widened when an idea popped into her head. "When we found her, she grabbed her gut and cried that her belly hurt."

Clay's brows lifted. "It's likely she has an infection. That's a major cause of both fever and this delusional state. We're checking for urinary tract infections now. It would cause frequent or burning sensation at urination, blood in urine, nausea, or vomiting. If that's the trigger, we can treat it with medication. Which one will depend on the specific infection she has."

Charli winced. "Sounds serious."

"It is. She's being treated for dehydration while we search for the root of the condition." He stood, hands on hips.

Charli said a silent prayer that whatever ailed the woman could be easily treated. "Thank you, Clay."

"It's what I do. Someone will be out soon with the backpack, and we'll keep you abreast of her condition." The tall man disappeared through the door.

Jaiden took Charli's hand. "I spoke privately with Clay earlier and told him that no one is to know about this patient's presence in the hospital. We've got a guard posted outside of the ER where she's being treated, and we will continue to post a guard when she's transported to her own room. There will be no press release about this."

Eli laughed. "You know the Sweetwater grapevine. I'm sure our neighbor, Nancy, and the rest of the residents who saw us cart that gal into an ambulance will talk this up all over town."

Wyatt nodded. "Far as anyone is to hear, this is Charli's cousin, who fell down the steps and required emergency care. Say nothing more than that. The less it's talked about, the better. I already called Irma and warned her to keep her mouth shut." Wyatt also knew Gran well.

Charli's brows rose. "Good thing. She's got poker tonight. You know how that group is. They love a good story and are the central hub for local chatter."

Sage put her palms together in a *namaste* pose. "People mean well, but this could interfere with the sheriff's murder investigation."

Eli gazed at his friend. "So, Wyatt, learn anything helpful on your trip to Detroit?"

Wyatt shrugged. "A bit. Apparently, our man worked as some sort of bodyguard. The company employing him is undetermined, very vague. No legitimate address or phone number that reaches them. What's on his card is bogus. We're not sure exactly what he did. Landlord said he paid on time and always with cash. He's lived there several years, upstairs from her and has a separate entrance. She seemed kind of a busybody type and kept an eye on his comings and goings. Said he would travel for days at a time; she assumed on business. Not many visitors. A female friend stopped by occasionally. Landlord never met her. Never spent the night. She assumed the gal to be married."

Jaiden scrunched her nose up. "I don't see how a guy can sleep with his wife every night and not know she's screwed around on him."

A pang of guilt hit Charli. Wyatt would know. He'd caught his first wife in bed with his best friend.

"It happens." Wyatt shrugged. "The victim maxed out his two credit cards. No bank account we could establish. We're trying to determine what he did with his income, besides pay rent."

Leo leaned forward. "Must've had some sort of money-sucking habit."

Jaiden frowned. "Doc said he tested clean. His liver was in decent shape, so not a heavy drinker or druggie."

"Gambling?" Charli rolled her eyes.

"Perhaps," Leo answered. "I've got the people securing player card data from casinos in and around Detroit and Windsor."

Charli groaned. "All these persons of interest. What you need is a convictable arrest."

Jaiden chuckled and patted Charli's hand. "Don't we know it? Patience my dear friend. Patience."

Eli asked Leo, "So, what did you two learn from the homeless along the riverbank? You find the guy's shoes and wallet yet?"

Wyatt grunted. "For not being involved, you two sure know enough about this case. I expect complete discretion on your parts. You know the consequences."

Charli nodded and smiled, then blew the sheriff a kiss. "You've got it, Wyatt."

Eli smirked. "Of course. We wouldn't do anything to screw this up for you, just want you to find the killer and put him away as quickly as possible."

Jaiden glared. "You realize evidence points to that woman in there."

Charli winced. "I know how it looks, but I honestly don't see how that frail female could've killed that man. Maybe she stabbed him, but we never found a gun. I know the victim died of a gunshot wound."

Wyatt shook his head. "Is there anything you don't know, Miss Busybody?" His gaze shot accusingly toward Jaiden.

Both deputies shrugged and pushed their palms up in denial.

Charli took his criticism in stride. After all, the head lawman in the area knew his job well. Regardless of her relationship to Wyatt, she needed to tread lightly. As sheriff he performed his job expertly, as did Jaiden. Charli wouldn't risk getting her bestie in hot water with her boss, and she didn't want to screw up their investigation.

"Wyatt, Jaiden had nothing to do with this. She has used the utmost discretion where evidence is concerned. I'm a part of this since I found that hair pick. I have a right to ensure my fiancé is safe. Eli lives in the house where the person who stabbed that man lost it. It appears she did that. In her condition, I don't believe she's the murderer. That guy must've attacked her, and she wounded him. You heard Clay. Large hands gripped her arms and created those bruises. Same for those on her legs. Sounds to me like he tried to rape her. I believe, if she hadn't gotten away, she'd be on Doc's slab in the morgue."

Wyatt glared at her for a few seconds. One of his best interrogation tactics was dead silence. She refused to succumb to the psychological trick, so sat quietly and let him measure her with his eyes.

Finally, he broke the calm. "What about your knowledge of the GSW? Cause of death has not been revealed to the press. We only told them we discovered evidence of foul play."

Charli glared right back at her friend. "Wyatt Gordon, you know as well as I do; secrets get out in this little town. I have my resources and used them to learn about the gunshot wound."

Wyatt rolled his eyes upward. "I suppose you do. I get it. It's not like there's a person in town you haven't befriended. Knowing your grandmother, I assume she had a lot to do with your findings. What the hell. Irma knows better than to divulge information about this case to her friends. I expect the same from you two. This information stays out of the Sweetwater grapevine."

Eli snickered. "Our lips are sealed."

Charli chucked beside him and made a zipper motion across her lips.

Wyatt stood. "All right then, I am heading back to the office. You two behave yourselves."

Charli accepted his hug, and he shook Eli's hand. Sage's long, ebony ponytail swung with movement. Her slim, runner's legs stretched tall as she rose to her feet.

"I need to get home. Listen, if there's anything you all need, give me a buzz. Once you get back to work on your house again, I'll stop over and smudge the place—drive out any evil spirits that linger there."

Eli snorted a smile. "Sure."

Charli shrugged, not about to refuse any sort of help. "Couldn't hurt. Who knows what other entities live in the McGregor mansion?"

Sage laughed and waved as she left them. "Exactly. No harm. No foul. See you all soon."

After the door shut behind Sage, Leo tittered. "Funny. That gal has started to sound downright southern. No accent, other than that New Yorker thing, but she said you all and everything."

They had a hearty laugh. Each had a special reason to adore the New Yorker turned southern belle.

Eli met Leo's gaze directly. "So, spill it. Did you learn anything about the murder victim in your visit to the homeless camp?"

Leo took a long breath in and sturdied his shoulders. "Actually, we did. Several people said they heard shouts that day, a few hours before the victim's discovery. The voices weren't what we expected—that of a woman and man—but two guys shouted at each other. A couple said they heard a bang like a gunshot. Then the argument ceased. No one admitted they had explored the wooded area to find out what happened. Probably afraid to get involved in a drug deal gone bad or some other sort of brawl."

Charli studied Leo's face. "So, none of them hiked to the area and stole the guy's shoes and wallet."

Jaiden caught Charli's gaze. "They did not, but one fella said he'd seen another homeless man with 'spiffy hard shoes,' as he put it. He identified the guy as Spike. Apparently, this Spike fella is a loner. He hangs around there sometimes but keeps to himself. One woman said she thought him to be a homeless vet, maybe had PTSD. According to her, he acts kind of skittish."

Eli stared at the deputies. "Did you try to find this Spike?"

Leo frowned. "Sure did. We got a description of the guy from those who remembered him. He was nowhere at the transient camp, so we tried the two homeless shelters in town. One manager recalled the fella. He said he had shown up there for a meal and bed last week around the time the of vic's discovery. The man said Spike's shoes were much newer and nicer than the rest of his clothing. He had on camo pants and an overshirt with a black tee beneath. He had a dark, worn camo jacket with a hood. His shoes were shiny, and he recognized them as an expensive, high-fashion brand. Spike had dinner, and they gave him a bed."

Jaiden stepped in when Leo took a breather. "I spoke with one man who said he bunked beside Spike. That guy said he woke up during the night to find Spike counting some bills from a wallet. He stuffed the cash into his pants pocket and trashed the wallet. The guy waited until Spike slept. Then he took the wallet from the garbage can. He still had it and handed it over. The vic's—credit cards were still intact. The fella considered selling them, since he had no idea how to use them, but he hadn't gotten around to it. He handed it over, and we put it into evidence."

Charli snickered. "Did you apprehend him?"

"No. It's not illegal to fish out trash from a receptacle. Nor is it a criminal offense to consider committing a crime."

Eli frowned. "So, you didn't find Spike?"

Leo nodded. "Actually, we did. The shelter manager said Spike showed up the following evening, ate supper, and then asked for a cot for the night. He acted stupid-drunk, so they sent him away. It's against their bylaws to house an inebriated resident."

Jaiden smiled. "Since neither of the shelters would take him in, and he wasn't at the riverbank, we tried the old Ft. Washington Hotel."

Charli grimaced. "Isn't that where drunkards and derelicts live?"

Eli snorted. "Yeah, and I heard they sometimes rent rooms by the hour to working girls."

Leo puffed out a sigh. "You're both right, unfortunately. We parked around the corner and hoofed it to the building, crammed in between a newsstand and old barroom that stays packed from their 6 a.m. opening to closing at 2 a.m."

"Who knew so many hit the bottle that early in the day," said Eli.

Leo shrugged. "Lots of folks with issues, I guess. Anyway, we checked the tavern, but Spike wasn't there. The bartender said he'd seen him stroll toward the hotel. Spike carried a bottle wrapped in a paper bag. As we approached the entrance, the door propped open to the darkened lobby. To the right spanned a long hallway, and to the left a staircase led to the second floor—a dirty dump, as you can imagine."

Jaiden squirreled her nose up. "Absolutely frightening. Anyway, we heard a thump, thump, thump, then a shuffle. A guy who met Spike's description stumbled to the entrance and propped himself against the doorjamb. Disgustingly dirty, he had smudges on his face and paint chips stuck to his sweaty cheeks. Guess he rolled down the steps, hit the floor, and picked them up in the process. His eyes were glassy. He stunk to high heaven, and he wobbled where he leaned."

Charli said, "Guess there's no rule against being drunk as a sailor on leave at that high-class establishment."

Leo chuckled. "Apparently not. Anyway, we approached, identified ourselves, and invited him to a party."

Jaiden laughed. "Seriously, we just explained we needed to take him in for questioning concerning a homicide. He didn't look surprised or resist."

Eli scowled. "You didn't book him for murder?"

Leo shook his head. "Not yet. We put the guy in a cell to sleep it off so we can question him when he's sobered. He could be our killer. He acted coherent enough to identify himself as Harold Evans, a Marine veteran. Served in Afghanistan from 2001-2007. Must've seen some stuff." He gazed at Charli. "Sorry, Charli, I didn't mean to get carried away. It just gets to me sometimes. I hate that a vet lives on the street."

Charli sighed. "It's okay, Leo. War is hell."

He nodded. "We fingerprinted Sergeant Evans, and he left his DNA on things he touched. My cruiser needed serious detailing after we hauled the guy in. Geez, he reeked."

Eli pursed his lips. "So, this Evans is your murder suspect?"

Jaiden bit her lip. "Could be. It could've been a simple mugging. Evans might've tried to take the victim's wallet. If they got into a scuffle, it likely resulted in the vic's gunshot injury."

Charli inhaled deeply. Whoever shot that man was still at large. Would the danger never end? "Did he have the murder weapon?"

Leo frowned. "No, we have searched everywhere we can think of. Scoured the woods, dived in every dumpster in the vicinity, and even offered a reward at the homeless camp and shelters for news of its whereabouts."

Jaiden sulked. "The perp could've tossed it into the river—Ohio or Licking. Both are close."

Charli's protective instinct took over. "You searched our house for it before. I assume you'll do that again, since we found the woman in the attic."

Eli's groan sounded exasperated. "Yeah, will we ever our house back? We need to make up for lost time on the renovation. Our goal is to get it at least listed for sale before our December wedding."

Jaiden nodded. "The crime scene unit is going over the attic, tunnels, and the woodlands around the fishing lake, looking for evidence. They didn't cover that side of the hill where your house is situated, only the northwestern side toward the crime scene. We were not aware of the other entrance to your house. During the previous search, we had no clue the mansion might be involved. Now this female has been discovered, we're sure it is."

Charli exhaled. "Neither did we—not until we did some research and talked with our neighbor. Nancy Underwood's parents frequented the speakeasy that operated at the McGregor House. Once she grew up, they'd told her stories of the fun they'd enjoyed there. Lucky us. Not only does our house have a notorious history. We now have a secret corridor, secluded tunnel entrances to the residence, and we've unwittingly housed a murderer…murder suspect. I just pray you don't find that piece on our property."

Jaiden gave her an understanding, sympathetic smirk. "We'll soon find out. At the very least, you've hosted a person of interest." She glanced at her phone. "If CSU had found the murder weapon, they would've immediately texted Leo, Wyatt, and me. No word yet."

Chapter Seventeen

Charli phoned Gran to explain why she and Eli hadn't shown up for dinner. They stuck around the hospital until the nurse advised the patient to rest comfortably in her private room. A deputy stood guard. She would be sedated for the night. They could see the young woman the next morning, and Dr. Clay Barnes would give them an update on her condition when he did his rounds.

Around 7 a.m. the next day, Charli dressed and went to the kitchen. Eli and Gran chatted at the island and sipped coffee. "Oh, man, can I use a cup of that. It smells wonderful. Think I could get it intravenously?" She strode to the carafe and filled a mug with the steaming brew.

Gran chuckled. Her slender buttocks propped against the counter. "Good morning, my little adventurer. I understand you and Eli had a bit of fun yesterday."

Charli groaned. "Not sure I'd call it fun, but yes. We had an adventure all right."

She admired the fabulous, retired rock star. Gran, as she knew her. Irma, as their small town knew her. Starr Bright, as the world remembered her.

Gran never appeared outside her bedroom sans silver bob and makeup perfectly designed. Her eggshell colored linen slacks matched her cashmere V-neck sweater. A choker of pearls wrapped her slim neck, nearly devoid of wrinkles that might hint at her age.

"So, lovers, what's the schedule for the day?"

Charli leaned on the countertop beside her beloved grandmother. "The medical staff should've completed several tests on the woman Eli and I found in the attic of McGregor House. She's been moved to a private room. A…guardian is stationed outside her door. The nurse said we can see her this morning, so I guess we'll be off to the hospital." She studied Eli's expression.

He smiled, and Charli's day instantly brightened. "I called to check on her and got the room number and directions."

Gran met Charli's gaze. "Eli said you don't believe this gal is responsible for that man's death—the one found in the woods a few days ago."

"I don't. She might've stabbed that fella, but I don't think she is evil. Authorities searched through her things and haven't found a gun. Secondly, she seems to me to be a gentle soul—not capable of murder."

Eli frowned. "That doesn't mean she didn't kill him. It could've been self-defense. Even the mildest person might resort to drastic measures if their life depends on it. The wooded area where they found him is near the river. Whomever did the deed could've tossed the weapon into the water."

Charli nodded. "I suppose that's possible. After all, she clearly fought that brute off for some reason. Poor thing must've been terrified enough to stab him. Wyatt's investigating the victim's past to find out what motive she might've had to knife him and why he came here. She's obviously familiar with the area, since she located an unknown-to-us entrance and a hidden room. So, she'd know where the riverbank ran in relation to the crime scene."

Eli gritted his teeth. "Leo said divers are scouring the river bottom along the forest, at least out as far as anyone might've been able to throw the gun. Being weighty, a pistol wouldn't drift far, but it might be stuck deep in river bottom muck. They will also search the bottom of the lake near the icehouse in case she disposed of it there."

Charli glared. "Or someone else did."

Eli nodded. Gran shrugged.

"Anything's possible. The killer could be someone we're not even aware of yet. Or it could be that homeless vet Jaiden and Leo apprehended."

Charli sighed. "Possibly, but they didn't incarcerate him. They only detained him so he could sober up and be interrogated. He had the dead guy's wallet and cash, and he wore what they believed to be his shoes. Maybe he robbed and killed the man."

Eli's mouth twisted to one side. "They need to find out why the victim entered the woods in the first place."

Charli exhaled with a puff. "Hopefully, we can learn more today after they question the homeless man." Maybe they'd share their findings, though it seemed unlikely.

Gran poured herself another cup and refilled Eli's. "It's a dad burned shame that a guy serves his country, puts his life at risk for all of us, and ends up penniless to live on the streets."

"I agree with you there, Gran, but some people choose to live that way. We can't save them all." Her mind rolled, trying to determine what she might do about that situation. "Right now, we'd best check on my new 'cousin.'"

She strolled to the door and tossed her backpack around one shoulder. Eli followed her.

Behind them, Gran called, "You two stay out of trouble. That means don't get involved in the police investigation. We've had enough suspense and mystery already in this family."

****

Fifteen minutes later, they strolled the halls of Sweetwater General. Eli pointed. "There's her room."

Deputy Leo Sanders sat reading a magazine outside the door. He looked up as they arrived.

"Morning, y'all. Looking to visit your 'cousin'?" He snickered.

Charli's chin rose. "Yes, how's she doing?"

Leo smiled. "Better, I think. Doc's not been to see her yet this morning, but she communicated with the nurse. Seems to be coherent or at least more so."

Eli nodded toward the closed door. "Okay if we go in?"

"Yes, you're on the approved list." Leo frowned. "Holler if she gives you any problems."

"Will do." Eli tapped on the door and pushed it open. He followed Charli inside.

The blonde, dressed in a checkered hospital gown, sat upright in the bed with a sheet over her legs. A news program played on the television set mounted to an opposite wall. She looked toward her visitors.

"Good morning." Charli smiled. "You certainly look better."

An intravenous line strung from a plastic fluid bag suspended from a metal stand beside the bed. The hose disappeared beneath a bandage attached to the woman's right forearm. Transparent liquid dripped from the bag through the tube and ran into the woman's arm. Dark circles highlighted her sunken eyes. Today they were less glassy. She appeared more alert and calmer.

Charli approached the bedside. "I hope you rested well. I would've stayed, but the nurse advised me you'd be out for the night. I'm Charli Owens, and this is my fiancé, Eli Lange. We own the house where you were staying."

Recognition showed in her pale blue eyes. "You're the angel who found me. I remember. You were so sweet. I felt safe with you there."

Eli pulled a chair near to the bed beside Charli and one for himself. "Mind if we sit?"

She smiled. "Please, make yourselves comfortable. I'm glad to see a couple of friendly faces."

Charli sat in the chair Eli had moved for her, and he took the other. "Are you still in pain? You said yesterday your belly hurt."

The blonde placed her frail hands on her stomach. "It's much better. The nurse said they gave me some strong antibiotics, and my chart confirms I had a UTI. They also gave me intravenous fluids. I'm dehydrated and haven't eaten for a couple of days."

Eli smiled. "How long do you think you were in that delirious state?"

The stranger shrugged. "Not sure. A couple days, I guess. I didn't feel well and hit my head on a branch when I was…in the woods." She winced. "I should've been more careful."

Charli laid a hand on the bed. "Were you running from someone?"

Silence swallowed the room and pulled air out of it.

Charli held her breath, waiting. It seemed an eternity before the girl in bed spoke. Her hands twitched where they lay against the covers.

"Yes, a man attacked me." She paused as though willing her heart to stop racing, but urgency in her voice contradicted calmness. "Do you know what happened to my backpack? I need to find it. It's very important."

Charli sighed at the change of subject. "You clutched it so tightly we couldn't take it until you fell asleep. The nurses brought it out to my friend, Deputy Jaiden Coldwater. I believe she took it to the station."

Her pallid skin grew even more ashen, as her face screwed up in an agitated expression. Her hands jerked against her abdomen, and her whispered voice sounded shrill. "I must have that bag. It's a matter of life and death—mine. Please, help me get it back."

"Your bag is safe." Eli frowned and sat erect. "Are you in danger?"

Yesterday they'd choked her fearful demeanor up to delirium. She no longer seemed delirious. Tears pocketed her eyes, and her knuckles whitened as they gripped the sheet. Her shoulders appeared to tighten. Breath burst in and out of her, and she blinked rapidly as she shivered.

"Yes. They want me dead. I thought I'd be safe here. I mean, there…in the mansion. I don't know how they found me, but that man came to take me—."She licked her lips repeatedly, gasped, and expelled air as if in pain. "—to kill me."

Charli flinched back in her seat. "Really? Are you sure?"

She appeared to hold back a scream or tears. A hand flew to her head, as though dizzy. Holding her breath for a few seconds, she gulped down air and jerked at the sound of the door opening.

Deputies Jaiden and Leo entered the room.

"Morning y'all." Jaiden beamed as she glanced first at Eli and Charli and then at the woman. "You look much better today."

At their entrance, the woman mumbled what sounded like "Got to get it. Get it," but Charli could barely make out the words. Upon being addressed directly, she looked at the deputies. "You have to return my backpack. I need it. It's important."

Jaiden stood beside Charli, and Leo circled to the other side of the bed near Eli. He smiled and spoke calmly and softly to the frightened girl.

"Ma'am, your belongings are safe. We have them under lock and key at the sheriff's office. Nothing will happen to them. We assure you of that."

Jaiden took over. "Yes, ma'am. We took your backpack, among other things, to safeguard and to check for evidence. You were in no condition to answer questions when you were found, but it appears we were searching for you all along. You have been a person of interest in a recent case."

She looked like she would cry, as her head bent forward. "You have? Me?"

"We weren't sure exactly who we were looking for until Charli and Eli here found you. We only had DNA evidence and a blonde hair to go on."

Jaiden bobbed her head. "Your condition, that is the bruises, indicate you were in a physical altercation. Did you get into a fight?"

Tears spilled over the patient's lower lashes and drizzled down her cheeks, now clean. She barely nodded.

"Yes, a man grabbed me. He tried to hurt me." Her voice scarcely above a whisper.

Leo's stare was unexpressive. "Are you acquainted with a Mr. Clancy Mulhaney?"

Her eyes widened. "I am not."

Jaiden pushed a picture of the dead man toward her. The head and shoulders view of him on the morgue slab hid his injuries and autopsy incisions.

"Do you know this man?"

Her head rocked back and forth in denial. "I don't know him, but we met. He attacked me in the forest. I went out to buy food. On my way back to the mansion he grabbed me almost as soon as I entered the wooded area. I'm not sure if he followed me or if he was already there waiting for me. We fought. He smacked me across the face." Her hand lifted to her jaw.

Charli winced at the idea of that big brute manhandling this poor woman. That explained the bruised cheeks and arms.

The girl let out a little sob. "He overpowered me and threw me on the ground." She paused and gulped down a breath. "He said he wanted to have a little fun before he did what he'd come to do—kill me." Another pause. "I screamed and cried out, but no one came to help. I tried to fight him off, but he was too big. He pawed at me and ripped my jeans down to my knees. I begged for my life. It didn't faze him. He said he had a job to do, and he wouldn't get paid unless he completed it. Said his boss would kill him if he failed."

"Good grief," Eli gasped. "This wasn't just an attempted rape or theft. What the—"

"What happened then? We'll get to the why's later," Jaiden said.

"He held me down with one big hand, kneeling between my legs, and tried to undo his pants with the other." A little cry escaped her lips. "While he struggled with his zipper, I yanked one chopstick out of my hair bun and thrust it as hard as I could at his throat. I missed but hit chest. Blood spurted all over. He screamed, spouted a bunch of cuss words, and clutched his wound. He scrambled to his feet, yanked the stick out, then dropped it. I snatched it up. My fingerprints were on it. He kept squirting blood as he scrambled for a hanky from his coat pocket.

While he was distracted, I grabbed my backpack from where it had fallen. It caught on a branch and ripped. I ran as fast as I could, pulling my jeans up as I went. My hair stuck to bloody goo all over my face. I sweated something fierce but just kept going. I ran and ran, afraid to go to the riverside tunnel I'd used before. I weaved in and out along the riverbank, not wanting to give away the entrance, in case he followed me. My heart throbbed in my head so loud. I slapped through brush and couldn't tell if he trailed me or not but didn't want to take any chances. I zigzagging around the hillside all the way to the icehouse on the other side of the mansion. Somewhere along the way I hit my head. The branch knocked me on my ass. I might've passed out a few minutes—not sure. I got up and kept going."

That explained the goose egg on her head. This poor creature had been through it. Charli's heart went out to her. She hadn't been wrong. This woman acted innocent.

Leo leaned forward. "What did you do with the firearm you shot Clancy Mulhaney with?"

She scowled. "I don't know what you're talking about. Is Clancy Mulhaney the man's name? I didn't mean to kill him. Well, I guess I did mean to. Just didn't think. I simply reacted…to defend myself. I didn't shoot him. I never even had a gun. If I killed that man, I did it with a hair pick."

Jaiden glared. "Are you saying you did not shoot Mulhaney?"

Her brows lifted as she shook her head. "Absolutely not. If he's dead at my hand, it's from stabbing."

"So, you know nothing about a firearm?" Clearly, Leo and Jaiden didn't buy the woman's denial.

"No, I have never fired a gun before. I don't have a clue even how to load one, much less shoot one." Fresh tears streamed down her face.

Charli reached for one of her hands. At first the woman started to jerk away. Then she allowed her to hold her hand. It quivered in Charli's.

"It's okay. That man won't hurt you again."

Jaiden nodded with a severe expression. "Mr. Mulhaney is deceased. The murder happened the day he attacked you. Police found your hair pick at the scene—not the one you stuck him with—the other."

The blonde touched her head. "It must've fallen out during the struggle. I didn't think about it. Only by reflex, I picked up the one he discarded as he put pressure on his wound. I was so scared; I didn't care what happened to him. I just got the heck out of there as quickly as possible. I figured if he survived the stabbing, he'd chase me down, but he must not have tried."

Eli bit his upper lip. "Guess not."

Jaiden showed the woman anther photo. "What about this guy? Have you seen him?"

She pouted. "No, never. Was he hurt too? Did he work with this Mulhaney?"

It must've been the homeless Spike.

Leo took the question. "Doubtful, but we're not yet sure. We have him in custody and will question him this morning. We wanted to check on you first."

"So, you've never encountered this man, Harold Evans. Some call him Spike. You never met Mulhaney until he attacked you?" Asked Jaiden.

The woman drew in a long breath. "Actually, I saw the man you called Clancy Mulhaney a few times before. I guess he must've followed me here...looking for me."

Jaiden's eyes steeled. "Is that why you hid in the McGregor House?"

"Yes, they sent Mulhaney to kill me." Her eyes squeezed shut, and she gripped her belly as if in pain.

Jaiden glanced at the ceiling to the left. She took a couple of deep breaths before changing the subject. In the stillness, the shaky woman clung to Charli's hand and squirmed in bed.

Charli leaned toward her. "Does it hurt? Do you need the medical staff?"

She shook her head but didn't speak. Finally, Jaiden asked, "Are you able to tell us who you are? How did you know about McGregor House and the secret entrances and room?"

Charli sat on the edge of her chair in suspense. She glanced at Eli. His attention focused on the stranger as well. Everyone seemed to fidget or stiffen.

After a short pause, the woman looked up from her lap. "My name is Della Louise McGregor from Chicago. I worked for the Chicago Police Department as a sketch artist. It gave me the opportunity to use my talents and left time for me to pursue my art."

"McGregor," all the visitors said in unison.

Charli scowled. "Your name wasn't on the deed when Eli and I purchased McGregor House. My impression is that all heirs had to sign. It took a couple of weeks to get all the signatures from those spread across the USA."

Della's eyes closed and slowed the flow to one lone tear that dribbled down her cheek. After a lengthy inhale and exhale she looked at Charli. "My father Michael, along with others, inherited part of the house from my grandfather. Papa signed the deed a couple days prior to his death."

Charli sighed and touched Della's hand. "I'm sorry for your loss. Your dad was Michael Lawrence McGregor from Detroit, Michigan?"

The woman nodded and dabbed at her tears with the back of her free delicate hand. "Yes. Papa had been ill for a while—pancreatic cancer. I left Chicago almost a year ago to tend to him at his home in Detroit. Nurses came in for a few hours a week so I could work enough to make ends meet. I couldn't find work as an artist in Detroit. I took a part-time job at a bottling company."

Eli grimaced. "I'm sorry for your loss, Della."

"Thank you. At least I had that time with him." She sniffed with several blinks.

Jaiden leaned a hand against the bedrail. "Is that why you were familiar with the tunnels, hidden passageway, and secret room in the house?"

Della nodded with a sad smile. "Yes, we visited Grandpa Harlan often as a child. My cousins and I played in the attic. We were warned against going into the tunnels, but we explored them anyway. I knew them very well. We spent hours roaming those woods on hillsides to the north, east, and south of the mansion. Sometimes

147

when the owner didn't have fishing customers, we swam in the pay lake. He closed for fishermen in winter, and we skated there when it iced over."

Leo stared. "Why? What and who did you hide from?"

Della flinched and withdrew her hand from Charli's hold. Her jaw clenched. Eyes opened wide and darted about. Her hands shook, and she leaned back. Panic displayed in her bloodshot eyes, and her voice became shrill. "Where's my backpack? I need my things."

Jaiden patted the bedrail, probably to refocus Della's attention and still her fears. "No worries, your backpack and other things are safely locked up at the sheriff's station, as I mentioned before."

Clearly, Della wasn't yet thinking straight. "No, no, no, I must have my backpack."

Charli ached to help her. "Della don't worry. Whatever happens, you're safe with us."

Jaiden spoke with calm authority, "Ms. McGregor, your personal possessions are held securely. I can assure you of that. However, you are a person of interest in an open investigation. We will discuss this further, once you feel better. Right now, your medical condition takes precedence. If there's something you need us to know to keep you safe, please tell us now."

Della's jumpiness subsided somewhat, but she acted as though every nerve was alive and sensitive to touch and sound. She jerked at the slightest noise. Her shoulders sagged, and her voice quaked. "I know too much...or I think I do. They must've found out I took it. They came for me at Papa's memorial service, but I ran."

"It's okay, Della. We'll protect you. A guard is stationed outside your door. When you're thinking more clearly, you can explain. For now, allow the doctors to care for you. Try to relax and rest." Leo said calmly.

Jaiden's face didn't reveal her opinion about this strange woman, but it was certain she meant to ensure their main suspect didn't get away. "We are investigating a murder case. There is evidence you were involved."

Della's brows furrowed. Tears dried to a crust around her hollow eyes. "I killed him, didn't I? I stabbed him and ran when he attacked me. I tried to elude them, but they must've figured out Papa came from here. I didn't know where else to go. I guess Mulhaney followed me here. They're not done with me. They'll come for me…again."

Charli winced. "They? Who is after you?"

Della's face scrunched up. Her eyes filled with fresh moisture waiting for the opportunity to break free. "I don't know them, but they know me…and that I know too much." Her eyes squeezed shut, and she sighed then opened them. Her head rocked back. Eyes closed a second, as though she tried not to faint. Her head lifted to Jaiden's gaze. "He's dead. Isn't he? I killed him."

Della gave a heavy sigh. "Was Mulhaney alone? I didn't see anyone else, but I didn't look."

Leo frowned. "We haven't found evidence he traveled with anyone, but he didn't live here."

Della snickered. "Let me guess—Detroit?"

Leo nodded but didn't elaborate.

Della blinked several times, as though she pushed dizziness at bay, obviously, not completely coherent.

Jaiden looked sternly at the irrational patient. "Don't worry. We will talk more when you feel better. Right now, focus on getting better. We will ensure your safety."

Della glared. "They know I know, and they want me dead."

Jaiden twisted her head to the side. Her eyes rolled but not so the patient could see. Obviously, she believed this woman paranoid due to her condition. Guards provided safety for Della, but also because she'd been identified as the prime suspect in a murder case. Leo came to his feet to stand beside his partner.

Jaiden's head rocked forward toward the patient. "Don't contact anyone for now. An officer is on guard outside your door. You are safe. We'll check on your condition tomorrow. Perhaps we can talk more then."

As dusk replaced sunshine, and the day drew to an end, Charli and Eli sat quietly, allowing Della time to rest. Hopefully, their presence comforted her, not being alone. Soon after the deputies left, Dr. Clay Barnes arrived. He greeted Charli and Eli and then read Della's chart.

Clay shined lights in his patient's mouth, eyes, and ears, took her pulse, and then chuckled. "Looks to me our patient has made a rapid recovery. You're doing very well, ma'am. I don't suppose you can give me your name, now you're coherent. You were checked in as Jane Doe, and Charli is noted as your cousin. I know for a fact that's not the case."

Della smiled at the handsome surgeon. "Della Louise McGregor, and I'm sorry for the problems. I do have medical insurance. Please, don't make...my cousin...Charli leave."

"No worries. That's not my concern. The sheriff's department handled hospital paperwork. You will remain Jane Doe until Sheriff Gordon notifies us otherwise. If it's okay with you, I'll call you Della when we're together."

Della smiled. "Thank you."

Luckily, they'd decided to allow Della to remain anonymous for the time being.

The tall, slim physician caught his patient's stare. "With your delirium and high fever, we suspected an infection. It is and of the urinary tract. You were seriously dehydrated as well. We gave you fluids and a strong antibiotic. Tests show your head injury resulted in concussion."

"Will she be okay, Clay?" Eli asked.

"Sure, sure. Your temperature is near normal now, so clearly the antibiotics are doing their thing. Your delirious symptoms are getting better and may or may not reoccur. You should feel more and more coherent. I'd suggest you get plenty of rest. Stay calm, drink lots of fluids, and continue medication. If all continues to go well, we can discharge you tomorrow—assuming your progress continues."

Highly unlikely, the sheriff's department would release her. Della would surely go to jail.

Clay glanced at his friends. "Charli, Eli, you should go home now and let our patient rest. Charli, you're on the list of who can see the patient. If you'd like, you can come back tomorrow during visiting hours. We'll give Ms. McGregor a sedative so she can sleep."

"Thank you, Clay." Charli smiled at Della. "You're in good hands with Dr. Barnes. This handsome surgeon isn't just a local physician. Clay's surgical expertise is a blessing to our small town. He fills many medical roles at Sweetwater General, due to our low staff numbers. Doctors fill in wherever needed."

Eli stood and took Charli's free hand. She followed her fiancé's lead and strolled toward the door. "Della, I'll be back in the morning. Don't worry about a thing. Just rest.

Chapter Eighteen

The next morning Charli and Eli arrived to find Leo and Jaiden talking with the guard at her door. Leo shook the officer's hand. "You can take off now. We've got this."

They're here to arrest Della. Charli inhaled and held her breath. "Can I see her?"

Jaiden gave Charli a friendly hug. "Sure, go on in. We'll be there in a few minutes. I need to speak with her nurse first."

Eli wrapped his arms around Charli's petite body. Her head reached to just below his chin. "I'll leave you here and go check on the bathroom tiles we ordered for the house. If you need me before I return, just give me a ring."

"Okay, thanks, Eli. See you soon." She tiptoed to give his soft lips a peck. Charli peered into the hospital room. "Della, are you awake? Okay if I come in?"

A much perkier Della answered, "Absolutely. Thanks, Charli. I hoped you'd come."

Charli approached the bed where a fully-dressed Della sat. Her feet dangled from the side. "Of course. I told you I would."

Della smiled. "Thank you."

"Deputies Leo Sanders and Jaiden Coldwater are here to see you. I'm sure they want answers if you're up to it."

Della sighed heavily. "Might as well face them and get it over with. Doctor Clay told me earlier he ordered a prescription for me but said I could be discharged."

Charli blinked. "Yes, Jaiden is checking with your nurse now. I want you to know, you can trust them. Jaiden, Leo, Sheriff Wyatt Gordon, they are good people. They're all friends of ours."

Della gave a somber nod. "Good to know. I trust your opinion."

Leo entered the room, and Jaiden followed. "It's good to see you looking better, Ms. McGregor. Dr. Barnes said you're able to be released."

She nodded. "Yes. Thanks. Look, I know you want some answers. Can Charli stay?"

Jaiden stepped forward. "Yes, while we wait for your papers, maybe you can explain a few things for us."

Della nodded quietly. "I'll try, but I'm not sure where to begin."

Leo smiled. "How about telling us how you ended up in Charli's house?"

Della breathed in heavily and shoved air out in a surge. "I needed a place to hide and remembered how to get into the McGregor mansion through tunnels from my childhood. I didn't mean any harm, and I'd be happy to pay Charli and Eli rent for the time I stayed in the attic."

"That's not necessary. Because of you, we discovered the second tunnel and an attic. You owe us nothing." Charli mentally noted to contact Bubba so he could check the roof from inside the attic.

Della acted apprehensive. Charli asked, "Is there something else?"

Della sighed. "When Papa died, I was afraid to go home to Chicago."

Jaiden frowned. "Why? What were you afraid of?"

Della appeared to choke down a lump. "I saw something I shouldn't have gotten involved in. I'm not sure what exactly, but I know too much. They figured it out, and they came for me at Papa's funeral. I was talking with mourners at the front of the room. I recognized two thugs from the warehouse who came in. I got scared, asked my cousin for the keys, and told her I had to go. She didn't ask questions. Guess she saw panic in my eyes. She just handed them over. I promised to text her a location where she could pick the car up later. I excused myself, ran out the back door to her automobile, and got out of there as quickly as possible."

Leo scowled. "How did you end up here?"

Della shrugged. "I wasn't sure where to go, so I just drove around and around. Finally, I left my cousin's car in long-term parking at the Detroit Airport. I took a shuttle to the terminal then another to a downtown hotel. From there I took a cab to the bus depot and caught a ride to Indianapolis. After the night in Indy, I rode a bus to Memphis. A waitress at a truck stop introduced me to a semi driver who gave me a lift to Cincinnati. I took a cab to downtown Sweetwater and hoofed it from there."

Jaiden snickered. "That's a convoluted route to Sweetwater from Detroit." Clearly, she didn't buy Della's game.

Della smiled. "Yes, but I wasn't sure how to lose them. I just knew that if they caught up with me, they'd kill me. I figured out where to go along the way."

Jaiden cocked her head away, and her eyes rolled up. She smiled toward Della. "That's a lovely story. You'll have to entertain us with it a bit more once you're out of here." She glanced at her partner. "Leo let's go check on Della's discharge papers." She spoke to Della, "Charli can keep you company while we do that."

Without waiting for a response, the two of them left the room.

Charli leaned forward. "Della, you realize they will take you to jail. Right?"

Della's eyes closed. "I figured as much. I killed that man in the woods. They believe I did it, even though they claim he died from a gunshot wound. I swear, Charli, I never shot that man. I didn't even see if he had a gun. He was so much bigger and stronger than me. If he had one, he never saw reason to pull it out. He just overpowered me."

Charli laid a hand on the distraught woman's forearm. "I believe you, Della, but they have an open and shut case. They'll just continue the search for that gun, so they have even more evidence against you. You say that man followed you here, and that there were two thugs at your dad's funeral. I'm confused. Why were they there and who were they?"

"One of them was the guy from the woods. That's why I know he followed me. I recognized him at Pa's service and again when he yanked my pants down." Della's eyes closed and her shoulders sagged. "If the police find a handgun buried or sunken to the bottom of the river or lake, fingerprints will surely be distorted. Even if mine were never there, they'll believe they were. I don't know what to do. I'm going to prison for a crime I didn't commit."

Charli's heart ached with the need to help her new friend. "Tell me more about what happened to you in Detroit. Why were those guys after you?"

"It was from the bottling factory. I only worked

there a few months while Papa was ill. It was my job to open cartons of empty laundry jugs and load them onto conveyor belts in the automatic filling assembly line. I noticed on the first of every month empty jugs arrived heavier than those we received other days. I loaded empties, and they moved down the line to be filled, capped, caps tightened, and then they dropped back into empty cartons that had been moved from my station to the last one. Someone sealed filled cartons of product. Then a forklift driver loaded those containers onto pallets, took them to the loading dock, and dropped them into semis parked there."

"That sounds efficient and normal enough." Charli listened intently and tried to figure out the issue.

Della nodded. "Yes, it is. On the first of each month a unique trucking company showed up. I wouldn't have noticed except that this shipping line always sent a helper for the driver, even though they delivered to a location in Detroit. Those deliveries didn't need helpers. They never did any work, just hung around and watched the process. The guys always looked creepy and burly—kind of like bouncers at a nightclub—big, scary, dudes. The fella in charge of docks was kind of sweet on me. I had to pass his station to clock in. He was nice, so I sometimes stopped to chat before I punched my ticket. I noticed a manifest in his hand one day and saw the delivery location for one of the outbound orders. I asked him about it. He said the customer had a standing shipment only on the first of every month. They always used the same transportation company."

"Who was the dock manager?"

Della smiled. "His name is Clarence Boyd. Clarence has worked there for fifteen years."

Charli wrote the name on an open pad on her phone. "Do you recall the shipper's name?"

"Sure, it was Crane Motor Lines. The manifest stated they were a delivery for Detroit Detergent Distributors at 357 West Forbes Street, Detroit, Michigan. I looked the address up online, and it's near the bridge to Windsor in Ontario. There's a website for the distribution company. They advertise selling supplies to cleaning companies. The CEO is Dwayne LaRosa. There's a photo of him in a business suit. Nice looking middle-aged man. Kinda balding."

Charli frowned and made a mental note to double-check facts Della had just spouted. "So, why did you recognize the thugs from your father's funeral?"

Della's eyes squeezed shut. "They were two of the truck company thugs—driver's helpers. They did not know me personally, so had no reason to be at Pa's memorial except to find me. No one else from work showed up. It was just Papa's friends, neighbors, and a couple of relatives."

This did not sound good. "So why would they look you up?"

"I hung around and talked with Clarence one morning—the day I asked him about the manifest and freight company. One of those intimidating guys came around the truck bed and glared at me like he knew I'd stolen the crown jewels. His stare sent chills down my spine." She shook as though shivering, though the room was comfortably warm.

"That doesn't seem like enough to get you in hot water with those goons." Charli frowned.

Della shook her head. "Yeah, maybe not, but it put me on their radar—apparently." She paused and looked away, then back. "Later that day at lunch, I sat outside having lunch with one of the gals from the logistics office. Sue was her name. I asked her about the transportation company. She was surprised—said that the production company awarded all truckloads to specific shippers. Crane Motor Lines was not among the awards. That didn't sit well with her, but I assured her they took loads to this customer every month on the first. I don't know how many loads they delivered each month. According to Clarence, they were the only trucks loaded on those days. Sue said she'd check on it. I think she figured someone slid some business over to a friend or family without the producer's knowledge."

"Was that enough to have them come after you?"

Della frowned. "Apparently."

Charli's brows flew up. "You were really worried about this. How did you recall all of that?"

Della snickered. "I have a photogenic memory. I only need to see something once. If I focus, I never forget it."

Charli chuckled. "Funny, I have that same talent, but some days I am so stressed I can't remember my own name."

Della smiled. "I doubt that seriously. It's just a matter of concentration—or at least it is for me. I've just always been able to do it."

Charli snickered. "Yeah, me too. It's not a bad thing."

"Listen, Charli," Della leaned forward. "You've got to help me. I can tell, the police don't believe me. You're my only hope. If you don't help, no one will. I don't know what's going on. All I know is someone at the bottling company uses empty bottles to move something illegal."

Charli scowled. "That sounds odd, but it doesn't seem like you knew enough to get you in hot water. You must've done more than just notice these things."

"Unfortunately, yes. On my last day on the assembly line, I took something. They must've found out. I planned to get it to the police, but Papa died. I guess they discovered it was missing. They must've counted the damaged bottle bin and discovered one container missing. Figuring I took it, they came after me to get it back."

"What did you take?"

Della sighed. "We tossed damaged containers into a crate. The bottle manufacturer would later melt and reuse the plastic. I carried a box cutter in my apron and used it to slit open cartons so I could load empties onto the assembly line. We took turns at the end of each day collecting everyone's trash from the different stations and disposed of it in a large receptacle near the locker room. Then we'd leave the empty garbage cans there for someone to redistribute to stations the next day. I shoved one of those damaged jugs into the bottom of my trash can and covered it with refuse. As I gathered the other three stations' cans, I stacked them atop mine and then stopped off at the ladies' room. Inside a stall, I sliced off the bottom portion of the empty with my box cutter, shoved the remains back into the trash and covered it. I tucked the stolen section between my waistband and bra. My sweatshirt hid it. After I flushed and washed my hands, I tossed the contents of our waste cans into the large receptacle. I topped it with other garbage to make sure the bottle remains were concealed."

Charli's brows scrunched together. "How did you

get it out of the facility?"

Della shrugged. "The security guard checked my purse on the way out. The jug base was still beneath my sweatshirt. The waistband of my jeans held it against my stomach. I knew I could not return to the job. As it turned out, Papa had the same plans. I told him what I did that day. I'd already shared with him my suspicions. He was supportive and told me I'd done the right thing—even gave me the name of his friend who worked on the Detroit police force, so I could go directly to him."

Charli cocked one brow. "So, did you?"

Della shook her head. "I never had the chance. Papa died peacefully in his sleep that night."

She swabbed a tear away with her knuckle. Charli shoved the tissue box from her bedside table toward her. She took one, dabbed at moisture and blew her nose.

"He'd prearranged everything. All I had to do was make one call. They cremated him the next day. His memorial was two days later." She sighed and stared at the blanket that covered her. "There was nothing left for me in Detroit. I packed my things and called CPD, told them I would return to work. I figured I could let them handle the situation with Detroit locals once I got home. My bags were in my cousin's car. She planned to drop me at the airport after the service." She puffed out air, lips in an 'O.' "When I saw those men, I knew I'd never make it to the airport alive and couldn't risk my cousin being collateral damage."

Charli frowned. "Sounds terrifying. What is in that bottle base?"

Della smiled and her head shook. "I have no idea. Listen, Charli, I'm sorry I hid out in your house and got you and Eli mixed up in this mess."

Charli patted her hand. "No worries. We knew something strange was going on. Neighbors reported ghosts and prowlers around the grounds and inside. Eli even heard something. I guess that was you."

Della's head bent. "Guess so. I was kind of disoriented after I hit my head, and I was freezing something awful."

Charli smiled. "Dr. Barnes said that was your fever, and there isn't any heat in the attic. I'm glad to see your temperature is down."

Della smiled weakly. "Thanks. I appreciate that. Charli, I hate to ask you. I've imposed enough on you, but I need your help. The police don't seem to believe me. If you don't help, no one will. I thought I killed that man and was ready to face the consequences. If he didn't die from stabbing, then I'm innocent of his murder. I don't want to spend my life in prison for a crime I didn't commit."

Charli touched her quivering, cool hand. "I believe you, Della. I'll do whatever I can to help, but I don't know what to do."

Della appeared to ponder a few seconds. Then her eyes brightened. "I did some research in the days before Papa's death and checked into Detroit Detergent Distributors. Their website looks bogus. It shows a fancy warehouse and several loading docks. The owner is listed as Dwayne LaRosa. There was no business phone number, only an email address. I'm not sure why that name sounds familiar, but it does. There was no Detroit phone number listed for him. I found no complaints about their business practices. When I did a backward search on the street address from the website, I discovered another distributing company on that road. I called their number, and they said there was no such address or company located in the area. They claimed to own the land where the facility was alleged to be located and have plans for expansion to add more warehousing."

Jaiden and Leo entered. He pushed a wheelchair. "We have your discharge papers."

Jaiden handed them to Della. "Sign the first and third pages. Take copies of each one. After care instructions are on them. I have a copy for our files, so we'll make sure you have what you need."

Clearly, they were taking custody of Della.

Della gave her a penetrating look. "Is the bottom of a bright orange, plastic jug still in my backpack? If it's in there, you can't miss it. Please, don't let anything happen to that. It's important."

Leo smiled. "There was no such thing in your backpack when you were found."

"Oh, gosh! The bag ripped during our fight. Don't tell me I lost it when I ran from that man? You've got to find it. It's all the evidence I have."

Jaiden stared. "Evidence? What do you mean?"

Della's eyes pleaded with the deputy as she helped her into the wheelchair, and she handed Leo the signed papers. "I took it from the bottling facility where I worked in Detroit. It's proof something strange is going on there, and it's the reason that man tried to kill me. It's why he followed me here."

Jaiden handed Della a bag of her personal items. Della sat them in her lap and looked defeated.

"Della, I assure you, there was no such thing in your backpack. Nothing like that was found at the crime scene, in the tunnel, or the attic room. It must be a figment of your delusional state."

Della's eyes dripped tears. "No! You must find it. I don't know what's in it, but whatever it is must be extremely valuable. They're smuggling something illegal. You need to shut down that criminal operation."

Jaiden's eyes rolled behind the seated patient, but her voice remained easy-going. "We'll check into it, but Detroit is out of our jurisdiction."

Charli scowled and stood to follow them out. "How did they find you here? Sweetwater isn't exactly on the beaten path. It's not far from Cincinnati, Louisville, and Lexington but quite a ways from Detroit."

Jaiden pushed the wheelchair toward the door. "It's only about a five-hour trip from Detroit. Mr. Mulhaney drove his personal vehicle here. That's how we identified him."

Della grimaced. "Didn't he have ID on him?"

Leo took the question. "Actually, someone stole his wallet. We're uncertain who took it. We have a homeless man in custody who wore Mulhaney's shoes."

Della frowned. "I wish I could help you find his killer, but I don't know who did it. All I know is I stabbed him and tried to get away. Maybe the homeless man killed him for his wallet and shoes." It was a possibility.

Jaiden smiled. "When we get to the station, you can tell us everything you know. It's our job to solve the crime, and we will." Charli could see in Jaiden's eyes she believed she was about to take the guilty party to the Sheriff's Office.

Leo snickered. "We'll get to the bottom of this. No worries."

Charli followed the threesome out of the room and down the hallway. The deputies had two suspects in custody. Any crime committed in Detroit was the least of their worries. Charli was certain they had no intention of following up on what they obviously thought was Della's shot in the dark to divert attention from herself. Clearly, they bet for the odds-on favorite in this race.

Leo assisted her into the backseat of the cruiser parked at the hospital's front door. Della asked Charli. "What happens to me now?" Panic glassed up her eyes, and Leo shut the door behind her.

"Jail." Charli stood helplessly and watched the deputies take their seats. The vehicle rolled away.

Chapter Nineteen

The next morning, Charli sat at the kitchen island double-checking the data she'd acquired from Della the previous day. Everything the woman had said was accurate.

Eli waltzed into the great room, bent, and tilted her chin up so her lips met his. His taste was warm and minty, and he smelled of sandalwood bath soap.

"Good morning, my love." He smiled and strolled to the coffee carafe. "We still don't have custody of our house. Leo said we could go back to work on it after today. So, what's on our agenda, boss lady?"

She smiled at the handsome man who had stolen her heart and rocked her world. "You kind of like having someone else take charge, don't you?"

Eli's sandy mop of shaggy hair moved with his nod. "Sure do. I've had enough of upper management to last a lifetime. It's kind of nice having someone else figure out all the ins and outs of the business, so I can concentrate on the work I love doing."

"Well, as you said, we can't work on the house today. I have another project I can use your help with. How do you feel about a nice, long hike?"

Eli took a sip of his coffee, glanced out the kitchen window at the sunny autumn morning, and then smiled. "Sounds great. Got a park in mind?"

Charli stood and strode toward him. She leaned her

petite frame against his front and purred, as he propped against the countertop, "Not exactly a park, but a nice, wooded stroll for sure. I want to explore our property—the woodlands between the murder scene and icehouse."

He cocked a brow "Exactly, what are we doing this for? You're obviously up to something. This doesn't sound like a simple exploration of our forest."

She pursed her lips. "You're right. It's a search for what Della said she lost in the woods as she tried to escape from Mulhaney. Her backpack ripped. When she ran, she apparently lost the evidence she'd stolen from the bottling company. She says that man was after it when he found her—that and he was sent to kill her."

Eli's hands rested on her shoulders. "Let me get this straight. She had what he wanted, and that piece of plastic was worth killing her for."

Charli nodded slowly.

Eli blinked a couple of times. "And you want us to search for it?"

Again, she nodded. "Yes. It doesn't seem the sheriff's office is interested in exploring this lead, but Della is frantic about it. She swears she took an article from her old job that is evidence of a crime." Charli explained Della's suspicion illegal goods hidden in the base of filled laundry detergent bottles were shipped to a distribution facility in Detroit, and how Della knew the dead man.

"Why don't the authorities do this search?"

She backed away out of his arms. "First of all, they don't have time to chase down what they believe to be a distraction on Della's part. They simply don't believe her. Della and that homeless veteran are in custody. They're pretty sure they have the killer in one or the other of them. They can't waste valuable time searching for evidence of a crime in Michigan, when they have a murder case, they need to build a prosecutable case for."

Eli glared from across the room. "I assume, if I refuse to help you search those woods, you'll just go on and do it yourself."

She snickered in her most flirty way. "You know me so well."

****

A few hours later, they had parked on Sixth Street and trekked through the woodland, around the murder site to the end of the area marked off with crime scene tape. Charli glanced around.

"How about this. We can each search about an eight-feet-wide section at a time. I'll take this center of the hill area and search downhill all the way to the riverbank and then the next eight-feet upward to the center again. You can search that same width from here to the top of the hill. Then turn. Search the next line of sight down to where we meet in the middle. Let's move around the hill that way, and when the riverbank ends, I'll take it along the creek at the bottom of the hill. We can go all the way around to the icehouse."

"Sounds like a plan." Eli smiled and indulged his fiancé. "What if we find it?"

Charli slipped a cord with a whistle on it around his neck. "Just whistle. I'll come and meet you." She showed him a similar one around her neck."

They set off on their hike. A few hours later with nothing but sweaty bodies and exhaustion to show for it, they met in the middle. She tossed Eli a bottle of water from her backpack.

"Thanks, Charli, but are you sure we wouldn't be

more inclined to find Bigfoot than this bottle thing Della says she lost?" He dabbed at the sweat on his brow with a navy blue and white handkerchief.

"Don't give out on me now, Eli. We're about two-thirds of the way around the hill. Let's not lose hope. Della said she took a twisting, turning path to lose her pursuer. It could've fallen out anywhere."

Eli sighed and handed her the empty to stow in her pack. "It should be easy to see. I mean, it's fall but a bright orange plastic thing that size should be easy enough to spot." Della had described it as about six-inches across by about ten-inches wide and about two-inches tall.

"Let's get back at it." Charli waved a hand forward. "I'll reward you with a burger and fries from Sadie's Diner when we're done."

Eli glared down his nose. "Only if it includes blackberry cobbler and ice cream for dessert."

She grinned. "Whatever your heart desires, my love. Hey, look on the bright side. Not only do you get a good meal out of this. You'll get your cardio in today. Sadie's grub won't pack on the love handles before our wedding."

He groaned and trekked back uphill. "No worries there."

****

Half an hour later and multiple trips up and down hillsides, Charli spotted the orange bottle base. She blew her whistle. Adrenaline coursed through her veins, nearly making her lightheaded. She rushed to the spot where the object lay cradled in a leafless bush. Sitting her backpack on the ground, she pulled her phone from the chest pocket of her overall jeans and took photos.

Underbrush thrashed as Eli approached. "You found it? I was about to give up on this snipe hunt."

She pointed to the bottle bottom and took a plastic bag from her backpack. Using the bag to pick it up, she folded the item into it and zipped the lock on it shut. Then she stuck the bag in her backpack and slipped it back on.

Eli glanced around and then pointed. "There. Look at that branch. It's got something on it."

She pointed to a tree limb with bare spots where twigs had broken off. "This must be where she hit her head. It's about the right height, and there's damage here from the collision."

Eli nodded. "Yeah, that looks like blood on the bark."

Charli took several photographs of the branch then surveyed the surrounding area. "Here, look. The brush has been crushed like when a deer beds down. I'll bet this is where Della fell when she rammed into that tree. She might've fainted for a few minutes before she got up and continued her escape." Charli took a few shots of that area.

Eli looked from where Della must've fallen to where the jug section had landed. "It appears the base flew out of her backpack as she fell. It could've easily been tossed that far from the impact."

Charli photographed the distance. Then she pulled out some orange ribbon from her backpack. "Here, tie this to a stick and mark where we found the item." She pulled out another piece.

"I'll tie this around the branch she ran into. That way the deputies can find this spot easily."

Once they were satisfied, Eli stared into her eyes. "So, boss lady, can we go eat now? Or do we have to continue to scour the woods the rest of the way to the icehouse? That's about another five hundred yards through the woods on a straight shot—much farther up and down hill."

"Yeah, let's go eat. After I fill your gut, we can drop this and the photos off at the sheriff's office."

****

Later that afternoon they arrived at Wyatt's office. As they entered the bullpen, Jaiden got up from her desk.

"Hey, you two, what's up?"

Charli snickered and handed the plastic bag to her best friend. "Brought you a present."

Confusion furrowed Jaiden's flawless forehead. "What's this?"

"You know that crazy story Della told about a bottle base?" Jaiden nodded and held the plastic bag in her hands. "Well, she didn't make that up. Eli and I searched the woods for it, and this laid in a patch of dried-up brush. We discovered where she hit her head." She pulled out her phone and brought up photos of the branch and scene, then scanned through the shots. "We marked the branch and spot where we located the bottle section."

Jaiden groaned. "Charli, I told you to stay out of this. You realize this is tainted evidence."

"No. I never touched it. I was very careful about that." She pushed a few buttons on her phone. "I just sent you, Leo, and Wyatt the photographs we took. We put an orange ribbon around the branch and on a stick where this was lying. We didn't disturb anything—just wanted you to find it easily. It's our property. You can't be mad at me for a hike on my land. It's just fortunate I happened upon an item of value."

Eli snickered at the frustrated expression on Jaiden's

face. It was clear she couldn't decide whether to thank Charli, hug her, or scold her.

"Look, Jaiden, there is obviously something to this far-fetched story of Della's. It may or may not have to do with your murder case, but it's a valid concern for someone. Perhaps you can get this evidence to the right authorities. I'm sure the cops in Michigan would be interested in this. Feel it. It's much heavier than it should be."

Jaiden glanced at the ceiling, huffed out a breath and then glared at Charli. "Fine. I'll have CSU test it and see if there's anything concealed in the bottom of this thing. If so, I'll pass it along to Detroit PD."

Charli snickered. "That's all I ask. But in the meantime, you should realize this could have bearing on Della's case. If there's some type of contraband in that container, it could validate Della's claim that man came here specifically to kill her. She was defending herself."

Jaiden's head rolled around in a circle. "All right, alright. I'll keep it in mind. Now, the two of you get the heck out of my office before I book you for interference in an ongoing investigation."

Charli gazed up at Eli and shot him a sly wink as they dashed out the front door.

Chapter Twenty

The next morning Charli sat at her computer on the kitchen island. Eli entered from the bedroom hallway and carried his overnight bag. "Hey, babe, are you sure you don't mind me taking off for a couple of days?"

She smiled as she admired his long, lanky frame and casual stride. The man sure knew how to fill out a pair of jeans.

"Of course not. You need to pick up those antique dressers we bought in Cincinnati anyway. They will make the most adorable bathroom vanities for the house. You haven't seen Syd in a long time, and there's a football game tomorrow night in town. You might as well enjoy yourself. Spend some time with your old pal and remind him we expect him and his girlfriend to show up for the wedding next month."

"What are you working on? Wedding arrangements?" He peered over her shoulder.

"A bit of that and a bit of research about those companies Della told me about." She shrugged.

"Well, if you learn anything new, be sure to pass it on to Jaiden or Wyatt so they can follow up."

Her head tilted to the side. "Sure, but fat chance they'll bother. They're busy trying to build the district attorney's case against Della. A crime committed in Michigan is the farthest thing from their minds."

He bent and gave her a loving smooch. "Can't really

blame them. It's not exactly their jurisdiction. Wyatt would probably consider it a waste of his resources."

"Well, I talked with Jaiden earlier. They haven't found the pistol that man was shot with, and they've given up scouring the riverbed and lake bottoms."

"Guess they can only search so much. Who knows what the shooter did with it. It could be at the bottom of the Licking, somewhere downstream in the Ohio River—especially if he tossed it from one of the bridges. Or it could be in Lake Michigan." Eli picked his bag up and snuggled her under his arm. "It could even be buried somewhere."

She nodded gravely. "Yeah, I know. At least we know it's not in our forest, in the tunnel, or the house. Those areas have been searched to death." She gazed up into his deep chocolate eyes. "The killer could even still have it, especially if he thinks he's free and can't be caught."

Her arms slipped around his slim waist. Then she reached up and cupped his broad, square jaw. The dimples showed as he gazed down lovingly.

"I'll miss you, hunky daddy." She snickered at the use of her original nickname for him.

He pulled her close, lifted her off her work-booted feet, and rested her weight against his flat stomach. "I'll miss you too, Miss Hot Pants." Her preferred tank tops and cut-off jeans had been swapped out when autumn arrived for the much warmer, long-legged, bib overalls and flannel shirts. "Try to stay out of trouble while I'm gone. See you day after tomorrow."

Their lips met. She melted into his caress, hoping to make up for time they would be apart, their first separation since their engagement. He settled her back on her feet and sighed. "If I don't get on the road, I'll never make it to Cincinnati in time to pick those chests up before the antique shop closes."

"If you must. Just drive carefully and come home safe." She watched him stroll to the door. "Jaiden said we can have the house back tomorrow. So, when you return, you can take the dressers straight there."

"Okay, see you soon. Love you!" Eli waved one last time as he closed the door behind him.

In her bedroom, Charli gathered a few things. Half an hour later, she was ready. She took her small duffle bag filled with essentials into the great room and sat it beside her backpack on the kitchen island. She twisted toward the creak of the door opening.

Gran strolled in. She looked fresh and full of spirit. "Hey, Charli, how's it going?" Spying the bags, she frowned. "Going somewhere?"

Charli bit her lower lip. "I'm taking off for a couple of days."

One of Gran's brows shot forward. "Oh? Is Eli going with you?" She glanced around.

With a sigh, Charli shook her head. "He's on his way to Cincy on a business trip and to catch a game with a friend. I should be home by the time he returns the day after tomorrow."

"I see. So, does Eli know about this little journey you're planning? Is it a surprise for him, or are you taking care of wedding chores?"

If Irma Owens knew anything, it was Charli's tells. She would weasel the story out of her eventually. The woman was nothing if not persistent.

She might as well level with Gran. "I'm taking a little drive to Detroit to check on some data Della gave me. I've done all the research I can on the computer. I need to see a couple of things for myself...in person."

Gran plopped her slim behind into a barstool and patted the one beside her. "Okay, spill it. Tell your old granny everything."

Charli heaved an audible exhale. She explained everything Della had shared, what Charli had learned for herself, and questions that remained. She told how she and Eli had found the suspicious bottle base CSU kept for inspection.

"Gran, she has no one on her side. Della is about to face prison time for a crime she did not commit. She begged me for help. I can't just do nothing and let her rot in a jail cell."

Gran's gaze bore into hers. "I can't possibly allow you to go to Detroit alone, especially under these circumstances. That would be criminal on my part."

"You realize you can't lock me up or take away my truck keys. I'm not a child." Charli pouted.

Gran's gaze ping-ponged around. A *hmmm* noise came from her throat. Her hands wrung in her lap. "I suppose I can't stop you." She met Charli's gaze. "So, I'm going with you." She hopped to her feet. "Give me five minutes to pack a couple of things.

As she entered her bedroom doorway, she leaned backward into the hall and stared at her granddaughter. "I know you well enough to be sure you haven't packed appropriately. Go find a business suit. It can be slacks, skirt, or a dress, whatever. But you must look the part of an executive."

Charli didn't fight it. Clearly, Gran had formulated a plan which included Charli impersonating a businesswoman. Who was she to argue? The older woman knew more about getting away with pretense and how to act a part than Charli would ever know. After all, Gran was the one she always came to when she needed help. Why refuse it now?

Charli selected a classic navy pants suit, a pair of low-heeled pumps, and a red silk blouse to add to her duffle.

Gran awaited in the great room. "So, we're off to an adventure." She slid her free hand through Charli's arm.

Charli smiled as she allowed her grandmother to steer her into the garage to Gran's SUV. "It will make a better impression if we don't drive a pickup truck."

Charli couldn't dispute the point. She stowed her things into the back and took the passenger seat.

As she backed out of the drive, Gran chuckled. "Let's make a pact. No trouble. We'll just gather some information, snap a few photographs, and perhaps record a few interviews. No trouble!"

Chapter Twenty-One

Charli and Gran were near to Toledo when Jaiden called.

"Charli, I wanted to let you know, that story your 'cousin' told must've been true. We got the report back from CSU. The substance that weighed the jug base down was pure heroin. We turned over the sample along with Ms. McGregor's testimony to the Detroit police to follow up on. This crime takes place out of our jurisdiction."

Relief swarmed Charli's lungs. "So, will you release Della?" This could still have a favorable outcome.

Jaiden sighed heavily. "Soon as her funds are transferred in. The judge set a high bond to so she wouldn't be considered a flight risk. She had to obtain enough money through the probate judge who handled her dad's estate to pay the fee. She'll be out in a day or so."

Charli's renewed hopefulness plummeted. "You're still charging her with murder? This provides evidence that substantiates her case for self-defense."

Jaiden's voice remained professional. "It seems to, but the district attorney isn't yet ready to drop the charges. If this goes to trial, it might be up to the jury to determine whether it's self-defense or homicide."

Charli moaned. "Have you found the gun?"

"No, and we've given up the underwater search. If

it's in the Ohio or Licking River, it's somewhere downstream where it will be nearly impossible to find. We've searched the woods and found no evidence of it being buried. It could be anywhere."

"Well, Della sure didn't have it in her possession." Charli perked up. "The killer might've taken it with him when he or she fled, or he could've disposed of it somewhere out of the area. The homeless people told you they heard two men arguing—not a man and woman."

Jaiden's tenor softened. "That's true. The DA still wants us to continue building a case. Who knows. He might decide to try and plea bargain instead of taking this to trial."

Charli pushed out a breath. "I don't see how he can possibly prosecute Della for this crime. It's a clear case of self-defense. As far as plea bargaining, she seems adamant about her innocence. I can't see her agreeing to a few years in jail for a murder she did not do."

"Not up to me, babe. I'm just passing on the info." Jaiden's voice had a snap to it.

"I'm sorry, Jaiden. This whole thing just has me on edge. I feel so badly for Della."

"If you feel so badly, you might want to offer her somewhere to stay when she gets out on bail. She can't leave the area. I get the impression it took all her cash to pay the bail bondsman. She asked for a public defender."

"Who did she get?"

"Carlton Farmer."

"Whew! That's a relief. At least it's not some first-year attorney with no experience. Thanks for sharing the news, Jaiden. I appreciate it."

"No problem, Charli. I knew you wanted to stay informed. Bye now."

After hanging up, Charli told Gran everything Jaiden had shared. As they discussed Della's options and what they might do to help, Gran's phone rang. She hit the answer button on the steering wheel.

"Hi, Wes, it's good to hear your voice."

"Absolutely," Wes's deep, New York accent rumbled. "I've missed my woman. Geez, that sounds good—my woman." He chuckled low.

"Before you get too sassy, my love, I want you to know Charli is with me. We're in the car, and you're on speaker."

He laughed heartily. "Hi, my incredible granddaughter. How are wedding plans going? You gals out finishing up the details? Or are you shopping for that perfect Thanksgiving dinner you're going to cook for me?"

Gran's inhaled. "Wes, does that mean you'll be home for Thanksgiving?" As she spoke, her voice grew higher. "I hoped but was afraid to believe it could happen."

He chuckled. "I certainly will. There are still a few loose ends, and then I'm going home. Hot dang! That sounds almost as good as 'my woman'—home. I haven't had a real home since I was a little tyke. I look forward to it and to spending more time with my grandchildren. I haven't had much with Kyler yet. He will come home for the weekend. Right?"

Gran beamed. "That's the plan."

Charli added, "Kyler said he has a couple of exams today to finish the semester."

"Awesome, I'll see you ladies soon. Hugs and kisses."

Gran snickered. "Back at ya, sexy."

"Bye, Wes. See you soon." Charli watched as Gran hung up the phone. "I'm glad he didn't probe us about what we're up to."

Gran's head rolled to the side as though she released a tight muscle. "No worries. We'll be there and back before he gets home."

Charli sighed. "Yeah, same for Eli."

"Afraid to tell him you're sticking your nose into the case?" One of Gran's brows rose.

"If he were home, he'd be right here with me. I didn't want to spoil his plans. Besides, I've got backup." She winked at her grandmother.

****

Later that day they arrived in Detroit at the address Charli had read off Doc Baker's computer where he'd completed the ME's report. Hopefully it was the right place. Charli had assumed it was the last known residence of the victim.

"Jaiden told me the Detroit Police questioned Clancy Mulhaney's landlady. She didn't give them much help. Maybe we can get more from the woman."

They parked in front of the two-story, red, brick house in a low-to-middle income neighborhood. Similar homes of assorted shades lined the two-lane streets with aging vehicles parked along both sides.

Properties had been minimally cared for. Most had postage-stamp sized yards with barely enough space between buildings for slim sidewalks that led to the backs. Every few blocks the neighborhood boasted a corner barroom decked out in neon signage displaying assorted beer brands and catchy tavern names.

Gran held her head high and pushed the doorbell on the side entrance. A distant chime sounded inside. Then footfalls prodded toward the door. Lace curtains were spread apart and allowed the insider a view through the top plate glass half of the door. With a couple of clicks, the door crept open a few inches. A short, pudgy female face with white curls close to her head popped to the opening.

"Yeah, what do you want?"

Gran smiled graciously. "Ms. Crane, we've come a long ways to speak with you. I hope you will give us a few minutes of your time. We're here investigating the death of your tenant, Clancy Mulhaney."

The woman frowned, and more wrinkles formed on her forehead. "I already talked to the cops. Told 'em all I know."

Charli stepped forward, dressed in the suit Gran had recommended, decked out much more businesslike than she was used to. She assumed an attitude she hoped would pull the image off. "Yes, ma'am. We realize that, but Mr. Mulhaney was found murdered in our town. We are helping conduct the Sweetwater, Kentucky investigation. There are many unanswered questions. We promise not to take much of your time, but we hope you can shed light on some of those things."

The woman rolled her eyes and backed away. She swung the door open a bit further. "All right, since you've gone to the trouble to drive all the way from Kentucky, I guess I can spare a few minutes." She stepped back. "Come on in."

She strutted away. Obviously, they were to follow her.

Charli didn't miss the invitation but stepped inside before the old woman could change her mind. The television blared a soap opera, and knitting sat beside an easy chair. A tea mug on a side table appeared half empty in the dingy living room. Blinds were pulled shut, and a single table lamp lit the room.

Gran followed Charli inside and shut the door behind her. The women followed their hostess to a cramped kitchen decorated with food containers atop almost every surface. She pointed to a tiny vinyl-topped table shoved against the wall. Charli and Gran took two of the three seats. That left the one between them empty.

"Can I offer you something to drink? Tea, water, soda?"

"No, thank you. We're fine." Gran waved toward the empty seat, and the woman accepted it.

Charli assumed the lead. "What can you tell us about Mr. Mulhaney?"

The old woman shrugged her plump shoulders. "What's there to say? He was a good tenant. Lived here about five years. Always paid on time and in cash. Respectful."

Gran met her gaze. "So, he wasn't a partier? What about friends? Girlfriends?"

Ms. Crane tilted her head a second. "I don't know much about his personal life. He kind of kept to himself, private like. No parties. No loud, rowdy visitors. Hardly any visitors at all."

Charli frowned. "Hardly? He had company occasionally, then?"

Another head shrug came from Ms. Crane. "Rarely, but every few months a woman stopped by. They'd go to his apartment and spend a couple of quiet hours there."

Charli's brow shot up. "The same female each time? Tell us about her."

One shoulder rocked upward. "Yes, the same. Never

met her. No idea who she was. It was none of my business."

Gran gave her an understanding smile. "Of course, but surely you must've been curious. After all, you're responsible for this property. It's only natural you'd have concerns about anyone who spent time here. Didn't you find it peculiar that the woman just appeared every few months?"

Great tactic, Gran. Make her nosiness appear appropriate. "It doesn't sound like a serious affair if she only showed up every few months. Didn't you find that peculiar?"

Ms. Crane's shoulder hitched. "I suppose, and yes. I was curious. I figured she might be married, or something like that."

Gran's lips formed an 'O.' "Well now, I would've been worried if I were you."

Ms. Crane closed her eyes as though she considered her next words. "Actually, I took a mild precaution in case some jilted lover or husband showed up while she was here. One night while she was…'visiting' I took a photo of her license plate—just in case I needed it for the police or something." She stared away toward the wall, apparently to measure whether telling them had been the right thing.

Charli smiled casually. "That photo would be a great help to us in our investigation. Would you share it with us?"

Ms. Crane rolled her eyes with reservation, stood, went into another room for a second, and brought a flip phone with her. The woman pulled up a photo and tilted the screen toward Charli. "I ain't got internet on this thing, but here's the picture."

Charli eyed the photograph and took the cell phone from her. She manipulated the screen until the numbers were clearly visible. Then she pulled out her own phone and snapped a shot of the visual. Handing the cell phone back, she smiled at their hostess. "That's great. Thanks so much."

Ms. Crane sat back down, closed her phone, and laid it on the table. "So, what else do you want to know?"

Gran met her gaze. "What about his social life? Work? Habits?"

Crane's head shook. "I know nothing about his social life. He sometimes strolled down to the Corner Bar for a belt or two, but I never noticed him coming home drunk. Not sure about his work. He was some sort of security guard or something like that. He had weights in his apartment and worked out with them regularly. I could hear them thumping as he sat them down. Watched TV some but never had it loud enough for me to recognize what he was watching."

Charli was convinced the woman was aware of Clancy Mulhaney's every coming and going. "Did you notice anything strange about his trash?"

The old woman winced. "Trash? What do you think? That I dug through the man's garbage? Yuck." She gave a pretense of shivering that fooled no one.

Gran took it in stride. "The garbage collector would pick Mulhaney's waste the same days they got yours. As his landlord, you have the right to take measures to protect yourself and your property. If I were in your shoes, I'd have a peek inside, just to make sure my tenant wasn't cooking meth or something in his apartment."

Ms. Crane did an eye roll. "Well, I did steal a look a couple of times when his lid was ajar. Didn't want trash blowing out all over the place, you know. He'd sometimes toss a stack of old racing forms. Guess he liked to play the ponies."

Charli smiled. "That's not so unusual. I enjoy betting the horses occasionally myself."

It wasn't a lie. It would've been difficult growing up in Sweetwater without having a keen interest in racehorses, given professional racing and breeding ranches took up more than half of the area. Personal friends owned a few of them.

Gran stood. "Well, Ms. Crane, you've been very helpful. We want to be respectful of your time. Thank you so much for your hospitality."

Charli followed her grandmother with Ms. Crane coming up the rear. "Thanks for assisting our investigation. We do appreciate it."

As they stepped outside, Ms. Crane leaned into the small gap, as she pulled the door shut. "No worries. Just be sure the cops let me know when I can move Mulhaney's crap out of the unit. I need to get it rented, and he's only paid up until November 1."

Gran nodded. "We will be sure to tell them. Thanks again." She strolled down the sidewalk to their car parked on the street.

Charli followed and climbed inside. "Well, that was somewhat productive."

Gran started the engine. "Absolutely. What would you say to a cold one at the Corner Bar?"

Charli grinned. "Yeah, sure. Maybe we can learn more about Clancey Mulhaney's drinking, womanizing, and betting habits."

"Maybe. Either way, I could use an icy cold brew."

Charli chuckled. "Only one, Gran. You're driving."

Moments later, they strolled into the tavern Ms. Crane had mentioned. Dark and shady neon lit the area. A couple of lighted ceiling fans circulated the dank scent of cigars and stale beer around. The aging barroom sported an ornately carved, antique bar with a back wall lined with liquor bottles fronting mirrors that apparently hadn't been washed in many a moon. Metal wall tiles circa the 1920s had yellowed from nicotine, dust, and age. Green and white tile floors were cracked. Grout housed years of leftover traffic grime.

A wall-mounted television above one end of the bar area played a rerun of last week's local football game. Six empty tables were scattered around the room. A jukebox displaying tunes in vivid neon color occupied a wall beside a pinball machine exhibiting the figure of a busty female superhero. A visible back room housed an unoccupied pool table. Above it hung a plastic version of a stained-glass ad for a brand-name beer.

Two customers sitting on red vinyl barstools hunched over beer glasses and bottles. A forty-something bartender's black tee shirt displayed the Corner Bar white lettering across his puffy chest, as he wiped the scarred bar surface.

All heads craned at the entrance of two strange females. The patrons continued to eye them as the women took empty stools at the far end.

The barkeep strolled reluctantly toward them. "What'll it be, ladies?"

Gran spotted him a brilliant smile. "What's the coldest beer in the coolers, sweetheart?"

"Ah, that'll be Motor Mouth Brew." He snickered.

"Fine," she answered. "We'll have two of those and a couple of icy mugs if you have them."

With a nod he strutted a few feet, dug into a lower cooler, and pulled out bottles. He snapped the tops off, reached down and secured a couple of cold mugs from the ice chest, and brought them back, sitting one of each in front of the women. "That'll be eight-fifty. You want a run a tab?" His Michigan accent was strong, as was his cologne, but his body said otherwise, showing signs of neglect.

Gran pulled out a ten and placed it in front of her. "Keep the change."

Charli took the opportunity before he could walk away. "We were wondering if you could tell us about a customer of yours." She pushed her phone in front of him showing the photo she'd taken of Clancey Mulhaney that had appeared in the newspaper when he'd been identified. "Do you recognize this fella?" She used her most charming southern drawl.

"Yeah, I know Mulhaney. He came in occasionally. Didn't know him personally. Kinda kept to himself. I read in the paper that they'd found him dead in Kentucky. That where you ladies are from?"

Gran smiled. "Yes, we're from Sweetwater investigating the circumstances of Clancey's death." She sounded like she knew him personally.

"Yeah, well, not much I can tell you about him. He came in sometimes. Bought a couple of beers. Watched some TV. Kept to himself."

Gran beamed. "Yes, we'd heard he liked to drink here. He wasn't a drunkard though. Right?"

The guy pursed his lips. "Nah."

Charli sipped her beer. "We understand he had a girlfriend. Did they ever meet here?"

The man looked surprised. "No, never seen him with

a gal."

Charli nodded. "Did he ever speak about her? Talk with other customers?"

His head shook. "Actually, I've never seen him with anyone…except the boss sometimes."

Gran's brow lifted. "The boss?"

"Yeah." The guy gritted his teeth, clearly regretting he'd mentioned it. "I got the feeling he and the guy who owns this place had horse racing in common. They'd sometimes take a quiet table and…discuss it."

Gran picked up her bottle. "Is the boss in? Any chance we can speak with him?"

"Nope. He only comes in on Saturdays to take care of business and never works the bar."

Charli smiled as though it were inconsequential. "Could we get his name?"

The guy's eyes rolled upward. "Yeah, sure. It's Frank Capone." He pointed to the liquor license on the wall beside him.

Charli typed a note on her phone to have him checked out. "Thanks, that's very helpful."

She shoved a twenty-dollar-bill his way. He snatched it and pocketed the money. Then he rang up their beers on the register and secure his tip.

Gran eyed Charli as she swallowed a gulp of the cold brew. "Are you thinking what I'm thinking?"

Charli whispered, "If you figure Mr. Capone is a bookie, then yes."

Gran nodded, took another sip, then stood. Charli swigged down a long drink, then left the rest on the counter as she followed Gran out to the car.

Once inside, Charli texted Deputy Jaiden Coldwater.

—Research Frank Capone of Detroit, the Corner Bar. Bookie?—

—Tell me you're not in Detroit.—

—Run MI license #ACM-2938. Vic's girlfriend. Married?—

—Get your sweet behind home!—

Charli clicked her phone off staring at Gran. "Let's find a room for the night. We can check out the supply company tomorrow.

Chapter Twenty-Two

The next morning over a light breakfast at their hotel, Gran shared the plan she'd concocted during the night. They tossed ideas back and forth, and then strolled out to the parking lot to Gran's SUV. Gran started the engine and glanced at Charli.

"Heard from Eli?"

Charli sighed. "He left me a text late last night saying he was back at his hotel room, and their team won the football game. He will spend the day with his buddy and have dinner with his family this evening. He's picking up the dressers at the antique store tomorrow morning and will head home afterward."

"Did you let him know we're in Detroit?" Gran pulled out of the hotel lot.

Charli shrugged. "No. Why should I? It would only spoil his fun. He hasn't had a vacation in years. This is his last chance to spend time with his friends in Cincinnati as a single man. He couldn't do anything to help us out from there, anyway."

Gran's brows rose. "And of course, he wouldn't approve."

Charli's head tilted in an easy jerk. "Doubtful he would."

Gran smiled. "Oh well, too late now to change our mind. Sometimes it's just easier to say you're sorry than to ask permission. Not that you need permission from anyone before doing what you think is right."

Charli's heart warmed to the easy tone of her grandmother. "Thanks for being here, Gran."

Gran's hand left the steering wheel to pat Charli's leg. "I wouldn't be anywhere else, my sweet girl."

She exited the expressway into a dingy neighborhood of factories, small warehouses, and storage facilities. They drove along pothole pocked streets until the GPS advised them, they were there.

Surprisingly, the facility was tucked at the far end of a short street. A driveway along one side indicated deliveries were to follow the arrows. The building wasn't fancy—anything but. It was ill-maintained. There was no sign indicating what company occupied the property. A filmy row of four pane glass windows and a door were the only entrance along the front. The bridge to Windsor, Canada was visible from the tiny, empty customer parking lot in front.

Gran backed her vehicle into a spot so she could easily pull out as they left. Theirs was the only car there.

"Hard to believe this is the same business you showed me on that fancy website. This building bears no resemblance to the image depicted for Detroit Detergent Distributors."

Charli pointed to the small placard near the doorway. "It's 357, and this is West Forbes Street. This must be it. As we pulled in, I could see a line of Crane Motor Lines semis parked along the dock doors, and a few were along a far wall, as though waiting their turn for loading."

Gran stepped out and smoothed down her classic, designer, winter-white pants suit. The woman was stunning, and her silver hair gave her a commanding presence. "All righty then, let's do this thing—just as we planned."

Charli checked her outfit as she followed Gran to the entrance. Her head held high, assured her navy pants and blazer gave her a confident air, combined with the white shirt with blue and red pen stripes. She had chosen simple gold ball earrings, navy short-heeled pumps, and put her phone and necessities in the jacket pockets. She entered under the shadow of her much taller grandmother.

The small reception room had no seats for visitors, no artwork, and only a single metal door behind a small desk. A pimply, twenty-something young man sat there, attending the reception area. The nerdy-looking fella acted shocked to see the women enter his domain.

The flat-top desk was oak-designed laminate, only deep enough to hold a lap drawer. Its chrome, utilitarian legs gave a view of navy khaki slacks. Brown penny loafers hinted at the ankle that he wore brown socks.

The nervous-looking man stammered, "What…what are you doing here?" Obviously, they got very few visitors.

Gran's regal head held high. "We have an appointment with your company's owner, Dwayne LaRosa."

The guy glanced at the small laptop on his desk. "I…ah…there's no…We don't have a record of Mr. LaRosa having any appointments this morning. I'm afraid he's not accepting visitors."

Giving him a pointed 'don't mess with me' glare that Charli figured might cause the poor guy to wet his drawers, Gran's voice grew stern. "I'll have you know, young man, I came a long way for this meeting, and I assure you, Mr. LaRosa will see me."

The guy's hands visibly shook as he got up from his desk. He wiped them on his pants legs then opened the door behind him. "Excuse me a minute. I'll see what I can do."

Gran winked at Charli, who stood between her and the desk. Charli chortled and quickly grew serious as the door burst open again. The young fellow followed a rotund man about six feet tall. Barely any hair remained atop his head, and a ring of graying black hair circled it. His reddened face was bloated but otherwise nondescript. The buttons on his too-tight blue shirt appeared ready to pop, and their spread showed a white tee shirt beneath. He wore navy khaki pants and weathered leather loafers.

Nothing about this man's facade indicated him as an industry leader or as the person in charge of a major operation. If anything, he could be mistaken for a warehouseman, maybe responsible for picking and packing orders. He in no way resembled the figure shown on the company's website.

"Yeah, ladies, I understand you're looking for Dwayne LaRosa. I'm afraid there's been a mix-up. I'm LaRosa. I assure you I have no appointment with you today or any day for that matter. Now, if you will kindly depart, we'll get back to work." He acted as though he was readying to leave.

Gran's hands flew to her hips. Her legs spread apart. "Wait just a minute, Mr. LaRosa. I left you several emails, which you didn't bother to respond to. I texted you, and left you voice mails letting you know I'd be in town and would stop by this morning to talk business with you. I clearly told you that if that didn't work for you, you should let me know before yesterday. With no word to the contrary, my assistant and I flew to Detroit from Montgomery, Alabama, this morning with the specific purpose of discussing an offer of business with you. I am the CEO of the Midwest's largest industrial cleaning company. My people clean most of the high-rise buildings in major cities across the South and Midwestern US. I am looking for a new cleaning supplier. I've done some research on your company online, and it appears yours is the best option available. That is business you cannot afford to pass up."

Dwayne rolled his eyes. "Look, lady, I didn't get your emails, texts, or voice mails. Nor do we have the capacity to take on your business. We're not looking for expansion, and we cannot supply you with what you need. So, please leave my facility immediately."

A huff spat out of Gran's lips. "I will be reporting you for this indiscretion. I will not be treated in this fashion. This is no way to conduct business." She spun as though to go.

Before Charli could follow, chaos hit the room. The front door burst open wide. Four, armed, navy-clad people rushed inside, two men and two women. Navy windbreakers marked FBI in bold yellow lettering.

A male voice shouted, "FBI, you're under arrest. Hands in the air."

Multiple shouts exploded from the group, indicating everyone should stand still. LaRosa and his associate were told to put their arms in the air.

At the same time, the big man shoved Gran. She hit the floor on her backside in front of the desk. LaRosa snatched Charli and pulled her tight against his bulbous chest. One beefy arm wrapped tight around Charli's neck. His free arm whipped an automatic from somewhere behind and pointed it toward her. Cold metal sparked icy shivers from her temple throughout her body. Her feet slid unwillingly across the floor as he backed toward the doorway to the warehouse section.

The younger man had taken his seat at the desk while Dwayne and Gran had been arguing. His hand slipped into a nook beneath the desktop and withdrew a small revolver.

A familiar voice shouted, "Go ahead. I need the practice."

Charli's gaze flipped to the agent pointing her carbine pistol at the pimple-faced man. Recognition and puzzlement hit her at the same time. *FBI Special Agent Reggie Casse-Montgomery in Detroit?* Reggie worked out of the taskforce in Sweetwater.

The two male agents and the blonde woman directed their firearms toward Charli and LaRosa.

The woman's voice grew calm and coaxed, "Dwayne don't do something stupid. Your facility is surrounded. Your men in the back are being arrested as we speak. Don't make this worse for yourself by taking a hostage. Put the piece down now, before it's too late. Right now, we have you on drug trafficking. Don't add kidnapping to the charges."

The dorky receptionist's revolver clanged against the dirty tile floor and skidded beneath the desk. As he stood, the nerdy guy's shoulders sagged. Reggie rushed behind the desk.

"Hands behind your back."

He did as instructed. She snapped handcuffs around his wrists. His hands laid limp against the flat space that should've been his buttocks if he'd had any. She shoved him toward one of the male officers.

"Get this filth out of here."

The guy grabbed dork-man and pushed him out the front door.

"Let her go," the other male officer said. "LaRosa, you don't want to hurt this woman."

Charli gasped for air against her kidnapper's thick arm. Her mind raced, inventorying the contents of her pocket. Why hadn't she let Gran talk her into wearing a concealed handgun, like she did?

LaRosa reached the door. To turn the knob, he relaxed his grip on Charli. His automatic handgun remained terrifyingly against her skull. As he let go of her, her feet settled firmly to the floor. She lifted her right knee and slammed the pointy heel of her pump into the top of his loafer. The barrel shoved against her head, and she rocked left from the push.

A blast filled the air. Charli jumped leftward, away from LaRosa's trajectory. He hopped as though he were on fire, fell against the back wall and leaned there. As Charli spun around to face his direction, the female agent pushed her behind herself, and the male agent dragged her closer to the exit, using his body to shield her.

Charli could hardly believe her eyes when she finally focused on what had happened. Agent Reggie and the blonde female agent descended upon Dwayne. The reprobate subdued, he leaned against the wall, a look of agony on his plump face. He bent as though unable to stand erect. Both legs of his trousers dripped red.

Gran lay on her belly in her elegant, expensive, white suit, the receptionist's revolver in both hands pointed at LaRosa. She had only fired one round, but somehow had injured both of his legs.

Reggie bent and helped Gran to her feet, as the other agents took charge of cuffing and giving LaRosa his Miranda rights. Gran smiled at her rescuer and handed the firearm over.

"Thank you, Agent Montgomery." Gran bent, dusted off her pants, and straightened her jacket.

Reggie glanced at her fellow agents. "I've got these two." She stood still a few seconds, listening to the bud in her ear. "All's under control in the back. No shots fired."

Reggie put an arm through Charli's and Gran's arms and led them out the front door behind the other agents and their captives. "Ladies, you've got some explaining to do."

Gran rolled her eyes at Charli and snickered. "What about my vehicle?" she asked as Reggie led them to her SUV.

Reggie's hand shot out. "Keys."

Gran handed them over. Reggie tossed them to another agent. "Take care of Ms. Owens' automobile, Phil."

The agent snatched them out of the air and nodded. "Will do."

****

Half an hour later they were sequestered in a soundproof room with a mirror along one side. A single table separated them and the two female FBI agents. Surprisingly, they'd let Charli and Gran be debriefed together, hopefully evidence they didn't believe they were involved in the illegal operation.

Charli adjusted the collar of her blazer, hoping to relieve perspiration forming around her neck. It didn't work, so she removed the jacket and hung it on her chair's back. All the while, Reggie and the blonde agent sat across from her and Gran, looking like they were studying them.

Gran remained primly at her side, without moving, hands lying calmly in her lap. Her elegant suit showed signs of her adventure as she scooted around from her fall to obtain the receptionist's revolver. She didn't appear to let the damage to her wardrobe get the better of her. No doubt, the woman had found herself in more than one strange circumstance during her singing career.

If only a bit of Gran's confidence would rub off on Charli, whose nerves were shattered from the escapade. Her hands gripped tightly in her lap to keep them from quivering uncontrollably.

The blonde agent finally sat erect, her hands clasped lightly on the tabletop. "All right, ladies, let's get this over with."

Reggie sat forward as well, placing her hands on the table. She acted fine with the other agent taking control.

The blonde sneered. "What the hell were the two of you doing at my sting? We've had this operation under surveillance. You super sleuths could've destroyed months of hard work."

Charli had no idea how to begin, grateful when Gran took the lead.

"My granddaughter, Charli Owens—" her dainty hand did a flip to palm up toward Charli, "—and I were in town following some leads on a murder that occurred in Sweetwater, Kentucky, our hometown." Her gaze went toward Reggie.

The blonde nodded. "Agent Montgomery has filled me in on the murder of Clancy Mulhaney. Tell us why you are intervening and how you ended up in that warehouse today."

Charli rolled her eyes, praying to gain strength from the heavens. "A young woman friend of ours apparently stumbled on some sort of smuggling operation concerning a bottling house here in Detroit, where she—Della Louise McGregor—worked for a short time. Key parties to the crime noticed her discovery—whatever it was. They sent Mr. Mulhaney to silence her. She hid out in a house I am remodeling. My partner and I found her deathly ill. She admitted to being attacked by Mulhaney, who confessed he came to kill her. She stabbed him as she fought for her life. The puncture did not kill Mulhaney, however. After her escape, someone else apparently shot and killed Mulhaney."

The woman's head tilted forward. Her brow down, she glared. "That doesn't explain your presence. Go on."

Gran stepped in. "My granddaughter is getting to that. Ms. McGregor had confiscated evidence of whatever illegal substance these people were smuggling. We now know it to be pure grade heroin. She took the base of a laundry bottle from the bottling company's inventory with intentions of turning it over to the Detroit Police. Before she could do that, her father passed away. Obviously, the smuggling ring made a habit of diligently counting bottles, including damaged ones, because they sent Mulhaney and another thug Della recognized to her father's memorial service. They must've been there to silence her before she could alert the authorities. Luckily, she escaped and fled the area. Della hid out until Mulhaney tracked her to Sweetwater. She informed the local sheriff's office of all of this, but they did not believe her. They were convinced she'd shot Mulhaney with either her firearm or his and then disposed of it. The piece has not been located."

The blonde gave them a steady glare. "That's all very intriguing, but it still does not explain why you were at my crime scene."

Charli leaned forward, hands clasped in her lap. "The police didn't believe Della's story. Even if they had, they had no jurisdiction. The murder, however, occurred in Sweetwater. Far as they are concerned, they have the guilty party locked away. They have no authority or intention of following up on this lead. My partner and I discovered the evidence Della stole from the bottling company. We gave it to the sheriff. I have no idea what they did with it after CSU tested it."

Reggie snickered. "Actually, Deputy Jaiden Coldwater submitted the sample to CSU. Their test corroborates Della McGregor's story and proves the base of the jug to be filled with pure heroin, a fine grade we have tracked to Mexican origin. CSU released the item over to the FBI. This key piece of evidence tied together collusion between a string of businesses involved in the logistics of sourcing this poison for US distribution. This deadly, white powder contains fentanyl and has been flooding the streets in recent years. Agent Stone here has been working the case for the last year. She allowed me to assist with the operation.

Stone's head rocked up. "Yes, we were sure of the connection to a source in Canada that brought the drug into the states. Based on data from an informant from the bottling company, we knew that business and Detroit Detergent were involved, and that some unknown source smuggled it across the bridge from Windsor. We just weren't sure who and how. Dwayne LaRosa is a scumbag trafficker who distributes drugs in those bottles to dealers across the Midwest. We coordinated with Canadian authorities to simultaneously raid So Right Containers in Windsor, confiscate shipping containers as they were unloaded from vessels at a dock in Vancouver, as well as those already loaded onto rail cars that transported them to Windsor. At the same time, we raided LaRosa's operation, we took control of the bottling house where Ms. McGregor previously worked. Now we have Dwayne LaRosa and his cohorts in custody, we're going through his records to shut down those channels of wide distribution. We couldn't do this until we put together the front end of the syndicate's logistics. The bottle provided answers to many questions."

Reggie nodded at Stone and stared at Gran and Charli. "Yes, it proved how drugs got through customs, how they packaged it for distribution by the bottling company and the container blower in Canada, and how it got into Canada undetected. The heroin originally loaded in Mexico inside compartments in the center of barrels of concentrated laundry scents. These barrels were placed into shipping containers in the middle. Barrels of only laundry detergent surrounded the ones that held contraband. The containers were loaded onto ships. Drug dogs could not detect the illegal substance as concentrated odor of the items that surrounded it overpowered its smell."

Stone stepped up. "Ships unloaded in Vancouver and containers were placed on the rail where they were taken across country to Windsor. In Windsor, they blew the hooch into the base of specific laundry jugs. Then these 'empties' where placed in pallets in the center of semis. Barrels of concentrated laundry perfumes and detergent surrounded them. The untainted barrels' fragrance overpowered that of the ones which concealed drugs. They were driven across the border to the bottling house where your Della McGregor worked. There the containers were filled with scented laundry soap and immediately trucked to Dwayne LaRosa's distribution facility."

Reggie frowned. "So, ladies, now you know what a dangerous operation you have stumbled upon and that you are lucky to be alive today. You could've been shot or worse."

Gran stared without intimidation. "I was not about to let that man take Charli hostage. If that stupid fella at the front desk hadn't dropped his revolver, I would've pulled mine." She patted her chest, and her gaze shot upward. "You will return my sidekick, won't you? I've grown quite attached to my little semi-automatic pistol."

Reggie glanced without expression at Strong and then back to Gran. "Actually, Irma, you may not realize this, but you are not supposed to carry concealed into Michigan. You could be arrested for this violation. The FBI could permanently seize this baby. We have decided to overlook this infraction, considering how much help you ladies have been to our operation—even though you nearly blew the whole deal to hell when you showed up at the warehouse." She paused. "So, yes, we will return your pretty, little semiautomatic pistol before you leave here. Do not pull that weapon out again in this state."

"Oh, for heaven's sake, Reggie. Of course, I won't."

Stone intervened, "Ladies, you still have not explained your presence here today. Let's have it. Ms. Owens, would you like to take this one?" She glared into Charli's eyes.

Good, we're going to be freed.

Charli smiled at the controlled, but irate, Stone. "As Gran said, we decided to follow up on the leads that Della provided. We talked with Clancy Mulhaney's landlady, Ms. Crane. She told us Mulhaney bet the horse races, and he hung out sometimes at the Corner Bar. That's a small, neighborhood tavern a block from Clancy's apartment. Gran and I went there and spoke with the bartender."

Reggie rolled her eyes. "Geez Louise. Of course you did. So, what did you discover at this bar?"

Gran smiled with closed lips. "An enlightening experience, the bartender recalled Mulhaney. He came in sometimes for a beer, usually on Saturdays when the owner hung out in the bar. The liquor license on the wall showed him to be Frank Capone. Clancey kept to himself, never met up with women there or chatted up patrons. He sometimes talked quietly with 'the boss' at a corner table. We got the impression that Mr. Capone was Clancey's bookie. You might want to check into Capone. Perhaps Mulhaney owed Capone a large sum. He could've killed Mulhaney or had him killed to prove a point to others indebted to him."

Reggie snickered. "Thank you for the advice on how to do my job, Irma. We have already done so. Mr. Capone is indeed a well-known sports bookie. As for his having Mulhaney killed, that would be up to the Sweetwater Sheriff's Department to investigate. We are not here to solve his murder, but to dismantle a large, international drug ring. Jaiden texted me what she learned about Mulhaney's connection to Capone, however. Thanks for asking her to research it. It didn't help our case, but she knew we were going after

Mulhaney's employer."

Charli frowned. "So, you don't give a hoot about Mulhaney's murder, as long as it doesn't affect your drug ring?"

Stone sighed. "Ms. Owens, it is not the FBI's intention to step on the toes of the Sweetwater, Kentucky Sheriff's Department. A simple murder is not in our scope. Rest assured, we will share any data we obtain that might help in Sheriff Gordon's investigation."

Charli glanced at the ceiling and let out a quiet exhale. "We learned more from Ms. Crane. She seemed to be quite a busybody. In fact, Clancy had a girlfriend. She wasn't a regular visitor. Her occasional appearance at his apartment garnered enough suspicion on the landlady's part. So, she took a photo of the woman's license plate. If you allow me, I can show you on my phone. I texted Jaiden the number and asked her to find out who owned the car. The landlady figured the girlfriend was married or something like that."

Stone plucked Charli's phone from the basket on the table and flipped it to her. Charli pulled the shot up and handed the cell to the agent. Stone retrieved her own phone and sent the shot to herself.

Reggie glanced at the phone. "Jaiden sent me this number after she checked it. The vehicle belongs to Evan and Evette Avery, husband, and wife. Jaiden did a search on them and discovered Evan worked for the same security company as Mulhaney, a front for the operation—one of several. He and some others rode security on Crane Motor Lines shipments for LaRosa both from the bottling company to the distribution house and from there to distributors across the country."

Gran winced. "Did you arrest this Evan Avery in

today's raid?"

Stone's head shook. "No, and we're not sure why he's not among those apprehended. He must've taken the day off, or he could be sick. Now we have the DMV and his identity, we will follow up and locate Avery."

Charli's brow crunched together. "So, Mulhaney bumped uglies with his co-worker's wife? What a sleaze bag!"

Reggie nodded. "Jaiden showed his license photo to Della. She recognized him as one of the driver's helpers for the shipping company that delivered the suspicious bottles. She didn't think those short distance runs warranted a driver's helper. Apparently, she was correct. Those guys were there to guard the drug runs."

Charli smiled. "Yes, that's what she told me, only she didn't know what they were protecting."

Reggie smiled. "Well, now we know, thanks to Della's bravery and your perseverance and interference. Thank you, and I believe we are done here."

Charli's curiosity intervened. "Does that mean you'll head back to Sweetwater too?"

Reggie chuckled. "I'll admit, I'm used to doing the questioning. You are one stubborn little bugger, aren't you, Charli?" She laughed along with the Owens women. "Actually, Special Agent Strong invited me here to help with this raid. We have more work to do, but then I'll go home. Hopefully, it will be in time for Thanksgiving. Shae and I are supposed to have dinner with Sheriff Wyatt and Sage at their farm."

Strong stood. "Well, let's get these gals out of here, so we can work on the real criminals in custody. Ms. Owens, your gun will be waiting for you at the security desk as you leave the building. I'm a big fan. I have all your records—on vinyl, of course."

Gran stood and shook the agent's hand across the small table. "Thank you, Special Agent Strong. I hope we meet under better circumstances in the future."

Strong shook Charli's hand as well and left the three women alone. Charli put her phone back into her blazer pocket.

"Reggie, I forgot to ask about Mr. LaRosa's condition. I mean, after Gran shot him."

Gran snatched her phone and pocketed it as well. "Oh, yeah, how is that despicable creature faring?"

Reggie put a hand to Charli's back and ushered her toward the door. "Actually, you did quite well, Irma. Your bullet grazed one of his calves and lodged into the other. He's not a happy walker, but he'll be fine."

Gran frowned and feigned disappointment. "Too bad. I couldn't get a shot a little higher—more toward his privates. That desk obscured my view."

Their bawdy laughter as they stepped into the hallway caught attention of several men in navy suits who strutted toward them. It didn't stop them from chuckling, however. Finally, Reggie gained control of herself.

"Just between us, it would've served him right." She showed them to the lobby where Gran retrieved her gun and then out of the building. "Your car is parked to the left in front of the building. An agent is there with your keys. Thanks for everything, ladies. Let's never do this again."

Gran released Reggie's grip and Charli shook her hand. "Agreed."

"Safe travels home now." Reggie disappeared back through the front doors of the Detroit FBI Headquarters.

Chapter Twenty-Three

Soon after five p.m. Reggie finally released Charli and Gran. They opted to drive to Toledo, grab some dinner, find a hotel room for the night, and hit the road early the next morning, the day before Thanksgiving.

Finally, home at a few minutes before noon, Gran pulled her SUV into the garage. "Eli's truck is in the driveway, parked behind Kyler's. It looks like you need to come clean quickly, my girl."

Charli cringed in her seat as she released the safety belt and opened the door. "I dread this. Which will be worse, the confession or confrontation?"

Gran leaned over and gave her a hug and sweet peck on the cheek. "Might as well face the music. No sense in avoiding it. You can do this, Charli. Besides, Eli loves you with every fiber of his being."

They stepped out. Charli slung her backpack across one shoulder. She followed her grandmother into the great room. As much anxiety as Eli's reaction caused her, it thrilled her to see him again.

As the door opened, surprised shock soared through her. Instead of Kyler and Eli sitting there waiting for them, her grandfather met them at the door. Wes engulfed Gran in a strong hug. The handsome, silver-haired man picked the woman up. Together they swung around in a circle. Gran's feet flew as they whirled outward.

"My woman's home, and so am I. Finally, I'm here to stay." He settled her to the floor in front of him. Instead of letting her go, his arm stayed around her as they faced their audience.

Gran beamed with an ageless glow. Pure joy exponentially enhanced her stunning beauty. She trained that glimmer of joy on her grandson and reached toward him.

The tall, lanky young man stepped into the threesome embrace. She pecked him on the cheek. As he drew her arm free of Wes's hold, Gran ruffled the copper-colored hair, cut short now that Kyler played football for Louisville University. "It's been tough without your sunny disposition around here, Kyler. Welcome home."

The young man looked like a taller and male version of Charli without the unruly curls. Kyler hugged his grandmother and kissed her cheek. Then he stepped around his grandparents to pick his petite sister up. "How have you been, sis? I've missed you."

Charli gave him a kiss on his square jaw. "Not as much as I've missed you. I have no one to boss around without you here."

Kyler chuckled and sat her down. "Ah, sis, we both know you've been busy bossing poor Eli around. I'm surprised you haven't run that man off."

Poor kid doesn't know how close he is.

Regardless, she forced a little laugh and hoped she wasn't wrong. "No worries. Eli can hold his own."

Eli kept a distance from the group. He hung close to the lit fireplace that created a cozy atmosphere. If only his expression didn't look so off putting. He appeared to grit his teeth and visibly stopped the inclination. His shoulders rolled as though to shake tension from them. He took a deep breath, scraped a hand over his face, briefly closing his eyes, and his head swayed to the side. Facing the group, he stepped forward.

As he neared, he opened his arms. She stepped into them hopefully. He enveloped her and warmed the chill her concern held. If this was to be her last embrace from the man she loved more than life, she would breathe in every element of it.

He smelled of sandalwood with a hint of the beer he'd enjoyed with the fellas. The tension of his chest hinted at his frustration. The warmth of his body was impossible to miss, and it filled her with expectation.

He held her tightly as though afraid to release her. His heart beat fast and hard, and his limbs quivered in his caress. A low groan emitted from his luscious lips and eased to a heavy, quiet sigh. As his arms relaxed to let her go, she prayed silently for only a temporary liberation. A chill hit her. She shivered at being freed from his grip. With a hooded gaze, she met his eyes.

His speech sounded rushed and tense. "I'm glad you're home safely. When we arrived and found no note as to where you were, and your phone kept going to voice mail, I called Jaiden. She filled us in on what went down in Detroit."

So, he knew all about their adventure.

"I'm sorry about that. The FBI confiscated our phones until we were sent home." Her voice sounded unfamiliar to her own ears.

His chin lifted high. Arms crossed his broad chest. His jaw clenched, and he stood stiffly with rigid muscles. Lips pinched together briefly then he gave an unconvincing smile. "Would you mind joining me out front?" His glance shot from her to the ceiling. Then he strode toward the door.

She followed reluctantly, filled with remorse and trepidation. Her over-the-shoulder look at Gran received an apprehensive smile of encouragement. It did not bolster hope she hadn't screwed up the best relationship of her life. Once outside, she shut the front door behind her.

Eli paced in a tight circle then stopped abruptly. He gazed upward, then as though forced, toward her. "I'm glad you're home and safe, and I missed you so much it hurt. This first separation for more than a day since we've been engaged has been grueling."

With a pained expression, she stood, hands behind her back and gripped her wrists. "I missed you too. I'm so sorry if what I did worried or scared you."

He looked up and back down. "It did and thank you for saying that." His hand shot up and rubbed the nape of his neck. "I need some space to process all of this. I am angry. I'm frustrated. I want to scream at you and ask you why the hell you didn't tell me what you were up to. That would be pointless. I know why. You didn't want me to talk you out of it. You didn't want to argue with me over the phone. I don't want to say something I'll regret. I need time. Please, tell the others goodbye for me. Have a good Thanksgiving. I'll spend mine with Amanda, Frank, and Abbe." He didn't invite Charli but jumped into his truck and slammed the door…hard.

She rushed to the vehicle and banged her palm against the glass. Acting as though he didn't want to, he rolled the window down.

"Eli, I'm sorry. I'm sorry to have worried you, to have disappointed you. I'm sorry I didn't call and tell you about what I planned to do. I just didn't want to ruin your last chance to spend time with your friend before the wedding."

His head jerked away, and his palms slapped the steering wheel. He remained silent, as though considering his words.

"Eli, I'm fine. Gran went with me. She's fine. Please, forgive me. I love you. Don't do this."

He gunned the engine. "Bye, Charli."

She stood helplessly, drained of energy, as he backed out of the driveway and drove down the street. Numbly she watched without stirring until he rounded the corner and drove out of sight. Unable to budge for a very long time, she had no idea how long she had remained there.

Her phone rang. She clicked to answer at a photo of her best friend's face. "Hey, Jaiden, what's up?" No matter how hard she'd tried to sound upbeat, her voice did not comply.

Jaiden's thick Texan drawl came over the phone. "Tell me you're home safely."

"Oh yeah, why?"

"Well, sweet cheeks, I got the full rundown from Reggie. Your man got back into town and couldn't reach you. He called me for help. I couldn't lie to the guy. I figured it best if he had a chance for the news to settle into his handsome brain, before you got home. How are y'all fairing?"

Charli rolled her eyes and shook her head. "About like you'd expect. Not sure where we go from here. You just calling to check on me?"

Jaiden snickered. "Well, yeah, that, and I figured you'd want to know your 'cousin' made bail. Della told me she used all her dough and barely came up with enough to pay the bail bondsman. She has no cash and nowhere to stay, but she's not allowed to leave town."

At least this seemed halfway good news. "You at the station?"

"Sure thing."

"I'll be right over." She hung up and poked her head inside the front door. "Hey, everyone, I've got an errand to run. I'll be back in a little while."

Before anyone asked, she shut the door, opened the garage, jumped into her truck, and drove toward the sheriff's office.

Chapter Twenty-Four

Charli entered the bullpen of the sheriff's office to find Jaiden at her desk and Leo at the one beside hers. Wyatt's glass-walled office in the corner of the big room was vacant, as were the other deputy spaces.

Charli ambled over to Jaiden's station and sat in her guest chair. "Hey, guys, what's up?"

Leo stood and positioned his deputy hat on top of his crewcut blond head. "Not much for me, but I hear you've had an exciting week."

Charli snickered but said nothing.

Leo nodded and drawled in his soft-spoken manner, "I'm going over to Sadie's diner to grab a cup of joe. Want anything?"

Jaiden smiled. "Sure. I'll have a cup. Thanks, partner."

Clearly Leo wanted to give the women some space.

"Thanks, Leo. I'm fine."

After he'd left, Jaiden frowned at her pal. "I'm glad you finally made it home safely. I figured you'd want to know about Della's release. The judge set bail kind of high, and she barely scraped up the dough to cover the bondsman's fee. She can't leave town until this thing goes to trial...assuming it does."

Charli sighed. "Thanks for letting me know. I'll make sure she has somewhere to stay until then. Do you seriously think they'll try her for murder, even with all we've just learned?"

Jaiden's mouth squirreled to the side. "Look, Charli, I know you've done everything possible to clear her, but the fact is she looks guilty."

Charli straightened into her chair. "Maybe she defended herself, but she didn't shoot that guy. There's nothing to show she did that."

Jaiden pursed her lips. "It's not up to me. That would be for the prosecuting attorney and the judge to decide."

"I don't see how they can charge her with anything but self-defense, especially given the information the FBI and I dug up in Michigan."

Jaiden frowned. "Maybe, but it's out of my hands. Fact is, you didn't find evidence that proves her innocent."

Charli glared. "I thought one had to be proven guilty, not proven innocent."

Jaiden's shoulders slumped. "How did it go with Eli? He picked Wes up at the Louisville airport. He wanted to surprise y'all. When they arrived home and couldn't find any sign of you, no note or anything, they were worried. When they couldn't reach you and Irma, Eli called me. I couldn't lie to him."

Charli blinked. "I wouldn't expect you to lie. The feds had our phones for most of the day. When he called the last time, we were nearly home. I figured it wouldn't make things any worse to wait until we could discuss the subject in person."

Jaiden's brows lifted. "And?"

"And…He's royally pissed. Said he's having Thanksgiving with Amanda, Frank, and Abbe. When you told me Della has no place to stay, I texted him and

215

asked if she and I could stay at McGregor House for the weekend. There's not enough room at my house for her until Kyler goes back to university. Besides, with me not in the house Wes and Kyler will have more time to bond. They've only been together since Kyler arrived home and the day Wes and Gran drove to Kyler's college to tell him he has a grandfather who wants to be part of his life."

"There sure is a lot of crap coming down at your place. How are you surviving?"

Charli shrugged. "About like you'd guess. I'm determined to help Della. Eli is spending the weekend in Amanda's guest room, avoiding me like I have a contagious disease, and probably trying to determine how best to end our engagement."

"You think the situation will come to that?"

Charli lifted her shoulders. "Not sure but I hope not."

"Maybe he just needs cooling down time." The deputy spun around as a uniformed officer entered the room behind a disheveled Della in an orange jailer's sweatsuit. "Oh, here's your 'cousin' now." She nodded toward the newcomers.

Charli forced a smile. "I sure am glad to see you."

Della beamed as they reached Jaiden's desk. "Not as glad as I am to see you and to get out of this place." She glanced apologetically at Jaiden and the other officer. "Not that you didn't treat me well, but confinement is still no picnic."

Jaiden pulled Della's backpack from a drawer and placed the pink bag on top of her desk. She retrieved a small, purple duffle bag from the floor beside her feet. "Here are your possessions." She pulled a form and a pen from her lap drawer and laid them in front of the prisoner. "Go through your things and make sure it's all there…minus the section of that laundry container. That's with the FBI."

Della unzipped her bags and sorted through her meager belongings: a zip-lock baggie of personal care items, a pair of socks and panties, one pair of jeans and sweats, and a couple of short sleeved tee shirts.

Charli's heart ached for the woman. "Is that all you brought?"

Jaiden frowned. "The hospital cut her outfit off when first responders brought her into Emergency."

Della smiled sadly. "When you run for your life, you don't think much about what to pack. I just tossed a few things in and ran. I left most of my luggage in my cousin's car."

Charli sighed. "No worries. I need to run to the department store anyway to pick up some things for Thanksgiving dinner tomorrow. We can purchase a few necessities for you. You need some warmer clothing and a coat."

Della's brow furrowed, and moisture pooled in her dark brown eyes. "I don't have any money. I'll be fine with what I have." She bent and signed the document for Jaiden.

"Nonsense. We'll handle this. No argument."

Della swiped at her cheek. Charli made a note to help Della get back to her normal self. She needed some good grub, exercise, less stress, and sunshine. She hugged Jaiden as the deputy rose.

Jaiden pulled a packet out of her lap drawer. "Before you go, Della, would you mind taking a look at some photographs to see if you can identify any of the people in them?"

"Of course not."

Jaiden opened the envelope. "Good. You know, the FBI will want you to testify in their case against this drug ring when they go to trial."

Della nodded "Yes, Carlton told me so. I have no problem with that. I figured I'd be involved the instant I decided to snatch that laundry jug from the damaged bin."

Jaiden laid a few mug shots on her desk. "Know any of these guys?"

Della looked at each one and pointed to two. "These two men look familiar. They drove trucks for Crane Motor Company that picked up laundry on the first of each month. There were other drivers, but I didn't see all of them. I asked Sue in Logistics about the trucking company, and she said the laundry distribution company hadn't awarded them any business."

Jaiden's serious gaze went to her desktop then met Della's. "Sue was killed a couple of weeks ago in a hit and run accident."

Della's brows scrunched together, and her mouth opened with an exhale. She shut and opened her eyes. "I suggest someone investigate her death. I involved that poor woman and probably got her killed. I'd wager those criminals murdered her."

"I'll pass that on to the DPD and the FBI." She pointed to her computer screen. "Get this." She read from an elaborate website explanation of what the suspicious companies were supposedly about and what they did.

Charli snorted. "Sounds like a load of crap."

"LaRosa and his complex organization of criminals

will go away for a very long time. You were instrumental in making this happen."

Charli eyed her friend. "Shouldn't the DA look kindly on Della's case for all the help she's given? She's put her life at risk to do the right thing."

Jaiden winced. "I would hope so. It's out of my hands. I'm sure Della's attorney will keep her abreast of the situation. Carlton is one of the best attorneys in the country. He will represent Della's case well."

Charli smiled at Della. "Yes, Della, you're in good hands with Carlton Farmer."

Jaiden placed more photos on the desk. "What about these men?"

Della inspected them carefully. "I've seen that guy and this one. They waited for their loads the day I stood at the truck bay chatting up Clarence Boyd, the dock manager. Clancy Mulhaney strutted out from behind the semi with a glare on his face that nearly made me wet my pants. It wasn't the first time I'd noticed him, but the first time he'd paid me any mind." She shivered as though a chill ran through her.

Jaiden placed a few more photographs on the desk. "Know any of these people?"

Della looked at the shot of the pimple-faced nerd who had manned the front desk when Charli and Gran had dropped in at Detroit Detergent Distributors. She moved on to a few other characters Charli didn't recognize and stopped at the picture of a disheveled, scruffy Dwayne LaRosa. "I know this guy. Never met him personally. When I researched the distribution company, I found a picture of him on the website. Funny, he looked a lot more impressive in a three-piece suit with a tie and decent haircut."

Charli snickered. "Yeah, I saw that as well. My impression exactly. Let me tell you, that facility is nothing like what they show on that site. The nondescript building at the end of a secluded commercial drive didn't even have a name on the front. It was nothing like they advertise the facility to be."

Jaiden smiled. "I checked the company out too. My guess is they used a stock photo for the warehouse shot and did a photo shoot with a much better made up LaRosa so the company would give the appearance of a legitimate business."

Charli nodded. "Your impression is spot on. The only business they were up to was dirty business. Nothing clean about their laundry distribution." She looked to Della. "Do you see the men who were looking for you at your dad's memorial?"

Della's head shook, and her lower lip scrunched up. "No, but Mulhaney is one of them. The other isn't among these photos."

The next series of images Jaiden revealed appeared to be DMV sourced. "What about these folks?"

Della scanned them one-by-one. "Nope, don't know these four, but this guy is the other thug with Mulhaney at Pa's funeral. He acted as one of the driver's helpers I saw that day at the loading dock when Mulhaney scared me near to death."

The print she pointed at was of Evan Avery. The ones she didn't identify were of his wife and Mulhaney's lover, Evette Avery; Mulhaney's landlady, Ms. Crane; Frank Capone, owner of the Corner Bar and probably Clancey Mulhaney's bookie; the bartender who had served Gran and Charli; and a couple of other men Charli didn't recognize.

Jaiden left Avery's for last and pointed at it. "Just so you know, this man worked for the same bogus security firm that employed Mulhaney. Those guys are nothing more than muscle for the operation. Several of the others I showed you were also listed as employees of that shell company supporting LaRosa's illegal ventures. His name is Evan Avery, and we suspect his wife cheated on him with Mulhaney. Avery is in the wind, so just watch yourself."

Charli got a sudden chill. "What about Capone?"

Jaiden put Frank's photo back out. "This guy isn't someone you want to mess with either. He's a low-level criminal, and we haven't arrested him. Based on what DPD told us, he's got his own little hit squad to put pressure on business associates he feels need to learn a lesson. We suspect Mulhaney was into him for a good sum of cash for gambling losses. Stay clear of this guy and any others you feel the least bit eerie of. It's doubtful any of them will give a hoot about you, now the drug ring has dismantled, but it doesn't hurt to be cautious."

Charli's gut rolled. She took a deep breath as Jaiden secured the photographs. "That sounds well and good, but the men who run that operation must be powerful. Who knows how far their reach extends? They might not take kindly to anyone willing to testify against them. Shouldn't you have a protective detail on Della?"

Jaiden bit her lip. "The feds don't think it's necessary. They're confident they've arrested the major players. They expect to have Avery in custody by the end of the day. The chance of anyone giving a damn about Della is slim to none. You ladies go home. Enjoy your holiday. Eat too much turkey and pie and try to forget about crime and jail for a little while."

Jaiden's assurance apparently provided relief for Della. "You know, those trucks didn't need helpers. That looked suspicious. I saw the manifest Clarence held that morning. The loads only traveled across town, no stops along the way. Our forklift guys loaded the cargo. I'm sure the destination had people to unload them. All the helper did was ride along."

Charli's brows lifted. "And provide security for the drug shipment."

Della smiled. "Exactly. I figured there had to be more valuable goods than a truckload of laundry detergent being transported."

Jaiden smiled and shuffled the photographs back into the envelope. "I see why you were suspicious. It took some major guts to do something about it…like you did. My hat's off to you, Della. I wish you the best."

"Thanks for everything. What are your holiday plans?"

Jaiden hugged her tightly and then stood back. "Clay and I are having dinner at Wyatt and Sage's home. They invited Mom, Rose, and Cal. Wyatt's daughter, Hailey, is in from Boston. If she gets back in time, Reggie and Clay are coming, too."

Charli smiled. "Awesome. Sounds like Sage has a large group to feed—just as she likes it. She's a fabulous cook."

Jaiden patted her slim belly. "Don't I know it? I'll probably gain ten pounds just smelling the meal. Y'all have a great Thanksgiving." Doubt shaded her smile.

As they left Charli glanced over her shoulder. "We'll give it our all. Tell everyone Happy Thanksgiving and give them all hugs for me." She ushered Della out of the room, outside and to her truck.

Della settled into the passenger side and pushed a few tools out of the way of her feet. Charli hopped in, phone at her ear, and dialed Gran's number.

"Hey, Gran, I'll go to the store. Need anything, I might not think of from there?" She nodded and memorized the few items Gran cited. "Okay. No problem. Della and I will be home soon. She's staying us for a while."

Della watched as she fired the engine and pulled away from the curb. "I can't thank you enough for taking me in like this. Jaiden said you would. Carlton told me so also, but it's a lot to ask."

"Not a problem. We take care of our own here in Sweetwater." Charli drove the few blocks to the big-box store and parked.

"But I'm not one of your own. I'm a total stranger." Della's hands wrung together in her lap.

Charli stared seriously at her new friend. "Don't be silly. You are part of the Sweetwater clan. You're a McGregor. A lot of family history runs through your veins. Like it or not, you're from Sweetwater. You'll always be a part of this community no matter how far you roam. Besides, you're my 'cousin.' Remember?"

She chuckled and made a point to keep her tone and smile sincere and jovial. No sense in bringing Della down, mentioning her own romantic issues.

It took about fifteen minutes for the women to gather the few purchases on Charli's mental list. Then Charli forced Della to join her in the clothing department. She pointed to the rack of underwear. "Pick out some panties, a couple of bras, and warm pajamas. We'll spend the next four nights in McGregor House. The mansion might be a bit drafty."

Della tilted her head, eyeing Charli. "Oh? I thought we would stay at your house."

Charli nodded and tossed her a bag of socks like the pair in Della's duffle. "We are, but my kid brother is home for the holiday. It's a bit crowded there. He'll take off for college on Sunday evening. We'll move back in there once he's gone."

"So, we're staying at McGregor House with Eli?" Della asked.

"No, Eli will spend the weekend with his sister's family. It will just be you and me."

Della's brow wrinkled, and she bit her lip. "Okay, if I don't put him out. I'll bet you miss him while he's away."

She obviously thought Eli traveled to be with his family. No need to explain that. The truth would only confuse things further.

"Oh, yes, I will. It's fine, though." Time to change the subject. "Okay, now let's find you a pretty dress." Taking Della's hand, she dragged her along behind as she pushed the cart to the ladies' department.

"I don't need anything fancy. What I've got will do."

"Absolutely not. You'll freeze to death in those short-sleeved shirts. You need a nice outfit for when you make a court appearance, and you can wear it tomorrow for Thanksgiving." She sifted through a rack of dresses. "What size do you wear?"

Della told her and joined her to look for appropriate attire. They selected a couple of dresses. Then Charli insisted she try on some jeans and sweaters. While Della donned the items, Charli pulled out three coats that might suit her friend. Della modeled each garment for Charl.

They argued some about the cost. In the end, Charli won the disagreement. Della chose the coat Charli liked the best, a dark Kelly-green wool that hit her perfectly at the knees. They picked up a few personal care items. Then Charli paid for the clothing in their cart.

Once in the vehicle heading to Charli's house, Della cleared her throat and strained a fake smile. "I don't know how to thank you. I can't believe you're doing all of this for me. I will pay you back what you spent, once I get things settled." She hesitated. "What will your family think?"

Charli drove into her garage and parked her truck beside Gran's SUV. "They'll be happy I'm doing the right thing, welcome you into our home, and hope that should I ever be in such a dire situation, someone would do the same for me."

Tears flowed down Della's pale cheeks. Her frail hand reached over and covered Charli's on the steering wheel. "Oh, Charli, I've never had such a devoted friend or met anyone quite like you. You're the most compassionate person I've ever met. Thank you for all you're doing. I do appreciate it."

Charli grinned. "No problem. I know you do, and you're welcome." She hopped out of the vehicle. "Now, help me cart these groceries inside. Pick out a clean set of clothing, too. Leave the rest of your things in the truck. We'll take 'em when we go to McGregor House after dinner.

Chapter Twenty-Five

At home Wes and Kyler bonded over a football game while Gran piddled around in the kitchen. "Oh, I'm happy to see the two of you. We need to get a good start on those pies for dinner tomorrow." She accepted a bag of groceries from Charli and put items away with a nod toward the men. "Della, welcome to our home. That young fella over there on the sofa is my grandson, Charli's brother, Kyler Owens. His handsome cohort is the love of my life and Charli and Kyler's grandfather, Wesley Drake."

Charli sat her other grocery bag on the bar and pulled items out as the men hopped to their feet and joined the women at the kitchen island. Smiles enhanced their handsome faces as they extended their hands toward Della.

Wes beamed. "It's so good to meet you, Della. I've heard a lot about you—all good, mind you."

Della blushed as she sat her shopping bag down and accepted Wes's hand. "Thank you, Mr. Drake. It's a pleasure."

"The pleasure is all mine, my dear. Please call me Wes. Mr. Drake makes me feel like an old man."

Della smiled. "Whatever your age, you hold it well, Wes." She met Kyler's eager smile. "Charli told me about her handsome, talented brother. She's quite the fan." She accepted his hand.

Kyler didn't hesitate to draw the woman a few years his senior into a hug. "Della, we don't stand on ceremony here in Kentucky, and we hug family. It seems you've been ushered into our clan while I was away at school. It's good to meet you, and don't believe everything my sister says. I'm really a nice guy."

Della chuckled as he released her from the friendly embrace. "It's all good, I assure you."

Gran took over. "Now, you gents get the heck out of my kitchen and back to whatever mischief you've got going over there. We gals have work to do."

With a bit of good-humored grumbling, Kyler snagged a beer for Wes and a soda for himself. Gran snapped his rear end with her dishtowel. With a chuckle, he strutted over to Wes, and they settled onto the living room sofa.

Della took in the room as she unloaded staples from her sack. "You have a lovely home, Irma and Charli, and a unique decorating style. I've never seen guitars displayed on walls in a residence before. I take it one of you plays." Her gaze was on the glass-case enclosed, electric guitars hanging on the wall above the fireplace.

Charli watched her grandmother with pride as she stuffed items into cabinets. "Gran is quite famous. You may've heard of her. She was Starr Bright of the Terrestrials, a rock singer with several decades in the limelight. She's retired now and only performs at special events. Mostly, she writes songs for other artists."

Gran wagged her brows toward them. "Yep, these old, arthritic fingers aren't what they used to be. I'm delighted to be out of the touring circuit and here with my family. I do appreciate the artwork of such gorgeous, well-crafted instruments however, and the dear friends who gifted them to me. They are works of art worthy of being seen."

Della's eyes were wide, and her mouth fell open. "I'll say—man, you have known some amazing talent. That's an impressive cast of superstars and the best guitarists ever to play a stage."

Gran smiled proudly. "I cannot disagree."

Della drew closer to inspect the inspiring display. "My mother was a big fan of your music. She had all your records. I grew up listening to your songs. You are extremely talented."

Gran winked. "*Were* being the operative word, dear—were. I'm blissfully retired."

Della smiled. "That's incredible. I'm so honored to meet you. Thank you all for inviting me into your home." Her head tilted toward Charli with moisture in her eyes.

Gran broke the emotional time bomb. "Well now, you might like a nice, long shower after your time in the slammer. Charli, why don't you take Della to my bedroom? She can use my private shower to freshen up. There are clean towels under the sink. Shampoo, conditioner and bodywash are in the shower, and there's a hairdryer in the vanity drawer. Help yourself to whatever you need in there and take your time."

"It would feel good to get cleaned up and not smell like a jailbird."

Gran beamed. "Good. While you do that, Charli and I will get a head start on pies for tomorrow."

Charli showed their guest to her grandmother's rooms. Gran stood in front of the stove, stirring sugar and cornstarch into a pot filled with blackberries. Charli went to the cupboard and chose supplies to make pie crusts. She rolled the dough out, cut several circles of it, and then placed them into prepared pie pans. After poking a few holes in the bottoms with a fork, she moved them into the oven Gran had preheated to 350 degrees. Then she crushed graham crackers for more pies.

While the women worked in sync, the men's conversation had moved to fishing. Wes beamed at the photos Kyler showed him of enormous catfish he'd hooked at Kentucky Lake and the Sniper he'd caught when Charli had taken him to Cumberland.

"If you're free and up for it, I'll book us a fly-in trip to a little place I've fished in Saskatchewan. It's a tiny island on a remote lake we would have all to ourselves. Our boat will be docked right in front of the cabin. I guarantee you will nab trophy monster Pike and Muskie. We should catch enough big Walleye to eat all week and then some."

Gran piled two baked pie crusts with glossy blackberry filling and added dough shaped leaves Charli had cut to the top. She stuck them back into the hot oven for a few minutes to brown those toppings and then retrieved them while Charli mixed pumpkin pie ingredients together. Once the blackberry pies cooled, she placed them into boxes lined with clean cloth napkins.

The men finished prattling about their fishing and hunting plans for the next year and strolled together toward the delectable scents in the kitchen area of the great room. Wes leaned toward the cartons Gran sealed tight.

"Yum! It's been many a year since I've had a home cooked Thanksgiving dinner."

With a plastic spatula Gran swatted his hand as he reached toward one box. "Hands off, mister, that's for tomorrow. Play your cards right, and you can have a chocolate iced brownie after dinner tonight. No more snacking. You boys have had enough for a while."

"Irma." His gaze portrayed anything but disappointment. The expression spoke clearly of awe he had for the extraordinary woman before him. "You always were a bossy, spunky, little wench."

"Wesley Drake, you silly son-of-a-bitch, you know darned well a winch is a tool for something that needs pulling up. Son, you've topped every other man in every category in the contest, far as I'm concerned. You don't need anything or anyone to pull you to the top. I'll take spunky and bossy—kind of like those two. Speaking of bossy, why don't you two rascals get the heck out of this house for a while, so we can put something on the tube beside sporting events? I need you to run an errand for me."

"What 'cha need, Gran?" Kyler stuck his head in the refrigerator.

"Get that big noggin of yours out of the fridge, boy. You've drunk enough to float a boat."

"What can we do for you, your bossiness?" Wes put a hand to his belly and folded his straight frame into a bow.

Gran cleared her throat. "That's your majesty bossiness, and I need the two of you to take this pie over to Amanda's for their Thanksgiving dinner. The dessert is Eli's favorite."

She picked up one of the blackberry pie boxes and handed the gift to Wes. She leaned over the countertop and gave him a sweltering kiss that made Charli's crotch tingle, reminding her how much she missed Eli.

"Yuck!" Kyler jumped backward. almost bumping

230

into the fridge. "Quit frosting the pumpkin there, Grandpa, you dirty dog. Old people smashing donuts ain't nothing I want to see."

Wesley glared inquisitively at Charli, his brows lifted high. "I suppose that means he wants me to stop romancing his grandmother?"

Charli nodded with a snort. "Yep, you've got that right, Wes."

Hands on hips, Wes studied Kyler. "Son, unless the woman objects, you might as well get used to this. I've got some time to make up for."

Kyler's head bent down. Lips pursed, and he blubbered out a fluttering breath. "Hot dang. I knew this grandfather deal might come with strings attached." His hands slapped his thin hips. "What the hell, go to town, you two. Just don't do '*it*' in the living room where all Sweetwater can witness you doing the monkey dance."

With a snicker, the young man met his grandparents' gaze. "We'll be happy to, Gran."

Wes picked up the pie box, reached into his pants pocket, and tossed Kyler his keys. "I've had a couple of beers. You best drive, son."

Kyler glanced at the item in his big paws. "Whoa, damn, you want me to drive your fancy ride?"

Gran sneered. "Watch your language, young man. I'm still your grandmother."

Charli didn't miss the Gran's smile and then her sneer. Her expression showed pride to see her grandson accept his newly announced grandfather as part of their family.

He shot out an apology. "Sorry, Gran."

Wes put an arm around Kyler's shoulders. "Well, it's just a car, son. It's meant to be driven, and you're the most capable one on this journey."

The women watched the two of them leave through the front door. Charli sighed.

"They seem to hit it off."

"Thank goodness. I feared they might butt heads. You know how young men are with father figures."

Charli snickered and put pumpkin pie mix into the shells. "Yeah, but Kyler took that out on me many years ago. I became his substitute mother and father. My guess is they will be great together."

Gran stared at her as she stood from putting the pies in the heated oven "I'm sorry I couldn't take that burden off your shoulders, Charli. You were much too young to bear such a heavy load."

Hopefully, Charli's smile showed her feelings. "I know, Gran. You did what was possible. There are no regrets. I needed Kyler as much as he needed me. He was almost a baby—my baby—in my mind. It is what it is, and it all turned out well…for all of us. I'm just glad you were here to back us up. No worries. You did your part. All is good."

"If only you and Eli resolved your issues. I hate you being apart for this holiday…right before your wedding. December 20 will come sooner than you think. Wait until you're my age, you will appreciate how fast time goes."

Charli sighed heavily, at a loss for words. Gran had said it all.

Della stepped slyly out from the hallway, where she'd apparently listened to exchanges in the main room. "Charli, so Eli isn't out of town with his family?"

Charli inhaled quickly. "Oh, Della, I didn't see you there. Well, yes, he's just across town at this sister's house for the weekend. He thought if he stayed there, it would be easier for all of us. That way you and I can have McGregor House until Kyler leaves."

"Yes, but don't the two of you want to have Thanksgiving dinner together? This is all my fault. I've driven your fiancé away during an important holiday, right before your wedding." Her hands flew up to cover her face. "Oh hell, I feel awful. I've taken advantage of you and ruined everything." She rushed into the great room.

Gran dropped what she worked on and moved to their guest, as did Charli. "Now, listen here, young lady, none of this is your fault. It is fine. Do you hear me?" She put hands on Della's shoulders and with her mere presence, forced the younger woman's head to lift.

Della met Gran's gaze with watery eyes.

Charli stood beside them. "Della, Eli is pissed at me because I concealed something important from him. Our spat has nothing to do with you. It's not your fault. It's mine. He feels I deceived him, went behind his back and hid my plans. I didn't see things that way at the time, but I understand how he does. If he'd been in town, he would've supported me one hundred percent. He'd have been right there by my side, as Gran was."

Gran's head moved slowly upward, and she stared at Della. "Della, this will all work out fine. Eli and Charli have their own burdens to tow, as do you, as do we all. They will work this out...assuming it's meant to be. Believe me. I'm an expert on this subject. If those two are meant to be together, they'll figure this out on their own. I believe in them and am sure they'll be fine." She hesitated until Della nodded. "Okay, now you have your own issues to work out. We're here for you...even Eli. We're behind you all the way. You're a part of our family now, like it or not. So, snap out of it, sister. We've got pies to bake." Gran strode away and back to the mission she'd been working on.

Charli silently put a hand to Della's back. Della wiped a lone tear away. She contemplated the vaulted ceiling. Charli snatched an apron from the countertop and tossed the garment to her friend. "Put your armor on, Della. We've got a fruit-filled battle to wage."

Dell chuckled and donned the garment over her fresh outfit.

Chapter Twenty-Six

Frank and Eli sat at the coffee table. Eli played checkers with Abbe. A football game was on the television. They'd been warned to vacate Amanda's kitchen, so she could prepare their Thanksgiving dinner the following day without distractions. She clearly didn't consider singing along to the radio station that played nothing but Christmas tunes distracting, as she belted out her favorite holiday song. The doorbell rang.

"I'll get it." He hopped up from the sofa, strode to the door, and blinked in surprise at their visitors.

Wes and Kyler stood, shoulders hunched and bundled against breezy fall weather. Kyler pushed a ribbon-circled white box into his hands. "Gran sent this. She said the pie was your favorite, and y'all should have it with your Thanksgiving dinner."

Eli waved the men inside with an arm, the other accepted the pie. "Come on in. It's chilly out there." As they entered, he shut the door behind them.

Amanda entered from the kitchen, adorable in her pink, ruffled apron over a sweatshirt and jeans. Short blonde hair framed her lovely face, looking ever so much like her big brother Eli. "Well, now if you aren't the sweetest surprise this side of the Mississippi, I'll eat my apron." She grinned and wiped her hands on that garment's front and then gave their visitors each a hug. "My goodness, Kyler, I thought it impossible for you to grow any taller, but you've proved me wrong. Just look at the muscle frame this young man has built since he left for college."

Kyler blushed. "Thank you, ma'am. I've been working out with weights. It's part of the football program."

Frank stuck his hand out to the men to shake. "Well, son, it's working. Come on in and sit a spell. We're just watching the game."

Amanda took the pie from Eli. "Umm, smells good."

Eli took their coats and hung them on a rack behind the door.

"It's blackberry." Wes nodded toward the item. "Seriously, I think she sent us over here so they could watch something besides football on the TV."

Eli chuckled. "Getting rid of you, huh?"

Kyler beamed. "Something like that."

Eli and Frank showed their guest to the living room.

"Abbe's been beating me at checkers."

Kyler sat on the floor beside the seven-year-old. "What do you say? Want to play me a game, Abbe?"

Amanda disappeared into the kitchen with the box and returned with a tray. She passed beers out to the older guys, handed an icy glass of amber liquid to Kyler, and a cup of chocolate milk to Abbe. "I figured you could use some refreshments. She placed a bowl of dry-roasted peanuts in the table's center. "Kyler, I hope you like cider."

Kyler shot her a bright smile. "Love it and thanks. Yes, someone around here must drive us home." He flashed the classy European sedan's emblem-encrusted key chain in his hand and then stuffed the treasure into his jeans pocket.

"Be sure to tell your grandmother and Charli how much we appreciate their thoughtfulness."

Wes hadn't brought Charli up, but Amanda included her in the thanks.

"I'll just go write them a note so you can deliver our thanks when you get home." She returned to her work in the kitchen.

The men watched the rest of another game, and their chosen team won. Abbe beat Kyler, or he let her, several times. Wes reached for Frank's hand and shook it. "Thanks for the game and company. We'd best get home though. The gals probably want to serve dinner soon."

Kyler peeled his long, lanky frame from the floor. Frank stood as Wes did. "So, does this mean you've moved to Sweetwater for good? Eli tells us you retired."

Wes nodded. "Indeed, and I'm thrilled to be here."

"Congratulations." Frank patted his new friend on the back.

Eli helped the men with their coats.

Amanda stepped in and handed Kyler the note she'd written. "Bye now. Y'all have a lovely holiday." She waved and disappeared into the kitchen.

At the door, Kyler stepped out and strode toward the car, clearly excited to drive his grandfather's elegant vehicle. "Bye. Happy Thanksgiving."

Eli touched the other man's arm. "Wes, I could use some advice. A sounding board if you will. Would you meet me Friday for a cup of coffee?"

Wes's brows shot up. "Sure, son. I'd be delighted to."

Eli smiled. "Great. Say nine o'clock at The Royal Diner?"

Wes waved as he left. "Works for me. See you then.

Now, don't down too much turkey. You hear?"

Eli chuckled. "Ditto, man. I can hold my own around the table."

Wes chuckled as he climbed into the passenger seat. "Don't I know it. I've seen you eat, son."

Endearingly, Wes included Eli in his newly claimed family and called him son. His words caused a swirling warm sensation in Eli's middle and a much-needed calming effect on his recently-developed nervous condition. His frustration with Charli's actions and the stress it caused, along with resulting tension between him and Charli, had gotten on his last nerve.

Not sure how we can get past this.

****

Thanksgiving Day the house had been decorated and looked lovely. The weather cooperated with sunshine and appropriately cool air. Their meal tasted delicious. Joy showed on all faces around the table but resonated a bit forced. Tension wavered just below the surface. Everyone acted like they were afraid they'd step into a pile of horse manure.

"Wow, sis, you look amazing. Who knew you could pull a dress off?" Kyler snickered when she appeared in the great room, decked out in the wine velvet dress she'd bought for the occasion, assuming she would have other holiday and wedding event occasions to appear in the extravagant indulgence. "We're used to you in cut-offs and work boots. I knew a girl hid somewhere in there."

She sped toward him. He slipped around the island and hid behind Gran, who swatted his behind with a dishtowel. "Now you behave, you young rascal. Charli is as much a lady as I am, no matter what she's wearing." She focused eyes on her granddaughter. "You look lovely, sweetheart. Don't let this smart ass yank your lead line."

Charli rolled her eyes dramatically and shrugged. "I'll let it slip this time, since I missed him so much."

She rounded the island. Seeing what was coming, he managed to squat enough so she could reach her target. She planted a sloppy kiss on her brother's cheek.

Wes sat at the counter, peeling a bowl full of potatoes. He let out a guffaw that showed his delight in the youngsters' antics. "Do they always behave like this, Irma, my dear? Or have these two reverted to their childhood?"

Gran blew her man a kiss. "Better get used to it. They're always up to some sort of nonsense."

Wes seemed to get a kick out of his family's shenanigans. Charli was certainly happy to have him in her life. She strolled around to his seat and slid an arm across his strong shoulders.

"Wes, this is nothing. We're on our best behavior. We wouldn't want to scare you and Della off."

Kyler snatched a chunk and popped the raw potato piece into his mouth. Gran smacked his hand with a ladle, and he jumped.

"Ouch! Watch it there, Gran. These hands are extremely valuable to the team. What would they do without their prize quarterback?"

Charli chuckled. "Yeah, wouldn't want them to lose every game with their second-string rookie out for the rest of the season."

Wes joined in the fun. "Go easy on him, Charli. The boy has done well when he has gotten play time. He's only a freshman. It's no more than you can expect."

Della joined them, and everyone commented on

how nice she looked. Color back into her face, her eyes seemed brighter. "Thank you." Her cheeks reddened. "Charli bought it for me." She spun around in the deep green dress. I love it."

During dinner the family chatted about the upcoming holidays. Kyler complained about work he had to do to get through finals before he could return home on December 18, a couple of days before the wedding.

Between large forks-full, Kyler grumbled. "It's a shame Eli's not here. I miss that guy and have been looking forward to more time with him. Next year with the two of you married, we should invite Amanda, Frank, and Abbe to join us for dinner." His gaze moved up from his plate and met his grandmother's pointed glare. He glanced around at concerned faces around the table. "What's wrong?"

Charli stared at her lap as she crushed her cloth napkin into a tight ball between stiff fingers. Fighting a burst of tears, she blinked and inhaled. With controlled movements, she wiped her mouth and laid the napkin beside her plate. She pushed her chair back as she stood, not meeting the gaze of the others.

She turned toward the hallway. "Excuse me." She stiffly made it to the bathroom and closed the door behind her.

Distance and barriers muffled voices in the big room. She didn't care what they said. Big huffs of air forced their way in and out of her heaving lungs between sobs. She let pent up emotions flow without resistance, not bothering to wipe moisture away until she spent every single drop that ached to come out.

She splashed water on her face and then patted dry

with a soft towel as she inspected damage in the mirror.

Good thing I don't wear much makeup. I've given my waterproof mascara a run for its money. Her eyes looked a little puffier than before her breakdown, but not as red as she'd expected.

As she returned and sat at the table, Wes was explaining how he'd arranged for his company to thrive after his retirement, and how he would continue to reap profits of his long music industry career.

The family made no comment as she joined them. Talk the remainder of the day avoided mention of her second failed attempt at matrimony or the name they were apparently afraid to speak again.

Charli forced herself to stay in the moment, to enjoy the presence of her newly found friend, recently discovered grandfather, Gran, and her much adored brother. She had lots to be grateful for.

****

The following day Kyler left with Della and Wes, proudly spinning Wes's luxury sedan's key chain around his slim finger. Gran curled up on the sofa with a cup of tea. Charli grabbed her string backpack.

"I'll see you later. What are you up to today?"

Gran smiled happily. "Not a dadburn thing, just watching movies and enjoying a bit of peace and quiet. Where you heading?"

Charli opened the garage door. "Courthouse and errands."

"See you later." Gran waved as Charli closed the door behind her.

****

Eli stood as Wes entered the diner. He motioned the older man toward his table by the window. "Over here,

Wes."

Wes accepted his friendly hug. "Good to see you, Eli."

Sadie Carson scurried to their side. The redheaded waitress pulled a pad and pen from the white apron draped over the skirt of her pink dress. "Morning, gents. It's right nice to see the Owens women's fellas hitting it off. What can I get you fellers?" Sadie's famous southern twang came out so strong outsiders sometimes had a hard time following it.

Eli handed her the menu he hadn't bothered to appraise, a sure sign he'd officially become indoctrinated to Sweetwater. "I'll have coffee with biscuits and gravy."

Wes eyed the restaurant owner. "I planned to just have coffee, but Irma highly recommends your biscuits and gravy. It would be foolish not to give the dish a go."

Sadie tilted her head, and the white waitress crown pinned to the top flipped with the motion. Sadie's persona perfectly enhanced the restaurant's retro theme. "Good choice." She spun on her heels. "I'll be right back with your drinks."

In mere seconds she rejoined them with a tray of beverages. She placed two glasses of water, straws, a black insulated carafe, a small pitcher of cream, and two cups of steaming, dark brew on the table between the men. "Your grub will be ready in a jiffy."

Eli wrapped a hand around his mug. "Thank you, Sadie."

The woman strode toward the kitchen. They prepared their coffee to personal preferences and enjoyed their first couple of sips. Sadie arrived with another tray. This time she sat two warm plates of light brown goo and two plates of hot biscuits on the table.

The delectable aroma made Eli's mouth water.

Wes beamed. "This looks amazing." His comment brought a proud smile to Sadie's pleasant face.

Eli picked up one of the delicate rounds of piping hot dough, broke it into small pieces, placed them in the gravy, and then added extra pepper. "I assure you, my friend, this delight is well worth the calories."

Sadie glanced around the table. "Can I get y'all anything else?"

Eli lifted a bite with his fork. "We're good. Thanks." The waitress disappeared.

The men chatted casually about Wes's retirement as they breakfasted. "Irma didn't steer me in the wrong direction with their culinary advice." The older man ate the delicious, starchy concoction with gusto.

As he put down his fork to signal he'd finished, Wes forced Eli's gaze to meet his. "That tasted amazing. Now, son, I don't believe you invited me here today just to consume a mountain of calories." He patted his slender belly. "What did you want to talk about?"

Eli laid his fork on the plate and topped it with his napkin. Placing elbows on the table, he tented his fingers and drew in a heavy breath. "I'm hoping you'll be my sounding board. I'm frustrated about what's happened between me and Charli. I needed someone to talk with about it."

Wes leaned back against the red vinyl bench seat. "I'm your man, Eli. After all you and Charli have done for me, I owe you big time."

Eli blew air out his nostrils. "You don't owe us anything, Wes. We only did for you what one does for family." The last word struck him hard as it crossed his lips. His acquired family seemed to slip through his fingers. He studied the table for a minute. "You know I've been distant since Charli took off for Detroit and put herself in harm's way." Wes nodded silently. "I am trying to figure out how I can ever trust her again. She hid her actions from me, and she could've been killed."

"But she wasn't. She's fine. If I got facts straight, you were out of town, in Cincinnati on a pleasure and business trip. Right?"

Eli nodded. His brows quirked momentarily with a pang of guilt. "Yes, but she should've called and told me what she had decided to."

Wes closed lips formed a smile. "I suppose that's true. If she'd called you, you'd have tried to talk her out of it. Wouldn't you?"

Eli nodded with a flick of his eyebrows. "For sure, but once Charli sets her mind to something, stopping her is out of the question."

Wes's head tilted slightly forward. "So, you and she would've argued but for nothing. You both would've been angry, and she would've gone anyway. That would've distracted her and potentially made her trip more dangerous. She had no idea she would step into a life-threatening situation. Charli had no clue about the FBI's plan to raid that distribution center. She didn't even think the authorities were investigating Della's story. It's why she became so adamant about going to Detroit—to do that herself. She hoped to uncover enough information to convince the police to check out other avenues of Mulhaney's life. You said it yourself; you couldn't have stopped her. What would you have done, had you been here?"

Eli wrung his hands on the table. "I...I guess I would've gone with her. I would've been there to protect her."

Wes snorted. "Experience tells me my granddaughter can handle herself. Besides, she is smart enough to not go alone. She told her grandmother, knowing Irma would insist on accompanying her. She doesn't need you there just to protect her. It's not why you are in her life. Charli wants you by her side as her partner—not just in business, but in life. She doesn't want you around so you can hold her back. She needs you to love her, support her, lift her up, and stand beside her."

Eli winced. "It's just that since we met, I've been present when she put herself in danger. I feel so guilt-ridden. I watched football, ate hotdogs, and drank beer while my woman was in a battle of bullets."

Wes chuckled. "Charli wanted you to go on that trip. She knew how much you looked forward to seeing your friend and having some personal down time before the wedding. She didn't want to ruin your plans." He hesitated for a few seconds. "Besides, if I got the deal straight, and I usually do from Irma, she's a straight shooter. Charli didn't hit a wall in her online research into Della's case until you were nearly to Cincinnati. That's when she decided to drive to Michigan and do some in-person snooping around. Their trip proved quite productive, and they brought back some good leads the sheriff's office is fact-checking."

Eli sighed heavily. "I should've been there."

Wes leaned forward. "Look, Wes, Charli enjoys you caring for her. She's not had any man to lean on for herself since her father died. She's used to fending for herself…and her brother. She loves you. You love her. Face it and get over this protection complex."

Wes was right. Eli had been the father figure for Amanda as they grew up without parents. He became the protector of his former secretary after her husband died and she grew old and frail. He took care of Amanda and Abbe while Frank was in Afghanistan. He hadn't thought about his reaction that way, but Wes hit the hammer on the nail.

Knight in shining armor wasn't the role Charli wanted Eli to play. She wanted him with her, for her, to stand beside her, and love her. She wanted him as her equal in all things. Was that enough for him?

Wes' lips squeezed to the side. "It sounds to me like you're angrier with yourself than with Charli. Eli, take it from me. The past isn't where you want to live. Forgiveness isn't for the other person. It's for you. Forgive yourself for something you had no power to change. Don't carry around a load of guilt. It's worthless and can ruin your future. You love my granddaughter, and you're miserable without her. She's bat crap crazy over you and as unhappy as you are. Forgive her and forgive yourself, so you can get on with the life you want. Don't give up what you and Charli found together for what happened in the past and you couldn't prevent." He glanced out the window. "Oops, there's my ride. If we're done here, I'd best be going." At Eli's nod, Wes stood, slipped on his overcoat, and reached into his back pocket.

Eli's hand shot up as he stood. "Breakfast is on me. Thanks for the advice." His arms opened, and Wes leaned into them for a manly hug.

"Anytime, son." Wes winked as he exited the door. "It's what one does for family."

The word sent an ache into Eli's chest. He took his

seat and refilled his coffee cup as he mulled over their discussion. Wesley was right. He spoke from experience. Eli knew what the older man had missed out on because of a lack of forgiveness of himself and Irma, and their failure to communicate.

How could Eli to fix this? He had some thinking to do.

The door flung open. A tall, lean blonde stormed in. Her familiar face beamed at the sight of him. She rushed to his table and slipped onto the bench Wes had vacated. Her gloved hands reached across the distance and took his. "Amanda told me I could find you here."

Wes's brows rose, and he stared at the stunning female he'd known since childhood. "She told me you and Danny were moving to town. Why are you looking for me?"

Gina removed her gloves and stacked them neatly on the table. "Danny just started his new job as head of operations at the Sweetwater Distillery. Danny's staying at the Sweetwater Inn in one of those rent-by-the-month suites until we can relocate. Our home in Fort Thomas has sold. Bo and I are living with Mom and Dad for now. We've been looking for a house, so we can move here and found the most adorable antebellum mansion. The rest of the plantation has sold off, all but the house and three acres."

Good for his friend, but Eli didn't understand. "So, what's the problem?"

She waged her perfectly formed brows. "Amanda said you started a new construction company here in town and you remodel homes. The house we're purchasing needs updating."

Eli frowned with a downturned chin. "I, we—me

and my partner—do remodeling, but we usually purchase and renovate to flip homes."

Her head tilted coyly to the side. "Well, Eli, nothing says you can't also take contract jobs. Please, please, please, do this for me. I don't know any contractors here, and I trust you."

Eli never could resist a female in distress. Charli was proof of that. Their relationship had begun that way. No wonder he had a hangup with Charli's safety. He heaved a sigh.

"Alright, Gina, I'll take a look and speak with my partner."

She snatched her gloves and beamed as she hopped to her feet. "Wonderful. Thank you, Eli. I knew you wouldn't let me down." She reached for his arm and tugged him out of his seat. "Come on."

His brow furrowed. "Right now? What's the urgency?"

She yanked his bomber jacket off the rack and hung it around his shoulders. He slipped arms inside and shrugged the coat into place. "I drive back north today. Mom works tomorrow. I need to get home to take care of my kids. It's a long drive. We don't have much time, and I've got the keys."

Eli laid enough cash on the table to cover his bill and a hefty tip. He placed the saltshaker on top of it. "All right; no time like the present."

He allowed the bubbly female to slip an arm around his elbow and lead him outdoors toward her white German station wagon parked in front of the theatre next door. Chatter about her children never stopped during their short stroll. She promised to show him photos of them once they reached their future home.

At the driver's side, she beeped the vehicle unlocked. He opened the door, and she slid in behind the wheel. He rounded the car to the passenger side. A row of three children's safety seats occupied the back seat, and a stroller lay folded neatly beside a purple travel bag in the cargo area of the SUV. It appeared Amanda's best friend since childhood had created herself a perfect life.

Who was Eli to turn down a family in need? After all, family was everything. His heart ached for Charli and his beloved, adopted clan.

"Amanda said your wedding is on the twentieth."

He watched the road as she drove just above the speed limit until they left the city limits. "Yes. We have a honeymoon planned for the day after Christmas. Assuming we finish McGregor House before the wedding, we won't commit to anything until the first of the year."

She smiled as she sped along the country road a little too quickly for his taste. "That is perfect. We should close on the deal between Christmas and New Years. You can figure out what you need to do the job. You'll have time to order material and line up any subcontractors you need to hire."

****

Charli brushed a curl from her eyes as she stepped out of the courthouse into a bright autumn day. She folded the permit the clerk had issued for concrete Bubba's crew poured the next day in the McGregor House driveway. Stuffing the document into her overall bib pocket, she glanced left.

Only one vehicle occupied the small sheriff's office parking lot, and the truck belonged to Wyatt. Jaiden and the other deputies must be out on patrol. Too bad. She'd thought of inviting her for a burger lunch.

Charli glanced right. The theatre marquee touted the latest film production, introduced for the holiday fast track. A sleek, high-end model, white station wagon caught the sun's rays.

Charli's heart must've stopped. She could no longer feel a pulse beating in her chest. A giant cluster of air stuck in her lungs, and her eyes watered. She stopped midway down the steps, frozen in her path.

A tall, slender female's backside faced Charli. The woman strolled beside a man barely taller than her. The gal's arm clung to his, as they meandered toward a fancy vehicle. She beamed at him with a passion that explained their connection better than words could, though the woman never stopped chattering. When the guy got a word into the conversation, she seemed to hang on to his speech as though her life depended on it. This was an intimate relationship if there ever was one.

The strange blonde sported a sophisticated up-doo and wore a tailored, purple, wool coat that hit her long legs at the top of her slim, black, leather, spike-heeled boots. She was class personified.

Statue-still, Charli observed Eli and his blonde woman arm-in-arm and then speeding off in her white vehicle, feeling ever so much like a voyeur. Gritting her teeth, she forced air out of her aching lungs and then took a renewing breath that made her almost dizzy.

She needed to get home. *Just make it home*. Things would be all right. No way could she have a mental breakdown on the courthouse steps in the center of town.

It took every ounce of willpower to keep herself together until she parked her truck in the garage and strolled into the house. She strode to the liquor cabinet, pushed around a few bottles, and chose amaretto. After selecting a tall tumbler, she filled the glass with ice and put the items along with a box of tissues into a basket retrieved from the countertop.

Gran entered from the garage. Her eyes widened as she took in Charli's contents. She moved toward her and took the basket. Sitting it on the countertop, she patted a barstool.

Charli knew better than to argue, and she didn't have the energy. She popped her behind into the seat.

Gran opened a cabinet and brought out two shooter glasses. She sat beside Charli, took the fresh bottle of liqueur, and opened it. She poured each of them a tiny glassful and handed one to Charli. "So, what has us sipping the good stuff at midday?"

Charli's eyes shut. She chugged the thick, sweet drink down and savored the burn. "Let's just say, don't spend any more money on wedding plans for me. Eli has moved on."

Gran rolled her eyes. "Good heavens, Charli. You know better. You and Eli will get through this tough spell and be fine."

She glared at her grandmother. "Not this time, Gran. It's over. Eli has kicked me to the curb and started over with a much higher-class female."

Gran frowned, apparently studying her to determine if she told a sick joke. "Well, I find it hard to believe he would cheat on you. Have you talked to him?"

Her lips pressed together, and her head rocked. "No need. I saw the two of them myself."

Gran squinted. "I'm sure there's some logical explanation, sweetheart." She refilled Charli's shot.

Charli's eyes watered up. She slugged down the full

glass and blew out the heat that rolled in her belly and coated her throat as it rose.

Voices sounded out front, and a car door slammed shut. Charli hopped to her feet and retrieved the bottle.

"They don't need to see me like this." She grabbed the basket and rushed down the hallway to her solitary bedroom.

She sat on her bed, and took turns mopping up the waterworks flowing from her eyes, blowing her nose, and guzzling gulps of fiery liquid straight from the bottle. About a half an hour later and a trashcan filled with wadded tissues, a soft knock sounded on her door.

She tried not to blubber. 'I'm busy, Kyler. Go away."

The door opened, and Jaiden stepped in, adorably exotic in jeans that appeared painted on her voluptuous curves. A purple, cashmere sweater displayed her ample, perky boobs. She kicked off her favorite, well-worn cowboy boots—not the dancing kind—the ass-kicking, horseback riding kind. "It's just little old me."

She plopped onto the bed and brought those fabulous legs up into a yoga pose. "Irma said you're day drinking. I didn't want to miss the fun." She placed two highball glasses in the basket that occupied a place on the bed beside Charli's bare feet. After prying the bottle from Charli's hands, she poured amber liquid into them and added a cube from Charli's tumbler of ice to each. She pushed one to Charli and sipped from her own. "Yum. Good choice."

Charli nodded and took a healthy, cool drink. "It's your day off. Why aren't you home, riding that handsome stallion of a fiancé for all he's worth?"

Jaiden didn't flinch at Charli's crude words. "I

would be giving him the slow bang, but Doc has three surgeries scheduled. He won't be available to dance the dirty until early evening. I figured by now you and Eli would've worked out your issues and be shacked up somewhere to make up for lost time by doing the horizontal boogie. What's going on, Charli?"

"You might want to see if you can get a refund on that maid of honor dress you bought. The wedding's off."

Jaiden swigged back the remainder of her drink, refilled both their glasses, and glared at Charli. "Bull. That man ain't stupid. He's like a stud in heat, wild and crazy over you. No way will Eli let you slip out of his hands and risk some other steed claiming his mare."

She flipped a thick tress of bone-straight hair off her shoulder, exposing the horse head tattoo on her neck. She'd worn the shiny mane loose, and silky raven hair blanketed her back to her waist.

Charli fluffed her pillows and leaned back into them, slipping her short frame downward onto the bed further. Messy, copper curls tickled her cheeks.

She took another swig and chuckled. "This stuff doesn't burn after you've had a bit of it. As for that man, he's just another pretty face and ain't as smart as we gave him credit for. I'd sworn off good-looking guys, thought I'd learned my lesson. I broke my own rule when I met him. Nothing great comes from losing your heart to a fancy fella. Yep, it's mud-fence ugly men for me—if I ever give another one a chance. For sure." Her words sounded slurred even to her own ears.

The Lord only knew how bad she sounded to Jaiden, who didn't judge. That was something Charli liked about her pal.

She reached up and fondled Jaiden's coal-black hair in her fingers. "It's so silky. You know, you're one sexy-looking gal, my friend. Old Clay Barnes is one lucky SOB."

Jaiden snickered and added the remainder of the ice to their glasses. She poured the melted water into Charli's and added more liquor to them.

Setting the drink on Charli's bedside table, Jaiden took a sip of hers. "You're quite the catch as well, Charli. Don't let anyone convince you that you're not."

Charli pouted. "Not enough. Eli tossed me to the side of the road and replaced me with a classier model. I saw them myself, so don't try to tell me it's my imagination."

Jaiden's brows lifted high. "Oh, yeah? I'll have to kick his sweet behind if that's so."

Charli chuckled. "I can see that. He's only about a foot taller than you."

Jaiden's head rocked back. "Hey, this is an ex-Texas Ranger you're talking about. I've whooped up on many a bigger dude than Eli, a lot meaner, too. I can take him."

Charli snorted with a laugh. "Yeah, you're a fierce little bitch. Aren't ya?"

Jaiden nodded. "Got that right, sista. Now, tell me about this woman."

Charli stared at the ceiling. "I'd like to say she is as ugly as a boar's ass, but that ain't so. Almost as tall as him. Slim. Long legs. High-class. Expensive clothing. Her hair coiffed in the perfect French twist. I'm telling ya, Jaiden, the wind whipped every which a way out there. From where I stood, not a single hair dared move out of place on her flawless head. Yep, I am yesterday's news. He has upgraded. They made an exquisite couple."

Water works spewed to high gear, and her words blubbered before she finished her speech.

Jaiden shoved a wad of tissues into her hand. She blew her nose into them and leaned her head back on the pillows.

Chapter Twenty-Seven

Sunlight streamed through the blinds and stripped the bed. Charli's hand slapped across her eyes to block the glow. She twitched herself awake.

Holy crap.

Every movement caused her pain. Someone inside her head tap danced to the thud of her heart, and it hurt like hell. What had died in her mouth and rotted away during the night, leaving a slimy film?

She forced herself to a sitting position, blinked away the cobwebs that clouded her brain. *Sweet.* Jaiden had covered her with the bedspread before she'd left her drunken friend. She rolled her shoulders and stood. A watery cocktail glass sat on the bedside table. She tossed the empty amaretto bottle into the trash.

Charli grabbed fresh clothing and slipped quickly across the hall to the bathroom. After swallowing aspirin with a handful of water from the tap, she slugged into the shower. Hot water streamed over her, awakening her ability to think.

She'd really tied one on yesterday. *Oh crap, Della.* She'd totally deserted her new friend.

She rushed through the rest of cleaning herself up, slipped into her clothing and followed the sound of chatter and laughter to the great room. Gran, Wes, and Della sat around the breakfast table in the dining area. Kyler carried a platter of pancakes over and placed the dish in the middle.

"Sis." He smiled. "You're just in time. I cooked breakfast." He took his place with the family.

Charli slipped into her chair beside Della and placed a hand on her arm. "Della, I owe you an apology. I had a bit of a meltdown yesterday and completely forgot about you. I'm sorry you had to spend the night alone at McGregor House."

Della smiled sweetly. "But I didn't. Your family insisted I stay here. Kyler gave up his bedroom for me and slept on the couch. He's quite a gentleman."

Kyler's face was a bright pink. He shrugged and cut into a slab of his cake.

Gran swallowed her first bite. "No worries. We know how to make do. Couldn't have that sweet gal sleeping over there alone when we have plenty of space."

Wes observed Charli. "Are you feeling better, sweetheart?"

The sound of his new nickname for her helped ease what tension remained from her alcoholic binge.

"I'm good, Wes. Thanks for asking."

Kyler pointed his fork, filled with chunks of pancake, toward Della. "Tell Charli your good news."

Della's eyes glistened. "You know Kyler gave me a ride over to Carlton Farmer's office yesterday for my scheduled meeting. Carlton said the district attorney determined that without the firearm used to shoot Clancy Mulhaney, he wouldn't have enough evidence to get a murder conviction. My bodily injuries at the time are clear evidence of a battle. My skin cells were under Mulhaney's nails, and it appears I fought for my life. They've declared my actions as self-defense. Charges have been dropped. I'm free to return home to Chicago now."

A heavy weight lifted from Charli's shoulders. Finding Della had weighed on her severely. Della hiding in McGregor House and related to the family who had inhabited the property since construction made her feel more like family than a stranger. They had struck a personal relationship from the start that quickly developed into a strong friendship.

"Wow, I'll really miss you. When are you leaving?"

Della smiled sadly. "I'll miss you too. My life, my job, and friends are there. My condo is empty now. The woman I sublet the apartment to moved out the end of October. It feels good to be free, to come and go as I please. My bail bond money was refunded. There's an envelope for you on the counter to cover what you spent on me for clothing and personal items. I sure appreciate your generosity. I can't imagine how I would've gotten through this ordeal without you all."

Charli placed a hand on Della's wrist. "That is the least of my worries but thank you."

Della placed her slim hand atop Charli's petite one. "No, thank you, Charli. You've been a Godsend." She sighed and lifted her hand. "There's a flight to Chicago out of Louisville on Sunday evening. I booked a seat. Kyler offered to drop me off at the airport on his way back to university. Don't worry. I'll stay in touch, and I'll return for your and Eli's wedding."

Charli puffed out a blast of air. "It doesn't look like there is will be one."

Gran and Wes's gazes met. "What's going on, Charli?"

"Eli has tossed little 'ole me to the side of the road like a used cigarette butt. Guess he couldn't deal with a strong-willed, independent woman as well as he'd thought."

Wes gave her a serious stare. "Don't go canceling plans quite yet, sweetheart. I have a feeling it will come together. Give it a few days. Whatever happens, things will work out for the best, regardless of how they might appear now. Look at me and Irma. We're the worst-case scenario. It took us decades, but we finally got our show together."

Gran smiled softly. "Charli, you're okay."

Charli shrugged and tried to focus on her plate. "Yep, sure." She got along fine before she met Eli. She'd be all right again…in time.

Gran sparkled. "I have an idea. We ladies need a spa day. Soon as we finish our meal, I'll call and make the arrangements."

She received a round of happy agreement. Settled.

****

After their luxurious day of mud baths, facials, manicures, and pedicures, at home they found Wes and Kyler watching an action flick on the television.

Gran laughed. "I'll make some popcorn. Come, girls, join us."

Charli looked at Della, and they shook their heads at the same time. "Thanks, Gran, but we're heading out now."

After goodbyes and hugs all around, the women strolled over to Charli's truck. Once settled, she backed the vehicle out of the garage.

"Feel up to a drink?" She glanced sideways at her passenger.

Della grinned. "Sure. Whatever you want."

"Great. I'll take you to a real, down home, country

bar. It's my favorite hangout." Minutes later, she pulled into the parking lot of the Ten Mile House.

Della gazed at the full lot of mostly newer model trucks and SUVs parked in front of an ancient but well-preserved log building. The neon light on the front and the large lit up sigh on a tall pole announced the name. Though the logs were thick, the sound of country music blared loud enough to be heard as they stepped out of the truck.

Della's eyes and mouth were wide in awe. "Wow, this is an authentic log structure. The building must be at least a couple of hundred years old, but it's so well preserved."

Charli looked over the tavern. "Yes, my friend Justin Henderson owns and runs it. His wife, Corrie, helps as much as she can. She's busy though—CEO of her family's conglomerate, The Adelle Corporation."

Della's nose curled up. "I've heard of them. They're involved in all sorts of things: banking, big-box stores, appliances, hotels, and probably more. But aren't they headquartered in New York City?"

"They are, but she works mostly from her office at Mane Lane Farm. The corporation owns the farm, famous for breeding and racing some of the best thoroughbreds in the world."

"Wow, that's so cool."

Charli grinned. "Yes, it is. The farm is just down the road. Corrie's brother, Levi Madison, runs the operation. He and his wife, Riley Powers-Madison will likely be hanging out here, too."

Charli glanced around the parking lot and spied a familiar vehicle. "Oh, I can't go in there. Eli's here…probably with his new arm candy."

Della stopped, her brows high. "Oh, yeah, that might not be good." She hesitated a minute. "Aren't you just a little curious?"

Charli looked at the truck. "Yeah, of course, but I'm not ready to face him. Especially not in front of a barroom filled with people I know. I'm sure by now the whole town is aware of our breakup. I don't want to feed the Sweetwater grapevine."

Della frowned. "I've an idea. How about I sneak over to the entrance and peek through the door window? Maybe I'll get lucky and see what Eli's up to."

Charli secretly thrilled that Della would do that for her. "Yeah, sure, suit yourself." She climbed into the truck cab, placed her hands on the steering wheel, and laid her forehead on its cool plastic-cover.

A couple of minutes later, the crunch of footsteps on gravel alerted her Della's spy session ended. The door opened. She jumped in and slammed it shut.

"Hump, your man sat at the bar with his back to the door."

Charli's brows lifted. "Doing what?"

Della winced. "Chatting up some blonde chick."

Charli's eyes shut and she prayed for strength. As she opened them, she fired the engine on and gunned it. "Let's go to McGregor House."

Della cocked her head. "Stop at that convenience store down the road. I feel like ice cream."

"Great idea."

Chapter Twenty-Eight

At McGregor House in Eli's makeshift bedroom in the dining room, Charli had set up the roll-away bed near his twin bed in a corner and between them a small table. She lay, propped on pillows against the wall behind it, a pint of her favorite ice cream halfway finished in hand. Della was in a similar position on the corner bed, working on her own flavor of choice. An empty carton of chocolate chip sat on the table.

Eli's television across the room played the ending of a sappy chick flick. The trash can beside Charli's bed sat half-filled with wadded tissues, and the box beside her on the bed remained only half-full.

Charli tossed the remote to her friend, expelled a low belch, and threw her feet off the side of the bed. "Excuse me." She burped into her hand. "You find something else for us to watch. I've had enough ice cream to choke a horse."

She picked up her empty. Della placed hers inside it. Charli pushed both lids into the center and shoved their spoons inside. She grabbed the half-full carton and put its top on. "I'll put this in the freezer. Be right back."

Her feet slipped into the fuzzy slippers Eli had bought her and she picked up her phone. She'd set the ringer to vibrate so they wouldn't be disturbed. Noting a missed call, she checked it. Jaiden's name came up. The evening had gotten too late to call her back, so she slid the cell into her pajama pants pocket.

All cried out, she pushed the impulse to shed more tears away and headed to the kitchen. The delectable dessert stowed in the fridge, she washed their spoons, and then shoved the cartons into the over-full trash can.

With a sigh, she pulled the full bag out of the can and tied the top. After finding the box of bags in the cabinet beneath the sink, she inserted a fresh one.

"I'll take the garbage out. Be right back," she called to her friend.

Charli headed through the mud room and out the back door. She carried her load around the back of the house to the side where the new driveway and parking area had been poured and to where the receptacle stored out of sight.

With her view of the street, her interesting, nosey neighbor appeared with Pookie at her feet. She must've been giving the little poodle a last chance to empty his bladder before bedtime.

Charli shouted loud enough to be heard across the lane, "Hi, Nancy, have a pleasant night."

The woman waved and smiled. "Oh, Charli, I didn't see you there. The same to you."

Charli strolled back indoors and locked the back door. She stepped to the refrigerator and chose a bottle. "Hey, Della, want a water?"

"No, thanks." Della's quiet voice indicated drowsiness.

Time to call it a night. Her phone vibrated as she passed the butler's pantry. Checking it, Eli's name appeared on the screen. She didn't want to talk with him now. Still holding the gadget in her hand, ready to drop the persistent thing the rest of the way into her pocket, she entered the dining room.

Blood drained out of her face, and her breath halted. She hit the record button and let the phone slip inside the pocket out of sight. She forced a strong inhale, rocked her shoulders back, and used as robust an attitude as she could muster into her words. "What are you doing in my house?"

The statuesque, burly man grunted. "I came to free the world of you two prying bitches. You've stuck your noses into my business and ruined my life."

Charli moved closer to the man who held an impressive automatic gun. Why hadn't she taken Gran's advice and worn a concealed weapon of her own? "Get this straight, big fella. You're a criminal. You ruined your own life. The feds know who you are, and they're looking for you."

He grumbled. "Yeah, I got the message when they raided the warehouse."

"They know you worked for LaRosa, even though you weren't there that day. It's just a matter of time before they find you." Della's soft voice quivered.

Evan Avery snorted. "They ain't gonna find me. I'm about to disappear for good. First, I need to take care of the two of you."

Charli swallowed a lump in her throat along with terror building up inside her. "Don't be ridiculous. They only have you on drug trafficking. Maybe not even that. You could say you had no idea shipments you protected for LaRosa were loaded with drugs. They might buy that defense."

She eased closer, staying as separate from her friend as possible, to make it harder for their intruder to train his weapon on both captives at the same time. Her gaze darted around seeking something to defend herself with. No such luck.

Avery waved his firearm. "Funny, bitch. That ain't going to work."

Della cowered near the fireplace. "Sure, it would. If you kill us, you'll get the needle or life in prison. Wouldn't you rather only serve a few years for trafficking?"

Charli nodded. "You might even get off easier than that, if you have something on LaRosa you could leverage with the FBI." Another baby step put her closer to the man.

She should've hit recall instead of record. Eli could've alerted the sheriff's office. He might not love Charli anymore, but he wouldn't want her dead either.

"You nosey bitches had to go snooping around in Mulhaney's life. You made your own bed."

Charli strained to keep her words steady. "What's that got to do with you?" Close enough to see the red in his puffy eyes.

He winced as though in pain. Tone flat and monotone. Posture stooped. As he spoke, his voice broke. "Detroit PD talked to my wife. She…she learned I wasn't on a run for LaRosa when her lover boy died."

"You didn't know she was sleeping with Clancy Mulhaney?" Della sounded tentative and filled with dread.

His eyes rolled as his head rocked upward. "Oh, hell, yeah. I knew. I just didn't want her to know I did. If you'd left well enough alone," his gun waved from Charli to Della. "Evette never would've figure out I was in Kentucky that day."

Charli sidled a step closer. "You're the one who shot

and killed him."

He nodded and glared at her with daggers in his eyes. "Son of a bitch was my partner, and he banged my woman behind my back. He deserved what he got." He paused and emitted an edgy laugh. "If you hadn't come snooping around, Evette never would've known I put her sleazy side-man down. She'd be alive today."

Geez. He murdered his wife. He'll never let us go.

Charli's stomach rolled. Her heart thudded heavily in her tingling chest. She shivered, and her icy fingers twitched at her sides. The ache in the back of her throat made swallowing difficult.

She needed a weapon. Her gaze darted around.

With a quick smirk, he lunged toward Charli. Gun in hand, he backhanded her. The crack sounded in her bones as his knuckles contacted her jaw.

Her slight frame tumbled backward. The large, sparsely furnished room held nothing to catch her fall. She struggled for footing to right herself.

His big foot shot out and knocked her feet out from under her. Her backside slammed against the wooden floor Eli had carefully sanded, stained, and varnished. Avery's fancy designer dress shoe slammed into her side. The snap of at least one rib vibrated through her skeleton and made its home in her brain.

The room went black.

Chapter Twenty-Nine

Eli shut his phone, having given reaching her one last try. He slammed the gear into park in front of the house and rushed out. The neighborhood seemed peacefully quiet. The only light shown through the building's tall widows along the middle of the side wall—the dining room he'd temporarily used as sleeping quarters.

He eased along the outside and peeked through the glass, making sure he remain hidden. Urgency in the voices inside indicated trouble.

With ice in his veins, Eli's spotted Charli's still frame on the floor in the room's center. She appeared to be unconscious. Della cowered near the fireplace along the empty wall. A hulking stranger hovered over Charli's delicate body, an ugly twist to his mouth.

Please, let her be alive.

Full-body tremors ran through Eli. His skin went clammy as he suppressed a primal scream. With flared nostrils, he shook his head in denial.

Enough with the worry. Act.

Eli backed away. Tall windowpanes reached from just above the floor nearly to the ceiling He couldn't pass them without being seen. So, he ran silently around the building. Reaching the back entrance, he unlocked it with his key as quietly as possible. After easing the door open, he slipped into the mud room, one of the areas they'd stored tools for the renovation.

He needed something to defend the women with until the cops came. Too bad, he couldn't keep his promise to Jaiden to wait for them to arrive. Charli needed him—now.

He selected what might be of help and slipped the hammer into his belt. Under his left arm he carried a tool, and in that hand a selection of new saw blades. After sliding a glove on his right hand, he picked one from the bundle.

Creeping closer to the dining room, he listened briefly from the entrance to the butler's pantry.

Della begged for her life. "Please, Mr. Avery, don't make this worse on yourself. The authorities only have you for trafficking. They have no idea you shot Mulhaney. One murder will put you away for a long time, but multiple ones with get you the death penalty."

With angry arrogance, their captor slapped Della with his words. "Shut up, bitch. You're already dead. You two idiots ruined everything. Detroit PD told Evette they wanted me for murder. and they have the ballistics to prove it. That's why she came at me with a knife. I had to kill her."

Della's voice held a minute level of hope. "It was self-defense."

"Whatever. Makes no difference. I got nothing except the need to gun down you two bitches. Then I'm gonna disappear for good."

Eli sped from his hiding position and whipped the sawblade in his right hand toward the hulking villain. The sharp knife spun as it whirled through the distance and slammed into his left arm and chest below the shoulder. Blood oozed from the wound.

Shock showed in the intruder's eyes, as they widened, and his gun almost fell out of his hand. He gripped the weapon tighter. As the big goon attempted to get his bearings, Eli slung another blade toward him. This one sliced into the guy's right thigh. Red spurted from the gash, and the man dropped his gun. He bent to reach it.

Della sprinted toward Eli. He sprang forward and yanked Charli's slight body from the floor, pushing her backward toward Della. "Get her out of here."

Charli muttered something, as she regained consciousness.

Della commanded in a quiet tone, "Help me, Charli. We've got to go."

Arm around her friend, Della half-dragged the woozy Charli in the direction Eli had come from. Charli appeared to be coherent enough to try and stand on wavering legs.

Eli kept attention on his opponent, who tried to pick up his shooter with one hand and stop the gush of life-giving fluid from his leg. His eyes burned with evil directed at Eli. Eli didn't hesitate to flip another whirling sawblade toward the man. The intruder tried to fend the spinning cylinder off with his free arm as he attempted to stand. The sharp item propelled into his left forearm, and another stream spewed from it.

Out of blades, Eli yanked the hammer free from his belt and flung the mallet as he'd done the axe at the county fair, when he had tried to hit the wooden slab to win Charli a teddy bear. The metal end struck the dude on the side of his head and clamored to the floor with a bang.

A loud thud came from the front of the house, as

hard-thumping steps sounded from behind him. Simultaneously, the thug lifted his gun, pointed the barrel at Eli's middle while Eli shot the nail gun in his direction. Nails discharged from the tool propelling across the distance and stuck in the guy's upper chest.

Wyatt's deep southern drawl came across authoritative and harsh from just behind Eli. "Put the gun down, Avery. You're surrounded."

Jaiden and Deputy Leo Sanders entered from the foyer. Serious-looking rifles pointed at the injured man. Obviously, they'd kicked the front door open—the thud heard from the front of the house. Avery's weapon clattered to the floor.

Eli laid the nail gun beside his feet and smiled at the three law enforcement officers. "I've never been so happy to see your ugly mugs." Hearing his words, regret forced a correction. "Jaiden, not you. You're actually a sight for sore eyes, a beautiful one."

Leo kicked Avery behind the knees. "Down, hands up."

The man knelt on the floor and complied. His lifeblood drizzled into pools on Eli's freshly refurbished hardwood.

Jaiden snickered and clasped cuffs on Avery and sighted Eli over a shoulder. "No worries, handsome. Where's your woman?"

He glanced behind him. Only Wyatt stood there with a rifle in hand. "I'm not sure. I pushed her and Della out of the room."

Wyatt shrugged. "Don't look at me. I came in from the back and didn't see them."

Eli passed the man. As the deputies pushed their bleeding perpetrator out the front entrance, his words echoed in Eli's ears. "I need medical attention."

And there came Leo's answer. "Shut your trap. You'll get what we give you."

Eli knew the words to be an idle threat. The deputies would arrange for Avery's immediate transport to the hospital.

He entered the kitchen, Wyatt at his back. Eli flicked the light on revealing a large room. The lock on the door to the basement appeared intact. They entered the butler's pantry.

Eli strode toward the back wall. "They must be in the secret stairway." He tried the release, and the door didn't budge. He knocked on the bookcase. "It's safe. Unlock the door."

A click sounded from inside. The shelving swung slowly toward them, opening to the hidden chamber. A disheveled Della stood there with a battered Charli leaning against her, one hand on the doorway.

Eli sped to his fiancée and scooped her into his arms. "Let's get you to the hospital." She didn't resist but melted into them like warm butter. "Della, are you okay?"

"I'm fine."

Wyatt helped their guest into the room. "Are you sure?"

Wyatt smiled and put a thick arm around the small woman. "We're getting you both checked out." He hollered to one of the deputies stationed outside. "Ben, be sure to lock this place up when you're done here."

By the time they reached the street through the front door, Jaiden and Leo had left in their cruiser, taking their injured killer with them.

Wyatt led Della to his vehicle. He opened the back

door, and Eli slid inside, Charli in his arms. Her head lay slackly against his shoulder, and her eyes were closed. Breathing came shallow, but steady, and icy cold. He snuggled her tighter against his chest, to share body heat with the woman he loved more than life. His eyes closed, and his head bent to relax against hers. Coppery curls tickled his nostrils, and he breathed her scent in, with a prayer.

Wyatt opened the passenger door and ushered Della in. Then he went around and climbed inside. Sirens blared and blue lights flashed from the lights on top of the car as they sped toward help.

Wyatt stopped in front of Sweetwater General's emergency door. With the vehicle still running, he rushed around and opened the back seat door as first responders rushed out to meet them.

Eli climbed out and laid his lightweight, precious cargo gently onto the gurney. Blue-uniformed medical staff secured the patient. He spoke evenly to the men. "She was unconscious but then came to somewhat. She's been very still and quiet for the ride."

Della said from behind him, "She was hit on the face with a gun. Then the man kicked her, while she lay on the floor. Fairly coherent, she helped me get her to safety but definitely remained foggy headed from what I saw."

"You need to get this woman attention as well. She's suffered a trauma. No bodily injury." Wyatt looked questioningly at Della, who nodded.

A nurse waiting inside the door as they stepped through, put an arm around Della. "Let's get you to an examining room, so someone can check your vitals."

Della followed the woman to a room just past the one Charli was wheeled into. The scent all hospitals seem to wear filled his nostrils, and with the odor came a semblance of hopefulness. Wyatt put an arm around Eli and showed him to the waiting room close by.

A television on the wall played a game show. Worn magazines lay rumpled on a small table, and the walls were lined with wood and vinyl chairs. He selected one the farthest from the noisy entertainment and slumped into it.

Leaning forward, elbows to knees, he rested his face into his hands and gave a silent prayer.

Chapter Thirty

The sanitary, medicinal scent only hospitals manage filled Charli's nostrils. Her headache excruciating, a heavy metal band beat a throbbing rhythm in her bones, resonating from her right jaw. Effort to breathe took all her energy and came with a stabbing pain to her right side. What did she drink last night—lightning?

Eli's steady breathing and the scent of his bodywash eased tension in her body. She forced her eyes open, expecting to see him curled on the pillow beside her. Instead, he stood over her. Blaring sunlight silhouetted his frame and caused her head to pound worse. She hadn't believed that possible. Fully dressed, he wore an anxious expression.

Reason set in. She recognized her surroundings—not her bedroom but a hospital room.

Figures moved about the small space, and Gran appeared with Wes beside her. Kyler and Della stepped forward. Concern on their faces evidenced she hadn't simply overindulged. Something was wrong.

She gasped. "What the—"

Gran's hand shot out and pacified her quivering one. "You're okay, Charli. We're all here with you. You've had a harrowing experience, but Doc Barnes said you'll be fine."

Wes smiled with a sigh of relief. "You had a close call, and we've been worried for you. It's good you've woken up."

Charli winced in agony. "Easy for you to say. Nothing feels good about this."

Eli smiled and caressed her forehead. "You gave us quite a scare. We've been waiting for you to regain consciousness. I take it you're in pain?"

She nodded painfully. "Got that right."

Kyler grinned. "Good to hear your voice, sis."

Gran pushed the button on the remote lying beside Charli. "Clay ordered a prescription for the pain but didn't want to medicate you. He feared drugs would delay your regaining consciousness. You should be able to have it now."

A female voice came over the com. "Nurse Brown. What can I do for you?"

Gran's voice bore no-nonsense. "Charli Owens is awake and needs the pain meds Dr. Barnes ordered. Can you see to that immediately?"

"We'll take care of it." The intercom clicked off.

Eli stroked her upper arm casually and continued the movement. "Do you recall what went down last night? You've been out of it since we brought you in."

She strained to remember. A vision of being cradled in Eli's arms. Her nose nestled against his chest. His near-shoulder-length hair ticking her cheek, and his square jaw's slight bristle against her forehead. She'd been blissfully happy in his arms.

Blinding beams disturbed her slumber as people pushed speedily along. Squares of fluorescent light from a drop-style ceiling lit endless corridors. Her body, one massive pain on some sort of cart, surrounded by strangers in blue scrubs. Commanding voices from people around her barked orders. Then nothing.

Her eyes opened and met Eli's. "Only the ride to the hospital with you and being moved to an extremely illuminated room."

Della looked on from behind Gran. "You don't remember our evening together?"

Charli studied her face for a few seconds, and memory returned. "Yes, we were eating ice cream in bed, watching a movie."

The reason for drowning her sorrows came with it. Her gaze shot toward Eli. Something made him withdraw his hand from her skin.

She told Della, "I remember taking the trash out. Nancy and Pookie were out for their before-bed stroll. She waved good night. I came back in and…Oh geez, Evan Avery had you at gunpoint. Oh, Della, I'm so sorry. He must've gotten in because I left the back door open." It all came back to her now. "He blamed us because he shot his wife. He intended to do the same to us." She gulped down a thick breath. "We tried to reason with him. He hit me—" Her hand went to her jaw.

Della nodded. "Yes, with his pistol. You fell, and he kicked you in the side. You went out for a while, but you came to when Eli showed up and lifted you off the floor. You were like a rag doll, and I knew I couldn't get you out of the house and far enough away that we could escape him if he came after us. So, I hid us in the secret stairway off the butler's pantry until the standoff ended."

Jaiden and Leo came into the room. "I heard the patient was coherent." She strolled to the side of the bed. Leo stood behind her.

Kyler smiled. "Kinda."

Charli looked at her buddy. "Sounds like I missed most of the fireworks. I don't understand how we got away, and Eli managed to bring me here."

Jaiden glared. "I got some news and tried to reach you several times but got no answer."

Charli nodded as little as possible to keep from causing the metal band drummer to change tunes. "We were busy." And she didn't want to talk to anyone.

"Yeah, well, when I couldn't reach you, I called Eli, and he tried you."

Eli's head rocked in agreement. "I had no luck either, so I left the Ten Mile House to come check on you gals."

Leo joined the story. "Yeah, we were clear out in the county at a multi-car pileup on the expressway when Jaiden got word from Detroit PD."

Jaiden winced. "Yeah, my contact there called to tell me they hadn't located Evan Avery yet, but they'd discovered his wife's body. She'd been shot, and a ballistics search of the round brought up Clancy Mulhaney's murder case, as well as several others. We've learned our Mr. Avery worked as a hired gun for LaRosa. Probably Mulhaney as well. The feds ran Mulhaney's weapon and got some hits, also."

Leo decided to help. "It appears Avery had it in for Mulhaney. As you discovered on your excursion to Detroit, Clancy slept with Evan's wife…often. Their trip to Kentucky in pursuit of Della provided an opportunity for him to take his partner out. Conveniently, his death made Della look suspect."

Jaiden added, "Also convenient if it drew her out of hiding. We didn't think he'd come for you but wanted to inform you…in case. When we couldn't reach you—"

Cringing, Eli bent his head toward Charli. "When I arrived at McGregor House, Jaiden rang me again and told me about Avery's wife, and that he was in the wind. She said the dispatcher got a call from Nancy saying she saw an intruder skirting McGregor House. They usually take her reports with a grain of salt but always check them out."

Jaiden's brows rose. "Yes, we figured Avery ran. We had no idea he would target you two...until—"

Eli grunted. "Until I looked in the window and saw what went down." He took a big, open-mouthed breath. "I hit Jaiden back and told her what happened. She told me about Nancy's call, and said they were far away."

Leo blustered, "Thank goodness for nosey neighbors, huh? Jaiden specifically told you not to do anything until we arrived."

Eli shrugged. "Sorry, pal. I saw what was happening. That big dude meant to kill them. No time to waste. Charli had been knocked unconscious...maybe dead already." His big hand came up and dabbed at wetness in the corner of his eye. "I couldn't just stand by and let bad things happen. I had to do something, if only to stall that SOB until help arrived."

Charli cocked one brow in question. "And you did." She still didn't understand how they escaped certain death.

Jaiden snickered. "You should've seen it, Charli. "By the time we arrived and the team barricaded the house perimeter bloody circular saw blades lay all around. The perp had nail-type staples in his arms and chest gushing blood. He brandished a firearm. Your man put on a little ninja show from what I saw. Eli stood opposite him with a nail gun aimed at the intruder. We subdued and apprehended the subject."

Leo smiled. "Eli showed Wyatt where you were

hiding out, and they got you quickly to medical help."

Eli smiled toward the blonde. "Della's quick thinking saved your life. All I did was help get you out of the line of fire and stall him as best I could until the cavalry showed up." He frowned. "I'm afraid the guy bled all over that beautiful shine I put on the dining room floor. I've got to research how to get bloodstains out of hardwood."

Charli chuckled best she could without causing further pain to herself. "You're both quite the heroes. Wish I could give you medals."

Kyler laughed. "Don't dead heroes in the military get those?"

Wes rustled the young man's head. "They still deserve an award."

Jaiden patted Charli's arm. "No need to worry about Avery any longer. He's going away for multiple murders, including Mulhaney's, plus abduction of the two of you and attempted murder. Sheriff Gordon has been working with DPD and the feds. He will likely let them extradite Avery to be tried first in Michigan, where he has been indicted on the bulk of those crimes. Just from those, he'll never see the light of day again. Then, we can try him here in Kentucky, to add to the massive list of offences."

Charli smiled, grateful to be surrounded by so many who cared for her. "Jaiden, I recorded his confession. At least, I hope it taped okay through my pajamas. I hid my phone in my PJ pocket on record the whole time."

Kyler opened the cabinet behind Charli and pulled out a plastic bag with the hospital logo on it. "Here you go, sis. They put your things in this."

Charli rifled through it, pushed the fuzzy slippers

aside, and pulled out the waist of her sleep pants. She snagged the cell phone and handed the device to Jaiden. "Hopefully, it's on there."

"Smart thinking, babe." Jaiden handed the phone to her partner. "We'll get this back to you when we're done with it."

Charli glanced at the wall clock. Just after noon, and Sunday. "Kyler, don't you and Della need to head to Louisville?"

He came forward, around their grandmother. "Yeah, sis, but we couldn't go until we were sure you would be okay." He bent his long frame and gave her a cheek peck. "Guess we should gather our things and hit the road." He backed away and glanced toward Della.

Della smiled and came closer. "Charli, you have been a godsend. I couldn't have survived this without you. I owe you my life, and I will never forget you." She backhanded a tear.

Charli took her hand. "Della, you've become more than a friend over this short time. You're part of the family. We will never forget you either. I owe you my life as well."

Della chuckled. "Let's call it even." At Charli's nod, she bent and kissed her cheek. "I'll come back for the—"

Charli interrupted. "Of course, you will. Thanks, and safe travels."

As the twosome strolled out the door, Kyler shot his sister a warning. "Sis, I'll be home in a couple weeks. Think you can stay out of trouble until then?"

She waved him out. "Get out of here. Be sure to ace those finals, young man."

The heavy door closed to his, "Yes, ma'am."

Gran hit the remote button again. "Nurse, where the heck is that medication? My granddaughter is in pain in here."

The voice responded, "Yes, ma'am. Someone will be right there."

Minutes later a pleasant, pink uniformed woman checked the machines and noted Charli's chart from the cubby at the foot of her bed. The nurse took Charli's vitals and changed the hanging bag. "This should make you a little drowsy. You need to rest, that is if you want to heal enough to go home tomorrow." She gave the visitors a pointed look. "It will dull the pain." She cleaned her hands from the wall dispenser next to the door and left.

Eli stared. "I'll come get you tomorrow."

Obligation? Pity? Guilty? Charli sneered. "That's okay. You have work to do. Gran and Wes can take me home."

Wes glanced at Gran, then Eli, and then Charli. "Actually, if he's working tomorrow, I promised Eli I'd help." Turning back to Gran, he smiled. "You don't mind. Do you, babe?"

Gran beamed at her lover. "Not at all. You go ahead. Eli needs you with Charli out of commission."

Wes's focus went again to his granddaughter. "Well, it's been a long night for all of us. You need to rest. So does your grandmother, and we haven't had a meal since dinner yesterday. Would it be okay with you if I take her home so we can get a decent meal and a catnap?"

Charli gave them a woozy smile. "Of course not. Go on now. Get some sleep."

After a round of hugs and kisses, the couple left her alone with Eli. She'd hoped he would've excused himself and left along with them. It was all she could do to keep her eyes open.

He fidgeted and stammered, clearly uncomfortable. Silence broke with Dr. Barnes' entrance. He greeted the two of them and gave Eli a manly hug and shake combo. After checking her chart and sanitizing his hands, Clay leaned toward his patient.

"Let's get a look into those eyes." He touched her face to help widen his flash lighted view, and then took her pulse and blood pressure, checked machine information, and inspected her fluid bags. "Okay then." He smiled broadly. "Not too bad for having been used as a soccer ball."

She snickered. "So, Clay, what is the prognosis?"

The tall, slim blonde nodded. "X-rays showed your jaw is badly bruised but not broken. A few teeth appear loose, and your mouth is swollen, as you know. That will all go back into place and tighten up as swelling goes down. You have two broken ribs, a bruised kidney, but no other internal injuries we know of. There's a bit of whiplash from the blow to the jaw. Take it easy on your neck. It will be sensitive for a while. I can give you a shot of cortisone if it's too uncomfortable. You've got a few contusions and abrasions but no sign of concussion. Are you hurting anywhere else specifically?"

She eased out a headshake and winced at a stabbing pain. "No, I'm good." *Maybe not.*

He grinned, knowing she was anything but good. "What you need is a week or two of complete rest." He gazed at Eli and back to her. "That's an order. I want you here in two days so I can have another look at you."

"Sounds good, Doc. You're springing me from this trap tomorrow. Right?" It's what the nurse had implied, but she needed confirmation from the horse's mouth.

Clay slipped her chart back into the footboard's tray. "Sounds good, long as you get through the night without complications." He shook the hand Eli stuck out for him and gave Charli a last wave as he left. "Now, get some rest."

Eli's mouth twisted, and his eyes rocked to the side. "Well, that's my exit cue. Guess I'll be going."

Charli's head bobbed softly. "Yeah, you've got tons of work to do on the house. Are you sure about Wes's helping? Does he know one end of a hammer from the other?"

Eli snorted. "Doubtful, but he's eager to help. I can use a go-fer, and he's offering free labor."

Charli snickered. "Keep in mind he's unskilled labor. Don't let him get hurt."

Eli waved a hand. "I'll keep an eye on him. No worries. Well, I'll be going." He hesitated. "Listen, Charli, when you feel up to it, there's something we need to talk about."

She closed her eyes pretending to succumb to drowsiness. "Yeah, sure." Her voice stayed soft and low as though falling into slumber.

"Okay then, bye. Sweet dreams." Soft footsteps grew lower, and the sound of the door swinging slowly shut came.

She let herself ease into the quiet, dark, lethargy her closed eyelids offered. Nurses and aides occasionally attended to the machines she remained hooked to, interrupting her sleep at a low level. They took her vitals from time to time and then left her to rest for most of the afternoon and night.

****

She awoke with an insistent growl of her stomach, the headache still there. Instead of the heavy metal band playing cymbals, a big band orchestra played a soft samba in her head. Her jaw ached. The cracked ribs fought back movement with piercing stabs, though tight tape helped keep them from further damaging her insides.

The door swung open, and a cleaning lady entered with a mop and bucket. Behind her, a smiling familiar face appeared in blue scrubs.

"Good morning, Charli. You're looking beautifully colorful today." Amanda strolled to her bedside and fluffed Charli's pillows.

"Really? Can I see?" She'd been wondering what the damage looked like but hadn't been up to seeing her face the day before.

Eli's sister pushed the bed table over Charli's knees and cranked the adjustable cot, so she arranged herself in a semi-sitting position. She slid the top over, opening the internal compartment, and lifted the mirrored base. "Here you go. "That's a lovely shade of green, and a bit of purple to."

Charli moaned at the sight of her shiny, swollen jaw and flamboyant hues across her skin around it. "Ouch, that will take some heavy makeup to hide."

Amanda checked machines and changed Charli's fluids. "I wouldn't worry too much. At least it's not broken. I'm sure the color will subside before the wedding. You will be a beautiful bride."

Obviously, Eli hadn't shared the news about their breakup and his new arm candy with his sister.

Amanda wrote something on the chart and laid a menu on the table. "Call that number and order some breakfast. Not sure what time they'll let you leave. You might as well order lunch as well. You need nourishment to heal. Keep in mind, Doc wants you on a soft diet for two to three days, until your teeth tighten up. He's in surgery all day but told me he'd look at your chart online and sign you out between procedures. I'll let you know when he's done that. You might want to call someone to bring you some clothes. It's getting cold out, so tell them to include a coat. You were admitted in your pajamas."

She left, and so did the cleaning lady. Charli ordered the meals. A few minutes later an aide brought her a tray with milk, oatmeal, and toast on it. Amanda popped back in while Charli scarfed down her meal.

She laughed. "I'll bet oats have never tasted so good." She laid Charli's sparkly, pink cased phone on the table beside her tray. "Jaiden Coldwater dropped this off for you. She said they're finished with it. She and Leo were heading to a call, so they didn't have time to come see you."

"No worries, and thanks." Charli finished her food and called Gran to give her a list of items to bring when she came to fetch her.

Gran's reassuring voice played music to her ears. "Okey dokey, sweetheart. I'll be there in a jiffy."

Chapter Thirty-One

At home with Gran, Charli was assigned to the sofa to nap, watch movies, read books, and not advised to move from there except for restroom breaks. Gran brought her a cup of steaming tomato soup and a grilled cheese sandwich for lunch, and she enjoyed them at the coffee table.

Wes arrived home after his day on the job. Gran stopped working on something and rushed to meet him as he hung his jacket up.

"How's my man today?"

He pulled her in his arms and gave her a passionate kiss. "It was a good day, but coming home to you is the best part. How's our granddaughter doing?"

They strolled toward the living room area of the great room, his arm still around her shoulders.

Charli sat up, having just awoken from a nap. "I'm good, Wes. Welcome home."

Gran must've noticed the pained look in Charli's eyes. "It's about time your pain meds are due." She broke away from Wes and went to the refrigerator, prepared a glass of ice water, and brought the drink to Charli.

"Thanks, Gran." She took a sip and then opened her medication bottle, looking forward to relief.

Wes smiled. "It smells wonderful in here. I'll go wash up for dinner." He started for the room he now shared with Gran.

Gran resumed what she was doing in the kitchen area. "Great. The table's set. I'll put the food out."

A few minutes later, Wes arrived wearing a clean shirt and a smile. "Man, I worked up an appetite." He took the seat at the end of the table.

Charli sat to his left, and Gran brought a steaming plate of dinner rolls to the table that was arranged with dishes. Once Gran seated herself, they loaded their plates with meat, mashed potatoes, peas and carrots, and dinner rolls.

Her stomach super empty, Charli swallowed a bite. "Thanks, Gran, for making meatloaf. It's one of my favorites. Everything you made is soft, so eating doesn't hurt my mouth. I appreciate that."

Wes nodded. "And it's scrumptious. I'm a lucky man to have such a great cook at my side." His hand slipped over Gran's, as she sat to his right.

"Why thank you, sir." Gran dipped her head in a royal motion and snickered.

Charli smiled at her grandfather. "Tell us about your day. Eli didn't work you too hard. Did he?" She focused on eating while listening to Wes.

Wes met her gaze as she looked up. "Not at all. I stayed busy all day, but nothing over taxing. Mostly, I did errands, fetched, and carried tools and supplies around. First thing, Eli gave me a list of items he needed to repair the front door where the Deputy Sanders kicked it in and that he needed to repair damage to the dining room, where that scoundrel bled all over the hardwood floor."

Gran swallowed a bite. "Did Eli get the stain out?"

He laid his fork down. "Yes. Removal proved more difficult than we'd hoped. I dabbed the blood up with a wet sponge, rinsing it out frequently with clean water. A good portion dried and seeped into the grain through the coat of polyurethane. So, he used a soft, wet cloth treated in mineral spirits. Next, he switched to the same chemical with fine-grade steel wool until residue came out. He wiped again with clean water and a soft cloth until the mineral spirits were gone." Wes picked his fork up and speared a bite of meatloaf.

Charli's head tilted. "Is that all?"

Wes downed his chewed bite. "No. He said he'll have to refinish the area tomorrow. The wood needs to dry for twenty-four hours."

Gran beamed with pride. "So, you're learning new skills."

Wes's shoulders rocked back proudly. "Indeed. Eli is a fountain of knowledge, amazingly skilled. He taught me how to remove a doorknob and replace the lock with a new one."

Charli smiled gratefully. "Sounds like the house can be locked up properly."

He smiled at his granddaughter. "Absolutely. Eli said the house should be finished and ready for sale in less than two weeks."

The good news brought sadness to her heart. "Awesome, I wrote the listing contract and sent documents to Eli to sign. He'll probably take care of that tonight and forward the paperwork to my broker, Roberta Roberts. She should publicize the listing this week. Keep your fingers crossed for a quick sale. We need to move the property and find our next project." *Unless Eli's tossing me aside means he'll move away from our partnership. If so, I'll be back where I was a couple years ago—no man, no partner, and no working*

capital.
Starting over.

****

Eli electronically signed the documents.

Roberta texted,

—I'll do my thing, if all is well, it will be on the market later today—

****

Charli sat on the couch, reviewing the listing online. The property looked beautiful with photos she and Eli had taken and had been priced right. The ad should attract a buyer quickly.

Eli only had a few minor tasks to complete to make the mansion ready to be handed over to new owners. Part of her proud and excited the project was nearly finished, another side of her grieved the loss of such a perfect home. She ached to keep the place and live there forever, filling the house with laughter, patter of little feet and joy, the life and family she'd hoped to create with Eli.

Gran and Wes entered the great room. Charli glanced at the time. The day had flown by. Wes strolled over to stand behind her as he adjusted cufflinks on his white shirt.

"You sure you don't mind being left alone tonight?"

She sneered. "Of course not. I'm fine. You two go on and enjoy yourselves. Gran's been hovering over me since I got home from the hospital."

Gran drew close to face her. "I feel awful leaving you alone. Wes and I bought the theatre tickets last week, before your…incident. If you're not up to an evening alone, we could probably still exchange them for next week's showing."

"Nonsense, you have plans. Go, have dinner. See

that play. I don't want to be a burden, and I'm fine."

Gran gave her a pouting smile. "You're no such thing. I love nursing you back to health, but if you're sure—"

Charli used her no-nonsense tone. "Positive. It would be a sin to waste that fabulous dress, Gran. Wes needs to take you out on the town and show you off on his arm. You always look amazing, but that wine colored, sequined gown drapes your curves like the dress was made for you."

Gran's knowing smile made her eyes gleam. "Actually, a little dressmaker I know in Paris designed the evening gown specifically for me during Fashion Week a few years ago. It's a classic look that will never go out of style."

Wes slid an arm around Gran's slim waist. "You are absolutely stunning, my love."

A chignon of tresses crowned Gran's head. Silver in her curls shined in the ceiling light. Charli hoped she would have inherited Gran's lush locks and wrinkle-free skin as she aged.

The elderly woman stuffed a tissue into a small evening bag that matched her garment. "Charli, I made you a plate. It's in the range's warmer whenever you're ready for dinner."

"Thanks, Gran. Wesley, you look very handsome, too."

He chuckled. "Thanks for saying so, Charli. We both know that Irma is the star. She outshines the sun."

Clearly, he was accustomed to Gran ruling the room whenever she entered. No wonder her stage name had been Starr Bright.

After the couple left, Charli tried napping. When

that didn't work, she gave reading a go. After two chapters, she couldn't recall what she'd read and put the book on the coffee table.

Sounds like it's time to eat. She laid a hand at her noisy gut and went to the oven to fetch her food. In the warming drawer, two plates were covered with foil. She flipped the warmer off. The doorbell rang. As she answered the door, a cold rush of autumn air blew in. She flinched back.

Eli's forehead wrinkled. He bit the side of his lip and frowned, then brushed hair from his face. "Hi, how are you doing?"

She stepped back and waved him in. "I'm good. Come in. I hadn't realized how chilly the weather is today."

He stepped inside, looking good enough to eat. "It is brisk."

Poor guy had no idea how hungry she was. She didn't even know until he showed up. Windblown hair framed his handsome face. His wide, square jaw showed evidence of freshly shaved whiskers, and his dimples creased as he feigned a smile. Shuffling his feet, his head tilted side to side.

She swallowed hard and sighed. "Yes, I believe fall has settled in. It should turn cold soon. I'm hoping for a white Christmas." –their holiday wedding!

"Um, yeah, me too," he stammered, rubbed his jaw, and acted as nervous as she was.

Enough about the weather. In the kitchen area, the oven drawer hung open.

"Have you eaten?"

His hand went to rub the back of his neck. "Ah, no, not since lunch."

She strode to the stove to turn her back and give herself a breather. "Gran left me two plates of food. She must've had a premonition I'd have company." The old woman never ceased to surprise her.

He rubbed his chin as he neared her. "Smells good. I could eat—never pass up an opportunity for Irma's cooking."

Charli pulled forks from a drawer, laid them atop the plates, and handed him one. She took the other and sat hers on the dining table. He followed and placed his across from her—not beside her.

"What would you like to drink?" She strode to the refrigerator. "We have sweet tea, soda, water, or beer."

At his, "Water, please," she retrieved a couple of bottles. "Want ice?"

"No, the bottle is fine."

Stiffness in the conversation was open attempts at stalling the inevitable. What next? Weather? Eli was there to break up with her.

She brought them to the table. Eli pulled her chair out, and she took the seat. He crossed around and sat down. Peeling foil from his meal, he smiled.

"Meatloaf, one of my favorites." Staring at the foil an overlong moment, he then looked up. "Thank you for this, by the way."

She shrugged and focused on her food. "No problem, just leftovers. Thank Gran. I sometimes think she's psychic. Other times, I believe she's a bit psycho."

They laughed together, almost like old times, and their chat relieved some of the tension in the room. Her shoulders relaxed, and they chatted quietly about work Eli and Wes had completed on the house as they ate. She told him how awesome the listing looked online and her hopes for a quick sale.

As they rinsed and loaded plates into the dishwasher, Charli's phone rang. The screen showed Roberta Roberts, her real estate broker.

"I'm putting you on speaker. Eli's here. That way you'll only have to explain once."

Roberta's deep tenor came over the speaker, and Charli laid the phone down. "Charli, Eli, your listing only went into the cooperative listing service today, but we've already received an offer on the property. I am emailing each of you the offer forms. It's a good deal, so I'm confident you'll want to accept it. If so, you know the drill. Electronically sign the documents and return them to me. I'll do the rest."

Charli's heart filled with excitement and despair equally. She took a long inhale. "Thanks, Roberta. I'll get back to you quickly." She went around the island to sit in the barstool in front of where she'd left her laptop. "Paperwork will be easier to read on my computer screen."

Eli came around to stand beside her. His gaze looked downward. She pulled the email up and went through forms with him page by page. "It's a good offer. Cash, not far from our asking price, no inspections or extra work requested. I don't think we can beat it." She talked through the options out loud.

His forehead wrinkled, and he squinted. "I guess we accept it."

As badly as her heart broke, they needed the cash flow to keep their business going and capital to purchase another project house. "Okay. We each sign, initial and date each doc from the copy Roberta sent us—you from your email address, and me from mine. That way it's all legal. Then we return them to Roberta. She'll notify the buyer." She doodled on a paper pad on the counter. "I wonder who the buyer is. Their agent represented them in the sale."

Eli frowned. "Who knows? It doesn't matter. Does it?"

Her mind raced. Trapped in indecision, she reweighed her choice. "It's probably someone famous, or a high-profile businessperson who wishes to remain anonymous until closing. The deed may go into a holding company, or the buyer's identity will be revealed in the public record. None of our concerns—they have cash and only need a week to close. It's a deal we can't afford to pass up." She clicked to electronically sign her version of the offer docs. "Guess I'd better start looking for our next real estate project."

Eli cracked his knuckles in a stalling gesture, giving the impression he wasn't eager to lose McGregor House either. Or did he hesitate because he didn't want to buy another property together because he was breaking up their partnership?

He waited, pacing around until she finished signing and sending her set of the paperwork. Then he twisted her laptop toward him and typed in his email address. The note with the offer came through, and he electronically signed the pages.

Eli slid into the seat beside her. "Charli, I wanted to talk to you about something."

Here it comes.

Her eyes closed in dread. Tension gripped her stomach. Breath caught in her throat.

He didn't stop over tonight to mooch a free meal. This is where he tells me in no uncertain terms the wedding is off. He's found a new love, and I'm history.

Eli rolled his neck, opened his mouth, stopped, and then looked away. "Amanda's best friend since they were kids is moving to Sweetwater. She and her husband, Danny Harrison, are buying an old antebellum plantation house. The land sold off to a developer all but the residence and five acres. He has started his new job at Sweetwater Distillery as head of operations. She's still in northern Kentucky with their children. Their home in Fort Thomas has sold, so they're staying with her mother until the house is in move-in condition. It needs some updating. Gina and Danny want us to do the job."

The air completely went out of her. This wasn't at all what she expected. "Oh. Well, we've never done a remodel for someone else, only focused on rehabbing vacant properties for flipping." She hesitated. "I don't know. What do you think?"

Eli smiled indecisively. "I viewed the house with Gina. She's adamant that we do the job and can be decisive when she wants something. The poor girl practically begged me. I didn't have the heart to say no. So, I told her I'd have to run the idea past you before committing."

"You like the idea?" Her head tilted.

He nodded. "This project wouldn't be the worst thing. Doing this remodel would give you time to research the market and find another property for us to purchase."

Floored he wasn't deserting her and the company completely, her hand fluttered around her lips and neck, a bit overwhelmed. "I'll need to see it."

Nodding, he grinned. "Absolutely. Soon as you're up to it, we can do a walkthrough, take notes, and work up a price. Chloe Roberts, Roberta's daughter, is the listing agent. She said we can pick up the key whenever we need it. Danny and Gina are closing between the holidays, so we could begin remodeling as early as the first of the year."

Chloe and Charli worked together at the agency for Choe's mom, Roberta. The idea rolled around and around in Charli's head. "That would work and give us time to order what material we need."

Eli stood, acting awkwardly like he wanted to get out of there while ahead, before she changed her mind. She escorted him to the door. At least his visit got one weight off her shoulders. Their business partnership remained intact.

"Well, your casual drop by was certainly productive."

He snickered as he donned his jacket. "I got a good meal out of it. Tell Irma thanks for me." His avoidance of any mention of how he felt about spending time with Charli didn't slip by her.

One disappointment down. The worst one to go.

"Will do. We have an executable contract on McGregor House and our next project lined up, hopefully."

He shuffled indecisively at the door, then pushed those big, broad hands of his into his jean pockets. "Well, give me a call when you're ready to see the Harrisons' house.

Had he resisted the impulse to kiss her goodbye?

No. Probably, regretted not completely tossing her to the curb. Maybe he figured she'd renege on the business deal.

One thing at a time.

Chapter Thirty-Two

Charli checked in at the receptionist's desk and headed for the hospital elevator. From the other direction, Amanda met her, sporting her nursing scrubs and a purse slung over her shoulder.

"Hey, gal, how are you doing? I'm returning from my lunch break. Three more hours of my shift." She sighed.

Charli winced. "Better than last time I saw you, but my neck is still hurting and gives me headaches."

Amanda punched the UP button, wearing a somber expression. "Oh, that's too bad. Dr. Barnes should help you. Make sure you mention it. I assume you're here for a recheck."

They boarded the elevator. Amanda pushed the second floor knob and the third for Charli. "Tell him I said hi."

The elevator stopped. Amanda stepped out but held the door. "I wanted to say how appreciative I am that you and Eli will be remodeling my friend Gina's house. She trusts Eli. You know, Eli practically raised me. Well, Gina is almost like a sister to me, so she looks up to him like a big brother. Knowing a trustworthy contractor makes a huge difference when someone is moving to a strange city where they know almost no one. She and Danny know you will treat them right. He's staying at one of those monthly rentals at Sweetwater Hotel. She's anxious to get the house ready so she and the kids can move here, too."

Charli gave her a deadpan expression, not wanting to commit to anything yet. "Well, it's a possibility. I haven't seen the place yet. Hopefully it's a job we can handle."

Amanda smiled and let go of the door. "Eli viewed it, and he's confident you'll agree. I can't wait to introduce you to them. She's so bubbly, a real live wire. You'll like her, I'm sure."

Gratefully, the door shut, so Charli didn't have to respond. She had ruled to not discuss potential work with outsiders. Even though Amanda had referred them, Charli didn't want to make a promise she couldn't keep. A job wasn't firm until they'd made a thorough inspection, checked current equipment prices, given a written bid, and received a signed contract from the owner. She didn't want to get the reputation of not fulfilling a commitment.

During her visit Charli told Clay about the issues with her neck and headaches. He gave her a painful shot of cortisone and told her to take it easy for a day or so, use ice, and that following his orders should help soon. Glad she'd backed off pain meds on her own, he recommended aspirin or ibuprofen for remaining discomfort.

****

Charli followed the doctor's advice and spent the next two days relaxing at home. She still hadn't cancelled vendors for the wedding. Gran and Wes kept insisting she give herself another week to recover.

Gran advised grimly, "It's too late to get your deposits back anyway."

Charli conceded, not having enough enthusiasm to make all those calls anyway. "Fine, but I need to contact them before they order supplies for the event."

Wes beamed. "If you're ready for some good news, Kyler called today. He's doing exceptionally well on final exams so far and studying his brains off to be ready for the rest."

The women glowed with joy. Charli needed something to make her feel better.

"We're very proud of our boy. Kyler's not only handsome, but a great football player, a good person. He's pretty, darned smart, too."

Gran's eyes shone as she took Wes's hand. "Some of that brilliance came from his grandpa."

Wes's chest rose with pride. Charli grew happier by the day that he had come into their lives. Understanding he'd finally found a home and family made their relationship even more special.

Chapter Thirty-Three

Eli unlocked the door of the fabulous antebellum mansion they were to remodel. Charli cooed with anticipation.

"Wow, this is a classic. If it's true the structure was built in 1802, the house has been extremely well preserved. The grounds are lovely—magnolia trees, lilies and rose gardens. No wonder they bought this place. It's incredible."

Eli showed her inside the enormous foyer. A huge, intricately designed, stained glass window crowned the swirling central staircase. The second-story ceiling displayed artfully carved decorative wood that brought the eye's focus to its glistening, crystal chandelier hanging what appeared to be about eight feet long and four-to-five feet wide.

Four double-wide panel doors along each side intermittently broke up wood paneling with matching crown molding, baseboard, and chair railing. The corridors reconnected behind the stairs and led to a back wall housing two similar doors.

Second-floor railing horseshoed around toward the front, leaving the area above the two-door entrance to the house open. A window above the entryway allowed the sun's rays to light the enormous entryway.

Charli gushed, "Good grief. This is a showplace."

Eli gave her a quick tour of the house. Then they

thoroughly inspected the areas they were to remodel. Charli took notes.

Eli shot photographs of areas. "The master bath needs refurbishing. This huge hot tub needs to go, all new tile, updated double vanity, and the Harrisons want a separated water closet and a walk-in shower built. We are to leave space to install a smaller, stand-alone tub— something the lady of the house can be comfortable in."

They strolled to the hallway, and Eli told her what Gina had requested for the two upstairs guest baths. Downstairs, the guest bath needed similar updates.

Eli led the way. "The kitchen is the largest project, and it's the priority. She wants new cabinetry, flooring, and lighting. Countertops should be granite in a dark grey. We need to build a central island with a second smaller sink in it, install a wine cooler there, with workspace on one side and ample seating for six on the other.

Charli studied the man she'd grown so accustomed to being in her daily life. Her heart heavy, she sighed. How could she go on, simply working with him, knowing he went home each night to someone else? A gaping cavern filled her insides that only Eli could fill.

"I guess I have it all, enough to price the job."

He smiled and made a few clicks on his phone. "Great. I just sent you the photographs. Mull the idea over and text me whatever research you need me to do to help calculate the cost."

She nodded, closing her notepad. "Will do. Once I have that and work up the client's estimate, I'll email the proposal to you to review. If you agree, feel free to shoot the contract on over to the Harrisons. It would be best to come from you, since you know them."

He showed her outside and locked the door. "Sure, that makes sense." His hand went to the base of her back, as he guided her down the veranda steps to the stone driveway and his truck.

His touch scorched his imprint on her flesh through her denim jacket, bib overalls, and flannel shirt. Charli willed the comforting sensation of his touch to stay. She ached to have him touch her skin—without interruption of fabric. Her mouth yearned for the tenderness of his lips.

Eli held the door for her. She climbed in. A hand against her tender ribs, she buckled the seatbelt. He came around to sit in the driver's seat and started the engine.

The heater came on, reminding her how chilly the weather had become. She'd been oblivious to it, her mind on Eli's slipping away from her.

Eli glared without putting the vehicle in gear. "Ribs still sore?"

"A bit, not bad."

"Are you sure you're up to this?" His head tilted with a brow lifted.

Depends on what this is. She wasn't certain at all she could deal with working alongside Eli by day and having him spend his nights in another woman's bed. The job presented another matter entirely. "No problem. We should complete the estimate in less than a week. Feel free to text that to the Harrisons, so they know when to expect it."

He shrugged and changed the subject. They talked about the impending closing on the McGregor house. The seller did not expect to come, so they just needed to stop at Carlton Farmer's office and sign documents a couple days later, and the sale would be a done deal.

They chatted about Kyler's progress with his finals before the holiday break and Wes's learning new skills as he worked with Eli as a laborer. As conversation became stilted, they each seemed to choose their words deliberately to avoid the issue brewing between them. The atmosphere was exhausting. A short drive to her home seemed gruesome, filled with unnatural stillness and humorlessness—completely unlike their normal banter.

****

The following day, Charli made a grocery run. At White's Market, she filled her cart with items she, Gran, and Wes had jotted down and a few things she found on sale. She arrived at the three registers stationed at the storefront.

Amanda rounded an aisle and pushed her cart behind Charli's. "Charli, how good to see you. Eli told me you've decided for sure to do Gina's project."

Eli might've tossed Charli aside for another female, but she still liked Amanda. Eli's sweet sister had done nothing to push her away. Her attitude toward Charli remained as warm as when she and Eli were together.

"That depends on the Harrisons. We're working on the bid. Once we present it, it's up to them to decide." One couldn't count on a job until both parties had signed a contract.

Amanda rolled her eyes upward. "Don't worry about that. Just figure out what you need to charge and shoot the proposal on over. I'm sure they'll agree. They're definite about wanting the two of you to do the work."

Reassurance coming from Amanda, but Charli couldn't count on it. Any manner of issues could prevent them from signing. In the meantime, she continued to look for another house Owens Construction could purchase.

Amanda pulled her wallet out, readying to pay for her purchases. She smiled at something there. "Charli, get a load of these adorable munchkins. They're Gina and Danny's boys. This little guy is Bo. He's almost one."

Amanda pointed to a photograph of three towheaded boys sitting together in a pile of toys. They looked like stair steps, one just barely bigger than another.

"This one is Cyrus. He just turned three. This little scamp is Chet, five years old. Aren't they adorable?"

"Absolutely." Charli admired the young ones. She and Eli had planned to start a family right away once they were married.

Another bashed dream.

Amanda fumbled with her wallet, probably looking for her credit card, and dropped it in the cart. The change purse fell open to a wedding pose of a blonde woman and tall, skinny, slightly nerdy-looking guy.

"Oh, I keep forgetting you haven't met Gina and Danny yet. This is their wedding photo." She rotated the picture toward Charli. "Once they move here, I should plan a welcome party so you and our other friends can meet them."

An icy inhalation filled Charli's lungs. She leaned forward to get a better look. The face and stature of the familiar woman sent a shock of frigid blood surging through her veins.

Holy crap. She'd misjudged Eli again. Her distrusting gut had risen from the grave Eli had helped her bury the son-of-a-bitch in. She'd let the green-eyed bastard resurrect itself.

Amanda stared. "You okay, Charli? The color drained from your face."

Charli squirmed. Her chest caved in. She coughed, speechless. Her voice sounded weak. "No, I'm good. Just a little headache." *Liar*. "Amanda, when was Gina in town last?"

Amanda's head tilted. She frowned and looked to the side. "Let's see. She and Danny came to dinner the day before Thanksgiving. He started work after the holiday. That's the day she showed Eli the house and then drove back to northern Kentucky. Why?"

Charli looked down, unable to meet the woman's gaze. and held a death grip on her purse. "Oh, I just wondered."

Thank goodness the cashier started ringing Charli's items up. She ignored her friend as she paid for her groceries. Pushing her cart away from the register, she gave a backward wave. "See ya later, Amanda. Got to run."

The chatty, tall, thin, blonde, wearing high fashion and flawless hair had been their new client—a married mother who considered Eli a big brother. Charli deemed herself even more inadequate than when she believed the woman had stolen her man.

Chapter Thirty-Four

Charli searched the listings, as she did every day, trying to find her company a new project house to purchase. If she didn't stay on it, the perfect one might slip through her fingers. She needed to be the first to view anything suitable as new listings came on the market. Having access proved to be one of the perks of obtaining a real estate license as well as being a contractor. The doorbell rang, and she went to answer it.

Eli stood there, shuffling his feet. "Hey, babe, how are you doing?"

She nodded and waved him inside against the brisk air. "I'm good. Thanks for asking." She spun toward the kitchen area. "Coffee, beer or water?"

"Beer sounds good."

He didn't wait for an invitation to sit but went straight to the island stools. She couldn't expect him to suddenly act formally. He had been practically part of the family, used to making himself at home.

After pulling two bottles from the ice box, she cracked them open and placed one in front of his chair, strategically beside hers near her computer.

"Thanks." He smiled and took a swig. "I see you're looking for our next project."

She nodded and took the chair beside him. "Yep, no luck yet. There are a couple of listings that are priced too high. I'll keep an eye on them in case they reduce the price."

He shrugged. "No worries. We've got enough work to keep us busy the month of January."

Stillness settled into the room. She drank from her bottle and then faced him. "How are you…I mean now we've closed on the house. Did you move back in with Amanda and Frank?"

His shoulder went up and down. "Didn't see the point. I've got thirty days to move." He bit the side of his lip, looked downward, and then met her gaze. "Listen, Charli, we keep beating around the bush. It's time we cleared the air between us."

Oh, boy, here it comes. She steeled herself with a heavy inhale.

"Babe, I'm sorry to have been such a butthead about your escapade in Detroit. I should've stuck around so we could talk it out then."

What now? She couldn't believe her ears.

"I've been so sick about what you went through…without me there. I became guilt ridden about you facing such danger with me not there to help. Instead, I had a blast with my friend, completely oblivious to what went down with the woman I love more than life."

She shook her head in awe. "Eli, you had no way of knowing. I didn't want to spoil your last chance to hang out with the guys as a single man. I wanted you to have a good time. I didn't even know when you left that I would end up in Detroit. I ran into a roadblock and couldn't make any headway in Della's case without driving up there to meet some people and ask questions in person."

Eli reached for her quivering hand. "I know that

now. I should've given you the opportunity to explain."

She huffed. "Well, I didn't want to argue with you about it over the phone, so I made the decision not to tell you. Knowing would've just ruined your trip, and you couldn't be there anyway."

Eli expelled some air. "I know. Wes explained how things went down, and you're right. We would've argued about it…whether over the phone or in person. I would've tried to talk you out of it."

She glared at him. "Seriously?"

"Of course, that would've been impossible. Once your mind is set, there's no changing it. If I hadn't gone on that darned boondoggle, I would've been here. I'd have gone with you."

"Listen, Eli, you can't be with me twenty-four-seven. I don't need protection. I can take care of myself. Besides, I took Gran with me."

He snorted. "I realize that." Then he snickered. "Come to think of it, your grandmother is much scarier than I could ever be. I know you were in good hands with her. You might've worked timing just right, so she'd insist on accompanying you. Am I right?" He gave her a sideways glance.

She laughed out loud. "I'm no fool, and I don't like traveling alone."

Eli took both her hands in his and swiveled her stool, so their knees fit together. "Can you forgive me?"

"Have you forgiven me?" Her head tilted, and she studied his expression.

His shook with the affirmative. "Absolutely. I can't hold being yourself against you. I love you just the way you are, bullheaded and all. Can we just go back to the way we were and finish getting ready for our wedding?"

She could hardly believe his question. "You still want to marry me?"

He beamed with a hopeful look. "More than ever and more than anything…if you'll still have me."

"Eli, there's nothing on this earth I want more than being your wife."

They melted into each other's arms.

Chapter Thirty-Five

Abbe's eyes widened, and she grinned as Charli and Jaiden entered the foyer where the seven-year-old stood with her mother, Amanda, Gran, Wes, Kyler. Music played inside the chapel and filtered through the double doors. "Wow, Ms. Charli, you look like a fairytale princess."

"Thank you, Abbe. Today I become your aunt. Since we're family now, you may call me Charli or Aunt Charli, if you wish."

The adorable girl in a full-skirted, floor-length, royal blue, velvet dress looked like an angel. Blonde curls surrounded her cherub face. "Okay then, Charli it is."

Her mother's short blonde hair caught the light as she knelt to her daughter's height. "Now, Abbe, are you sure you know what to do?"

Abbe shrugged and lifted the basket in her hand high. "Piece of cake, Mom. I've got this." The child's confidence was admirable.

Charli wished she moved with as much grace and poise. Not used to dresses, she'd chosen one without lots of fluff and sparkle. Her simple wedding gown had been designed from white satin. The bodice fit her body to the waist, and the neckline folded into a cuff to span from shoulder to shoulder in the front and down the back to her waist. Its A-line skirt flowed out to just above her feet. Foregoing heels, she'd chosen ballet shoes, wore no veil, and borrowed Gran's pearls. Jaiden had provided Charli's blue in a garter.

Jaiden took her hands. "Are you good?"

Her striking maid of honor looked even more beautiful than usual. The satin gown melted over Jaiden's curves, accentuated perky breasts, a tiny waist, and rounded hips and then hung straight to the floor. A back slit to her knees made movement easier. The royal blue color highlighted Jaiden's golden dark skin, honoring her Choctaw heritage. Raven locks draped straight down her back to her waist like a radiant, obsidian blanket.

Charli breathed an inhale and sighed. "Best I've ever been." Every nerve in her body alive and pulsing, she squeezed Jaiden's hand.

Kyler looked manly and grown up, and Charli resisted a tear threatening to muss her makeup as her brother extended an arm to Amanda and escorted her to her seat. He then returned to the vestibule. His hands went to Charli's shoulders.

"Sis, Abbe is right. You do look like a princess—a real, live one." He kissed her cheek. "Love you."

Her hand went to his smooth cheek. "Love you back, and I'm so proud of you."

Wes handed her a blue velvet box. "This is for you—your something new."

"Ah, Wes, you didn't need to do this. Thank you."

She opened the gift. A string of glistening pearls circled a rising base. A gasp exited her mouth.

"These are gorgeous."

Wes beamed. "I wanted you to have them." He lifted the necklace. "Here, let me put them on you." He stepped behind her and fastened the string around her neck.

Jaiden smiled. "They look perfect with your gran's earrings."

"Cool beans." Abby apparently approved.

The music changed a tune to signal the ceremony ready to begin. Jaiden touched Abbe's shoulder.

"Ready?"

With her nod, Wes opened the door for her. She strolled casually down the aisle dropping white rose petals in her path. At the front, she took a seat beside her mother and father.

Jaiden glanced up at the slim, best man. "We're on, big guy." She slipped her arm inside the one Kyler offered, and the twosome strolled side-by-side to the front and took their places, Kyler standing beside Eli and as tall.

The wedding march played, and Wes snickered. "If you're backing out, now's the time."

She laughed at his joke. "Not on your life." Her arm slid into his, and he opened the doors.

Her gaze met those of the handsome man at the front. Gran stood at the first pew. The packed room of guests faded to a cloud. Her grandfather escorted her toward her groom in an unhurried march. Her lover captivated her. Only he and she existed in a world of their own.

Wyatt had agreed to perform the ceremony. "Who presents this woman?"

Wes took Gran's hand and released Charli's into Eli's. "Her grandmother and I do." Wes and Gran kissed Charli's cheek then took their seats in the front row beside Della.

As Wyatt performed the quick and simple ceremony, Charli melted into her groom's deep chocolate eyes that seemed to convey the future they both wanted: a home, a strong, dependable, loving partner, and a family—stability that had been ripped from her as a teen with her parents' deaths.

Eli's normally disheveled, sandy hair somehow tamed for the occasion. A black tux and royal blue vest contained his rippling muscles and broad shoulders. The sight ignited a lusty fire in her belly in the anticipation of her hands and lips exploring at leisure every inch of his powerful physique.

The brief, traditional ceremony consisted of the exchange of rings and vows. Then Wyatt announced, "You may kiss your bride."

An eternity later, Eli's arms went around her. Their lips met in a sensual connection that sealed their eternal pledge to each other. Eli gave her a knowing wink as they pulled apart, acknowledging their change forever and for the better. They held hands and faced the audience.

Wyatt declared, "Ladies and gentlemen, I present to you Mr. and Mrs. Eli and Charli Lange."

The crowd cheered and clapped. Some snapped photos, and the newlyweds strolled out of the chapel. They greeted their guests as they left the church, each providing best wishes and a promise to see them at the reception. The wedding party stayed long enough to get a few formal shots in the church before they went to join the party.

Eli held her hand in the back seat of their limo. Gran, Wes, Jaiden, Kyler, Della, and Jaiden's fiancé, Clay Barnes surrounded the vehicle. She couldn't take her eyes off her groom. "I can hardly believe we're finally married."

Eli's gaze held hers. "I can't imagine life without

you."

Gran beamed at the couple. "Just make each other happy and never let go."

Wes's face held the same expression when he looked at Gran as Eli wore when he looked at Charli.

****

As the couple entered the reception hall, cheers, clapping, and whistles sounded. Tables were filled with their friends and family. They took their place at the head table, along with her grandparents, Della, Kyler, Jaiden, Clay, Wyatt, and his wife Sage.

Kyler gave a speech, and so did Jaiden. After toasting, the banquet hall owner, their spicy redheaded friend, Dovie Farmer, took the mic.

"The meal is ready to be served."

A flow of waiters and waitresses carried trays of steaming fried chicken, mashed potatoes, green beans, and cornbread to tables.

Charli leaned forward and around her grandparents to speak to her friend. "Della, we're so happy you were able to fly in from Chicago for our wedding."

Della smiled. "I told you; I wouldn't miss it."

After they'd eaten, the bride and groom visited tables and posed for photos as requested. Graceful Brightleaf Coldwater gave her a hug. The full-blooded Choctaw woman resembled an older, snowy-haired version of her daughter, Jaiden.

"Congratulations, my dear. Now, if you can convince Jaiden and Clay to take time from their busy schedules to get hitched, I'll be blissfully happy."

Charli chuckled. "I'll work on them, Brightleaf. I promise."

Beside Brightleaf, Senator Garrett and Adelle

Madison stood to greet them. Garrett gave her a fatherly hug, and Adelle snuggled her close with a tender kiss.

"We're so happy for you, Charli. You'll always be part of our family, so I guess that makes Eli our adopted son-in-law."

Charli beamed, letting her love for the elegant couple show. "Thank you, but you know, my life would've been disastrous if not for your generosity. Kyler and I would've ended up in a group or foster home, had you not interceded."

Garrett shook Eli's hand and drew him into a manly hug. "Irma's been part of Adelle's and my life since we were in grade school together. We couldn't allow her family to fall apart any worse than it had. It's what friends do for those they love."

Charli smiled. "And I love you and your whole family. I thought you might not make the wedding."

The distinguished senator slipped an arm around his wife's slim waist. "Nonsense. The senate is in session, but we took the company jet this morning so we could attend."

His graceful wife nodded. "We'll fly back to DC tomorrow."

Their son, Levi Madison, statuesque as his lofty father, stood beside his parents. A well-dressed Levi in a tasteful navy suit, rather than his normal jeans and tee shirt, had an arm around his wife's shoulders. Riley Powers-Madison, owner of The Power Agency, wore a navy off-the-shoulder gown that stopped midcalf. Her brunette bob had a single silver clasp to one side.

"Charli, Eli, we're so happy for you."

Levi hugged each of them and held Charli a pace away. "Best wishes, lil' sis," his nickname for her since she's lived with his family for a while after her parents' crash.

"Thanks, bro." She tiptoed to peck the broad cheek of the world-famous horse breeder.

The Madisons had been instrumental in getting Gran out of a three-year touring contract and had convinced several townspeople to qualify as foster parents so they could help care for the orphans while Gran completed eighteen months of commitments.

They talked to others who had taken the children in periodically, including Charli's friends, Bubba Larson and his recent bride, Candy; Coach Barry Barton and his wife, Nancy; and Roy and Beth Evans. They were like brothers to Charli and Kyler.

Charli left the room to prepare. Eli slid a chair to the center of the dance floor. She arrived and took her seat. Music played a striptease melody. Eli knelt before her, slipped her skirt over his head, and disappeared beneath the gown. He popped out with a puzzled expression on his face; and his hand held a pair of tiny, frayed, cut-off jean shorts. He stood and displayed them comically to the crowd's roar of laughter. Then he revealed the blue garter.

Charli stood. Jaiden handed her the bridal bouquet then took her place. Her back to the group of single females, Charli flipped the flowers over her head toward them. Jaiden jumped higher than the taller women surrounding her and snatched the bundle. She looked across the room at her fiancé and gave him a wink. Sounds of cheering and disappointment filled the air.

The men gathered. Eli first tossed the shorts over his head. Kyler grabbed the flying garment with a chuckle. Laughter rose in the crowd.

Eli then flicked the garter. The blue lacy thing landed square in Clay Barnes's broad, skilled hands.

Clay hooted and twirled the item around his finger. Strolling toward Charli's seat in the middle, he motioned for his woman to join him. Jaiden sat in the chair. Clay knelt before her, lifted her skirt, and guided the satin ring up her leg to just above her knee. The audience howled with amusement at the antics.

Charli and Eli cut the cake with its icing ribbon of blue connecting five tiers. Eli laughed when he noticed the topper. "I can't believe Dovie managed to find a groom and bride similar to us."

Charli pointed to the topper. "She had the cake decoration special made so the tall husband has hair like yours and the wife is short like me."

"She even has your honey-colored hair." He took her hand that held the knife. "You're not going to smash this in my face. Are you?"

They cut two small slices.

"Heck no. It's too tasty to waste. You doing that to me?" She linked arms with her groom.

"Nope. I don't want to spoil your makeup. It's rare to see you wearing any."

They fed each other a bite and finished eating the pieces themselves. Then they backed away from the table so Dovie could divide and serve the decadent dessert.

After an exhausting evening of celebration and dancing, the newlyweds said goodbye to their family and closest friends, then ambled hand in hand to the exit door. They waved to partiers.

Eli announced, "Thank you for being here to help us celebrate this momentous occasion. We love you all."

Charli blew them a kiss. In the lobby, they secured their coats. The limo drove them to the Sweetwater Inn, where Eli had reserved the bridal suite.

Charli sighed. "Finally, I have you all to myself, my husband." She tugged his lapels pulling him close for a tender kiss. "I have something for you." She pulled a case from her bridal purse.

He stepped back and accepted it. After lifting the top, he revealed a gold pocket watch with a glistening chain. He removed the time piece from the box and opened the front. The inside had been inscribed with *I'll love you always.*

"Charli, this is incredible. It's vintage. Right?"

She nodded. "Guess so. The watch belonged to my dad. Mom gave it to him when they married. I figured Kyler should have it, but in their will, our parents insisted it go to me. They left Mom's rings for Kyler. Their choice makes sense now I have someone worthy to give the watch to."

He held the timepiece to his chest. "It's beautiful. I'll cherish this gift always. Someday, the watch will go to our daughter—the first one." He took her hand and led her to a table where he picked up a red velvet container. "I have a present for you too, my beautiful bride."

She took the long, slim item. Lifting the lid showed, not jewelry, but paper. Thick paper stock looked impressive and important. She unfolded the legal document and gasped. Her skin tingled. Breathlessness forced a bark of laughter from her lips. Her voice shook, and her smile built as surprise set in.

"Eli, this can't be. It's the deed to McGregor House, and it's in our name. We just signed McGregor House over to the new buyers."

He spoke rapidly, bubbly, his voice light. Joy radiated from the glow of his eyes. "No, Owens Construction sold the house. I bought it. It's ours."

She frowned and plopped onto the bed. "I don't understand. I can't…we can't afford it. We liquidated the property so the company would have working capital. How—"

His arms swung in a fluid motion as he pulled her up and close. Laugh lines and dimples formed on his handsome face, and he chuckled softly. "But we can, Mrs. Lange. Man, I love the sound of that. We can afford it, Charli. Do you recall I sold my construction company in Cincinnati?"

Her belly settled against his bulging groin. He licked his lips, and a slow smile built there. His hands rested against the back of her waist, heat pulsing into her and stoking her internal fire. Her knees went weak, and warmth rose through her, as her chest flushed the way it always did when she was so close to this man.

"Yeah, sure. You financed some startup money in the company when we became partners."

He nodded, keeping eye contact, as he stroked her backside. "Uh huh, but my corporation sold for well over five-million dollars. Most of the capital is in stocks and bonds. When we needed to sell McGregor House, I realized I'd grown to adore the old girl, and how perfect the place would be to raise a family. I saw you loved the mansion as much as I did. I just could not bring myself to part with it. Besides, we need somewhere to live."

Charli glanced away and smiled. "We have my house."

He lived frugally off income from their partnership. She hadn't given Eli's financials any thought and did not realize he had so much money.

He nodded, shifting his feet. "Yes, but that house belongs to you and Kyler. Hopefully, Wes and Irma will stay there, at least until Kyler graduates and returns home for good; but darling, those two can use some privacy. We need that too. We need a home of our own."

Numbly, she nodded. "I suppose so."

His brows waggled, as he ground his erection against her middle and lifted her off her feet. Her legs wrapped around his waist, and he carried her to the bed. Laying her gently down, her legs remained open. He accepted the invitation and climbed on top of her. Nuzzling her neck and ear, he sucked the lobe into his mouth for a nibble that sent a flaming sizzle through her body and made her shiver.

He whispered, "What do you say, we get out of this restraining garb and get started making that family we want?"

She snickered as she trembled at his touch. "You're on, partner."

A word about the author…

This multi-award-winning, multi-genre author brings you the best in mystery and suspense with a dash of romance and a smidgen of history. The free-spirited world-traveler's diverse background and previous corporate career in marketing and global logistics, brings a rare perspective to her writing.

Appalachian-born coal miner's daughter Lynda, is part Cherokee. Her love affair with books, mystery, and American history stem from being immersed in the Mob's reign when Northern Kentucky prospered as a mecca for gambling and sin.

Lynda is published in mystery/suspense, contemporary and historical romance, MG mystery, children's books, and nonfiction.

Lynda Rees, The Murder Guru
Love is a dangerous mystery. Enjoy the ride!©
****

https://www.LyndaReesAuthor.com
****

If you enjoyed this story, leaving a review at your favorite book retailer or reader website would be much appreciated. Thank you!